BRENDA DUFFEY

NEW PANGAEA

AN EVOLUTION INTO THE FIFTH WORLD

NEW PANGAEA

An Evolution into the Fifth World

BRENDA DUFFEY

Contents

PROLOGUE

They forgot that they are all brothers and sisters cohabiting the same planet. They created borders to match this thinking and used their beliefs to create structures separating them. They started destroying these structures and the earth that sustained them all until a fifth coming united them once again as one family, one nation and one world – entering the Fifth World of a New Pangaea.

CHAPTER

1

A solitary figure moved in and out of the dark shadows created by buttes whose jagged arms thrust into the moonlight providing intermittent cover. The figure appeared, disappeared and then reappeared again in staccato movements across the blackened earth that surrounded the Kayenta Coal Mine operated by the Peabody Coal Company. The shadow made its way across an open field, moving slowly toward the blackened hills on the northern edge of the Black Mesa, an expansive highland plateau that stretched from southern Colorado into Northeastern Arizona. The figure seemed burdened by a massive, black body whose shape disappeared into the blackness of the Mesa. This was *Dailijiin*, Big Mountain to the Dine' or Navajo people living here, but another people had the ancient claim to the land.

The *Hopi –tu-* peaceful ones – had lived in villages throughout this part of Northeastern Arizona since the 11th Century. According to the instructions from *Maasaw,* they had lived as peaceful caretakers of the land – each clan sharing a responsibility for protecting their section of land. Title to the land was inscribed on sacred tablets given to leaders of the good people who had survived the destruction of the Third World with the help of Spider Woman who had brought them safely into the Fourth World. These sacred stones were deeds to each clan's settlements in the high cliffs of the First, Second and Third Mesas of the Big Mountain. To them, this was the center of the universe.

The Fire Clan held the title to the settlement now called Hotevilla near the Third Mesa. The original name of the village was Oraibi. The first settlers were led there by *Maasaw* – Master of the Fourth

World and Gate Keeper to the Fifth World. This Earth God of the Fourth World met the good people escaping the Third World. There, *Maasaw* had given the instructions to clan leaders to migrate to the farthest corners of the land in all four directions and maintain order and balance. *Maasaw* gave the Fire Clan leader a sacred tablet with a corner missing in the lower right-hand corner. When the time came to enter the final world of peace and harmony – the Fifth World – a leader would appear (*Pahana*) from the East – a long lost, white brother who would be wearing red and would have the missing corner of the stone. That time for a new Pangaea appeared imminent.

Spanish and American encroachment on the land for over a century had led to cultural decay and disconnection from the earth. Land was disappearing. Large tracts of land had been appropriated by American parties interested in mineral rights. Mining of these minerals was destroying the land, air and water. The Navajo had joined with the Americans and, with government assistance, this particular part of Hopi land was cunningly usurped from the Hopi and designated a Joint Use Area. Questionable leases had given the Peabody Coal Company permission to set up the coal mine north of Kayenta in the Black Mesa area. The figure continued its labored journey up the plateau.

The dark outline approached the area near a sign that said Peabody Coal Company. There the figure dropped the object under the glow of one of the strategically placed security lights surrounding the perimeter of the building. The light revealed the object to be a huge, black cross, but the figure remained in the shadow of a bulky crane that also protected him from the security camera above the light. The figure knelt and began digging into the soft earth with what appeared to be some type of walking stick, unaware of the silently approaching bird like figure stooped low to avoid the camera's eagle eye.

The bird like shape raised its giant wings and before the figure could turn around, the creature thrust what appeared to be giant talons into the man's back. The wounded figure screamed in pain, tried to turn but slumped forward beneath the raised bucket attached to the crane. The giant bird then grabbed the cross to strike the final blow. The bird stood there until all movement ceased. As quickly as it had appeared, it turned and seemed to look around before disappearing into the darkness once again.

*　　*　　*

Ranger George Yazzie walked toward the crime scene already marked with the familiar yellow tape to prevent the disturbing of evidence. The body still lay beneath the bucket of a huge, lifting crane owned by the Peabody Coal Company. Ranger Yazzie wore a light brown shirt with darker tie and slacks. He had a dark brown circular hat with the insignia of the Navajo Nation in the middle. Yazzie was one of 16 ranger/patrol officers based at the Navajo Police Department in Tuba City nearly seventy-five miles away. These ranger/patrol officers were usually the first to crime scenes and were charged with conducting the preliminary investigation. Since this was a murder on federal land, an FBI agent would soon be arriving from Flagstaff. For now, Yazzie was in charge.

George's family lived in Kayenta Township northeast of Tuba City near the Utah border. George had moved to Tuba City when he became a patrol officer in this expansive Black Mesa area of Northeastern Arizona. The ranger spent long hours in his white SUV with *Navajo Police* painted in green on the side doors, often driving six or seven hundred miles to investigate not only violent crimes but also crimes against the environment.

This area of the Black Mesa was in the Joint Use Area of the Hopi and Navajo Nations: Tuba City was in Coconino County, Arizona, on the Navajo Indian Reservation. The Peabody Coal Company had begun mining in the Black Mesa area in 1966 after securing questionable mineral rights through leases with the federal government and the Navajo and Hopi people who had inhabited the land for centuries. Controversy and public outcry had contributed to the closing of the Black Mesa Mine in 2005, but the Kayenta operation was still in existence.

George was tall, well over six feet, and had an athletic build. Dark skinned and ruggedly handsome, he was still single at 35. His job in a remote area afforded little time for socializing, but he had recently developed an interest in an attractive administrative assistant in the office, Jeanette Duffy. Jeanette's cameo complexion and thick, wiry copper hair confirmed her Irish ancestry. Although charming and friendly, Jeanette was aloof and discouraged any social invitations from fellow male officers- except for Robert Beneè.

George believed Jeanette's interest derived from the fact that Robert was even more aloof than she. George looked across the evidence scene at Robert, alone as usual, carefully combing through the crime scene to pick up any piece of evidence, however small and bagging it and labeling it for the forensics team. Robert picked up a black cross and what looked like a large, cottonwood branch. These items would be placed in the evidence boxes and taken back to Tuba City as well for further examination, including fingerprints.

Robert Beneè was from Gallup, New Mexico. Beneè was the sur name selected for his Navajo ancestors when they returned to their homeland after the Treaty of 1868 ended four years of resettlement in the Bosque Redondo area of eastern New Mexico. Resettlement was the name given by United States authorities, but the reservation was little more than a prison camp for the Navajo and their natural enemies the Apache.

Even for an Indian, Robert was exceptionally quiet and distant. Robert's dark eyes were impenetrable, and he never looked directly at anyone. *That stoic quality would challenge any woman*, he thought- *especially one like Jeanette who was used to being the center of attention.* "You'll need a hard hat, George!"

The words brought George back to the crime scene. The noise level of heavy equipment operating in the background made conversation difficult. Peter Munson walked toward George and handed him a bright yellow hard hat. "Company policy," he said. Peter was a short man with a wide girth. He buckled his belt below his waistline allowing for an overhang that bespoke of too much food and drink and too little exercise. Pete was the project manager for the mining operation. "How long before we can use this lifting crane?" he asked.

"What's the crane used for?" asked Yazzie.

"This is an excavator. We use the crane to scrape and dig up the overburden that covers the coal inside the rock; losing good time not being able to operate it."

"Well, your company's just goin' have to be patient here. The crane is part of the investigation and it can't be moved until we know if it was used for anything in this murder. I'm sure we'll need to interview the operator. Who is that?"

"That would be Eric Halverson. Came here from the operation in Black Mesa after it was shut down in 2005. Pretty pissed off about it. Eric stays to himself a lot, but he is one hell of an operator. Doesn't waste any time. I think Eric is inside. Maybe you can talk to him before you finish here."

"I could do that, but I'm sure we will have to take him and others to Tuba City for questioning when Josh gets here."

"Who's this Josh fellow?"

"Josh is the FBI agent Josh Overton who is based in Flagstaff; he is the head investigator for all felonies committed on land under the management of the Bureau of Indian Affairs. I'm sure Overton won't want this crane moved until he can interview anyone who was anywhere in the vicinity near the time of the murder. Crane can be used when the tape comes down."

"Not gonna do my ulcer any good," said Pete. "This happenin' with United Nations Investigators comin' to visit. Something about some Hopi artifacts bein' sold at a Paris auction. And those damned black crosses and rumors of crazy spirits haunting the place!

George wrote down "black crosses." "You think that black cross over there is connected somehow to those black crosses you mentioned?"

"Most likely," said Pete. "A few years ago a group that called themselves the Black Cross Alliance was goin' around puttin' black crosses like this one in front of the headquarters of the Peabody Energy and Emeren Corporation in St. Louis. Back in the fall of 2010 the crosses started showin' up in front of the Navajo Nation's Kayenta Mine in New Mexico.

That was about the time these nosy doctors from California and Oregon started doing investigations into lung diseases that they said were being caused by the dirty air. Matter of fact, one of those doctors just came back this summer – doin' "'more research,'" he said. Pete spat the words as though he were trying to get rid of some nasty material stuck in his throat.

"Where is this doctor and what is his name?" asked George.

"Dr. Statin or something like that." Pete rolled his eyes as he continued with a derisive chuckle. "Nerve of the fella calling himself a doctor; not much more than one of those herb peddlin' witch doctors in my opinion." George just silently nodded his head as he wrote *Dr. Statin* (?) in his notebook.

"What was that about United Nations Investigators and eerie sightings up here?

"Well, you know Chief Nat'aanii, don't ya? He's the chief ranger for the Hopi Resource Law Enforcement in Lower Moencopi Village, just south of Oraibi." Before Pete could elaborate, George remembered that Chief Nat'aanii had recently left to carry a petition to the United Nations to be delivered at the UN Session on the Rights of Indigenous Peoples on July 22nd.

"Oh, yeah, he's deliverin' that petition to stop the illegal sale of stolen Hopi religious artifacts in Paris, France – isn't that right?" asked George.

"Yeah, he just spoke a few days ago. Rumor is there are goin' to be some investigators heading this way soon." Pete watched as Yazzie jotted something in his notebook. "Hey, you don't think these two are related, do you?"

"Don't know, Pete. We have to follow all leads. We'll probably be asking all of you about these strange creatures you've been seein' around here. We'll also want to take a look at all your security videos from the past month. Crime scene investigators will need them as soon as possible to get them ready for viewing by the FBI."

"I'll get Maria right on it," said Munson. "Anything else, right now?"

"Nothing I can think of, but keep everyone out of the crime scene so long as this tape is up, and I'm sure Josh will want to talk to you as well when he arrives. Stay close." Pete grunted and called to Eric as he walked back toward the office.

Yazzie turned his attention once again to the crime scene. "What you got Beneè!" he shouted.

"We've about got all the physical evidence picked up and labeled. Appears the man was attacked here and probably killed with that huge cross over there." Robert pointed to the black cross that investigators were dusting for fingerprints.

"Once you finish here, head back downhill but stop and take a look at that pick-up truck at the bottom of the Mesa. Someone saw a red Cheyenne pick-up parked off 160. Dust the interior and collect any physical evidence first. See if you can find the keys anywhere. May still be in it. If so, just drive it to Tuba City."

Yazzie heard the voice of the medical examiner who was bending over the corpse. "What you got, John?" He asked as he walked toward the body.

John Cameron was in his early sixties. He had a ring of gray hair peeking from under the full brimmed hat that covered his bald head. The sweat was dripping down his forehead and along the sides of his face. He pulled a handkerchief from his lab coat to wipe his wet, horn-rimmed glasses that were slipping down his long, Roman nose.

"Pretty sure this is Ole Jack, the vagrant that roamed 'round the Little Colorado near the Grand Canyon picking up cottonwood branches to sell here," said Dr. Cameron.

The county medical examiner had turned the body face up to reveal a man about 40 or 50 years old. He handed Yazzie a set of keys that had fallen from the pocket of Jack's plaid coat. Yazzie put the keys in a plastic bag and then called to Robert. "I think these might be the keys to that pick-up!" Robert nodded and walked back to the pile of evidence. Yazzie looked at the corpse.

Ole Jack had a wild, unkempt appearance that made him seem older than he actually was. He had a thick, gray beard and hair pulled back in a ponytail. This look was common among the transients who roamed the isolated area around the Grand Canyon known as the Little Painted Desert. Ole Jack's skin was red and lined from constant sun exposure. George wondered what Ole Jack had been doing this far north. *Why had Ole Jack strayed so far from his business territory?* Yazzie had heard about Ole Jack; everyone living in this sparsely populated part of the county had heard his story.

Ole Jack had simply driven up to the Hopi Cultural Center on the Second Mesa about five years ago in his 1972 red and white Cheyenne pick-up truck. From then on, Jack had become a familiar sight driving his truck all along the state highways and dirt roads toward the villages that made up the Hopi Indian Reservation to sell his cottonwood to Navajo and Hopi merchants in the area.

Cottonwood was the preferred wood for making the highly popular Kachina dolls sold in every trading post and cultural center of both the Navajo and Hopi Reservations. Ole Jack would sell his cottonwood for a few thousand dollars and then disappear for months at a time until he reappeared with more wood to sell. The dolls were traditional gifts to Hopi children that had become highly popular with tourists from the time when Fred Harvey first established his chain of hotels along the Santa Fe Railroad route until the days of the automobiles that filled the Highway that became known as Route 66. What people knew of Ole Jack came from the stories told by the people who saw him at the Blue Coffee Pot. Jack's fondness for alcohol was well known in the area.

Ole Jack ate at The Blue Coffee Pot and was almost always "under the influence." Jack's truck was often parked for days on the vacant lot beside the abandoned Golden Sands Restaurant next to the Shell Station. Everyone knew he slept in his truck, but no one bothered him; they simply swapped stories about his checkered past at The Blue Coffee Pot.

Jack was the son of a Utah Mormon who had multiple wives; he had run away from this home as a teenager, spending most of his adolescence in youth detention and rehab centers until he had finally combined his love of nature with his business of selling cottonwood. *What brought him here?* Wondered Yazzie. Jack's overnight stays had coincided with the times when the Kachina spirits were out and about. George wrote, *"Connection to Kachina sightings"* in his notebook.

Kachinas were powerful spirits that could take human form and were active from the winter solstice in December until the end of the planting season in July. When revered, they used their power to bring good to the Hopi people in the form of rainfall, abundant harvest or healing. Masked dancers conducted ceremonies at intervals throughout this period to receive those blessings.

Kachina dancers entered the public square from the *kiva* in the center of the village. In this underground temple, the dancers put on their masks and prayed before climbing the ladder into the square; the dancers never appeared in public without their masks. The *kiva* was sacred; it represented the womb of Spider Woman through which the good hearted people of the Third World entered the Fourth World of Creation. At the end of the dances they returned to the *kiva* where they took off the masks and ceremonial costumes before returning to the plaza.

Kachinas resided in Old Oraibi Village from the end of July until the winter solstice. Recently, there had been reports of strange sightings of Kachina activity around the Kayenta Coal Mine; some people thought Ole Jack had something to do with this. George watched as Dr. Cameron continued with his initial examination.

Dr. Cameron pulled up the tee shirt that Ole Jack wore underneath a plaid jacket. The tee shirt had the symbol of the Broken Arrows Casino located on the Navajo Reservation near Winslow, Arizona. Ole Jack's wardrobe consisted of the plaid jacket and a collection of tee shirts and faded, worn jeans. "See these jagged marks around his middle? Appears Ole Jack was attacked by some type of bird of prey – a very large hawk, for example."

"Was that the cause of death?" asked George.

"Not likely, not enough blood spilled. See this protrusion on the back of the neck? That's the cause of death. Blunt force trauma, most likely from that cross over there. After all the physical evidence is collected, we will do DNA sampling in addition to fingerprints. We'll look for any DNA evidence on the body as well back at the morgue." Dr. Cameron turned to address the ambulance drivers. "Bring that stretcher here and a body bag. We need to get the body to the morgue in Tuba City so I can do some more tests."

Two EMT's wheeled a stretcher over to the body. Ole Jack was placed in the bag and lifted onto the stretcher. Dr. Cameron walked to his state issued medical examiner's car and yelled, "I'll see you guys at the morgue!"

George turned to the two lab investigators collecting evidence. "Bag everything up to take it back to Tuba City. We'll need to file a report as soon as possible. I'm going inside to talk to Pete and anyone else who may know something about what happened here last night. I'll also pick up recordings from the video cameras done last night. No need to stay at the lab because I'm going home after I interview everyone; we'll finish tomorrow morning. Overton should be here by then and you can give your reports to him. I'll turn over my notes to him at the same time since he'll be in charge after that." George sighed, wishing he could continue with the investigation himself. *Very strange things happening here,* he thought.

CHAPTER

2

Mehrrani (Rani to her family and friends) Bijan pulled her red canvas suitcase from her closet and placed it upon her bed. It was one of those beautiful, summer mornings in Albuquerque, New Mexico. The desert sun was still low on the horizon and had not yet warmed the air of this city in the high desert of New Mexico. There was a cool breeze drifting through the window of her old bedroom in the adobe house on Lomas Boulevard where she had lived since she was five years old.

Rani knew she had come from Iran with her mother after the Revolution in 1978, but her memories of her father and her life there were limited to the violent scenes that played out in terrifying nightmares that had haunted her well into puberty. Rani and her family had lived in Teheran, but her father had been from Khuzestan Province, home to the tribal Bakhtiar people who were migrant sheepherders. When the Revolution began in the fall of 1978, Rani's family was in danger because of their Baha'i faith.

Radical students influenced by extremist mullahs began to systematically round up any and all people associated with the exiled Shah. The Baha'i's were easy targets because of long held prejudice against this religion. Muhammad, Rani's father, was doubly fated. In addition to being a member of the Baha'i faith, he had been a personal assistant to Prime Minister Bakhtiar whose moderate government had lasted only thirty-six days after the Revolution began. A massive ethnic cleansing of members of this long persecuted faith in Iran began in earnest.

Baha'i's were rounded up and put into prison where they were executed if they refused to deny their faith and swear allegiance to

Ayatollah Khomeini. The streets of Teheran filled with angry mobs and the danger increased. Muhammad escorted his wife and daughter to the safety of their family home in Khuzestan Province on the eve of his daughter Rani's fifth birthday.

Feeling safe from harm, the family held a birthday party for Rani the next day, giving her a gift of a beautiful Persian, dancing doll. The doll was dressed in the bright colors of the Bakhtiari people and wore pink satin, ballet slippers. After the party, the family gathered around a fire in the center of the village to dance in celebration. Rani remembered the flutes and drumming being interrupted as a neighbor ran to her father and said, "They're coming for you! Quick, you must hide in our barn!"

"Take Bedar and Rani," he said. "Hopefully, they will be satisfied with just me."

"We won't go without you!" signed Bedar, clutching her husband's arm. A trembling, shaking, teary eyed Rani held tightly to her mother and doll, too afraid to say or do anything.

"You must go," said Muhammad. "I have already made arrangements to get you to safety, but now you must hide and stay alive no matter what happens to me! "Follow the instructions on this paper once it is safe to travel," he signed as he pushed his wife away and grabbed Rani for a last embrace.

Rani remembered running through the dark night clutching the beautiful doll her father and mother had just given to her. She kept looking back for her father but he disappeared in the evening shadows. Rani never saw him again. She and her mother spent the night buried under a bale of hay, afraid to move or even breathe.

After a night of terror, news came the next morning that Rani's father had been beheaded and butchered. There was no time to grieve or even give the husband and father a proper burial. Bedar and Rani were escorted in secret to Teheran where the Prime Minister was able to get the forged documents needed to get the family to his estate in Neuilly sur-Seine just outside Paris. Once there, with the help of the American Embassy, the two were sponsored by Bedar's sister, Slzdah, and her husband, Fahard, who had already moved to Albuquerque. Bedar and Rani had literally left

Paris with only the clothes on their backs, but the doll had never left her side. Rani sighed as she placed the doll in the suitcase. For a while, after the two had moved to Albuquerque, Rani could still smell her father's cologne on the doll. Those comforting smells had long since faded.

Rani studied the beautiful colors – peach, rust, blue, beige and gray; tribal colors of the Bakhtiari people. The doll was dressed as a beautiful Persian dancer. She held a tambourine and her full skirt reached to her ankles leaving only the tiny dancer's feet exposed. The last happy memory Rani could remember was the birthday celebration that had been interrupted by the neighbor's dire news. Rani's dark eyes moistened as she recalled that night.

Family and friends were in a circle dancing to the rhythmic music provided by the drums, flutes and tambourines. The memory of that dance still remained. Perhaps that's why Rani had joined the flamenco dancers that performed in Old Town after she started Rio Grande High School.

Rani's bond with her mother was much stronger than that of her American peers. The loss of her father and the resulting flight to another country had forged a bond between mother and daughter that seemed impenetrable. Bedar had been happy when Rani started dancing with her fellow high school students.

Rani was a natural. She had the long, lithe body of a dancer that brought grace and beauty to her performance. She also had a natural affinity for the rhythms that seemed to vibrate into her feet from the guitar and clapping of the accompaniment. Her olive complexion contrasted beautifully with the bright red, yellow and green costumes. Red was Rani's favorite color. Her raven hair pulled into a taunt bun at the nape of her long neck gave her the graceful appearance of a swan as she moved her feet in staccato beats across the floor. Serious and shy, Rani was happy she had dancing during those rough adolescent years when her mother had remarried and moved to New York. Dance and Rani's connection to the Native American culture, as well as support from her aunt and uncle had made staying in Albuquerque bearable.

From the first moment Rani had seen the tribal dances at the Indian Pueblo Cultural Center in Old Town, she had felt a sense of connection to these people and quickly developed a bond and sense of community with them. Shortly after Rani and Bedar had settled in Albuquerque, Bedar began going with other members of the community to a Hopi enclave within the Isleta Pueblo southeast of Albuquerque. Members of her faith were drawn to the tribal way of life and the drumming ceremonies that were similar to her Bakhtiari heritage.

As Rani matured she joined her mother on trips to the Isleta Pueblo. Beginning with her junior year at Rio Grande High School, Rani started going alone and fell under the tutelage of a blind elder named *He Who Sees with No Eyes.* The Oraibi settlement in New Mexico was more like the non-traditional settlement in New Oraibi, Arizona named Kykotsmovi Village than the one at Old Oraibi near Hotevilla, Arizona.

The non-traditionalists at Isleta Pueblo had more social exchange with other pueblo cultures as well as the *Kahopi* (non-Hopi cultures such as the Spanish and Anglo cultures) that had taken over their land. Therefore, Rani and her mother had participated in some ceremonies on visits there when Rani was still in high school, especially the coming of age ceremony when Rani turned 16. Rani had also learned *Tewa*, the native language of the pueblo people. The people at Isleta Pueblo joined her aunt and uncle as her extended family, providing the comfort and security Rani had needed when her mother had moved to New York.

Rani glanced at her high school year book lying on the dresser. She sighed as she remembered that summer before her senior year. That was the summer her mother married and moved to New York. Rani opened the yearbook and saw a rose pressed between two pages – a poignant reminder of her senior prom and Jake. Rani had met Jake the summer before her senior year. Jake was her first love – a handsome twenty year old flute player.

Jake was a descendant of one of the Hopi family of settlers who had moved to the Isleta pueblo after the split in 1906. Jake had moved to Rio Rancho, a city on the West Mesa near Albuquerque, after he had started working for the Intel Corporation as a computer technician. Rani and Jake dated during her senior year as well as her first two years at the University of New Mexico; Rani sighed when she remembered the break up.

Jake had wanted to marry Rani, but she was unwilling to marry before finishing her degree in special education with a focus on the hard of hearing. In addition, Rani knew she was going to New York after graduation because working for the United Nations seemed her destiny. Rani's break-up with Jake was the first in a long series of broken relationships. The break up was usually initiated by Rani when she sensed things getting too serious. She had built a protective wall that no one had been able to penetrate. The more attracted to the man, the faster Rani ran; she couldn't face the loss of another loved one. Loneliness seemed preferable to loving and losing.

Rani's native language was *Farsi,* but she had known sign language for as long as she could remember. Because Bedar was deaf she had relied on her daughter to help her connect to the speaking world after they moved to Albuquerque. Foreign languages came easily to Rani and she quickly learned English as well as Spanish, eventually adding the *Tewa* language of the Isleta Pueblo. This had made her a perfect candidate for working in translation for the United Nations delegates in the General Assembly in New York. Rani was delighted to find indigenous people from the American west were now part of the Assembly. Jake's need to stay in Albuquerque had provided the perfect reason for the break up. *There was always a reason.* Rani sighed thinking about the last time she had seen Jake.

Rani had seen Jake, his wife and young son when she had returned to Albuquerque for her ten year high school reunion. She hadn't thought much about not being married then. But now she was forty; Rani could feel the passage of time and the specter of her mother's death loomed closer. She found herself thinking more about the emptiness ahead when her mother and aunt and uncle were gone. That awareness had prompted her decision to move back to the Southwest. Rani shivered. *Maybe I should have stayed in New York and with Nate Harrison. Did I make a rash decision?* Rani carefully returned the rose to its place in the yearbook and resumed packing.

Just after celebrating her 40th birthday, Rani had decided she needed to finally separate from her mother and build a larger support network other than her mother and aunt. *Maybe that wall will come down in the process,* she thought. That's when she had applied for a teaching position in special education at Monument Valley High School near Kayenta Township in Northeastern Arizona.

Could you have chosen anything more different? But is it really different? She thought. Deep inside Rani felt a need to return to the desert. *What is taking me there?* It was too late for thinking about going back now. Rani placed the yearbook on the shelf in the closet – not because she regretted the memories; she just wanted to focus on new ones.

It was the last week of July and Rani had already signed a lease for an apartment beginning the 1st of August. She was flying from Albuquerque to Flagstaff, and once in Flagstaff, Rani would pick up the SUV she had purchased and drive through Tuba City, Arizona to Hotevilla-Bacavi. She wanted to visit Old Oraibi village and Prophecy Rock as well as New Oraibi in Kykotsmovi Village. She would then drive north to Kayenta Township in time for the start of the school year. *My contract is only for a year. I can always return to New York. I have to follow through. The desire is too strong.*

Standing here in her old bedroom, Rani was flooded with memories of her successful life borne of a violent beginning to a comfortable existence in the United States. Perhaps it was that beginning that still lingered on the edges of her subconscious that drove her to make the move. There was a feeling in her gut that there was unfinished business surrounding her father's death. Rani looked at the plain, cotton bag lying next to her suitcase.

Rani picked up the bag and pulled a jagged stone from within. Rani's mother had given the bag and its contents to her before she left New York. "Your father found this stone in the House of *Bab* on a visit to Shiraz after the house was destroyed," said Bedar. He sewed it into the hem of the doll's dress he gave you for your birthday and made me promise to get it safely out of Iran.

Bab was the spiritual founder of the Baha'i Faith; the name *Bab* meant the Gate, or Messenger, of the Messiah. The *Bab* identified the new Imam as a prophet from Shiraz name *Bah 'a u'llah*. This was heresy to the *mullahs* (religious teachers) who believed only in Muhammad as *Allah's* messenger. Therefore, both leaders had been persecuted along with their followers. The *Bab* had been executed in 1844. *Bah 'a u 'llah* had been persecuted and exiled to Turkey and Iraq before finally exiled to Akka, Palestine (now Acre, Israel) in 1868. *Bah 'a u 'llah* died there in 1892, and his faithful followers built a shrine there that is visited annually by Baha'i's now living all over the world.

Angry mobs had demolished the *Bab's* house after the Revolution. Rani's distraught father had gone there just after the demolition and had discovered the stone on top of a pile of rubble created by the bulldozer. The portrait, created by an ink stamp that permeated the stone, was of an Indian in a headdress of black feathers. Muhammad had dropped the stone into cotton, drawstring bag, which he had taken home to give to Bedar before the family fled Teheran.

"Your father said this had some importance and we were to take it with us on our journey to the West. Remember the petro glyphs we visited all over New Mexico and eastern Arizona when we lived there? Somehow, I think this stone resembles those ancient carvings. Since you are moving back there, I am giving it to you in the hope you will find some answers." Rani heard the front door close followed by the click of her aunt's heels on the tile floor below.

"Rani, are you packing?"

"Yes, Auntie. What do you need?"

"Nothing, I just came home from the market and wanted to let you know I am preparing some of your favorite Persian foods for dinner before Uncle and I take you to the airport this evening."

"That would certainly be delightful. I have really missed your cooking. There are so many good Persian restaurants in New York that I haven't felt like making home cooked meals." Rani's mouth watered as she remembered wonderful *Nowruz* celebrations of the past and the delightful foods that were part of the springtime celebration akin to New Year in America – chickpea cookies, *baklava* and *kuku* (eggs deviled with fresh dill, parsley and spinach).

Knowing Aunt Sizdah was home put an end to all the remembering and Rani finished filling her two suitcases and overnight bag and walked downstairs to keep her aunt company while she finished dinner. The first thing she did was grab a chickpea cookie from a plate on the counter and the two laughed. Both wished Rani's mother could be there with them.

CHAPTER

3

Rani absorbed the stillness that engulfed her on this remote stretch of Arizona Highway 264 connecting Tuba City with what was left of the Hopi Indian Reservation. She had flown into Flagstaff via U. S. Airways and picked up the SUV she had ordered on line from Albuquerque. She then drove to a grocery store where she could stock up on some fresh produce for her two day trip to visit villages that were part of the Hopi Indian Reservation. Her plans were to drive to Tuba City in Coconino County on the southeastern side of the expansive Navajo Reservation where she would stay for three days before continuing her drive to Kayenta Township to begin her teaching assignment. In recent years the Navajo Reservation had become larger through contrived leases that declared former Hopi land on the Black Mesa a Joint Use area with the Navajo Nation.

Making Hopi land a Joint Use area allowed the Navajo to extend the sale of mineral rights to the Peabody Coal Company which was expanding its operations in this coal rich Mesa. Health concerns and water issues had helped shut down the Peabody mining operation on the southern part of Hopi land around the Black Mesa, but the population was still dealing with the repercussions that threatened their way of life that had existed for centuries. Tuba City was centrally located between the Hopi Third Mesa and Kayenta Township. Rani wanted to visit the Third Mesa before moving into her apartment in Kayenta Township where she would live while working at Monument Valley High School. Therefore, she had decided to stay in Tuba City at the Navajo Nation Inn while exploring the Third Mesa. The Inn had everything she required for her stopover visit.

Rani settled into her comfortable room after a quiet meal in the adjoining restaurant that served traditional Mexican foods along with American selections. The taco salad had been tasty and filling. Apparently, Rani was not the only female traveling alone. She noticed an attractive woman about the same age as she sitting at a small table in the corner of the restaurant. The woman was so absorbed in what she was reading she hadn't even noticed Rani. Her khaki, cargo pants, tunic and hiking boots were in contrast to Rani's red floral, loose fitting sundress. *Must be some kind of archaeologist*, thought Rani as she left the restaurant to return to her room.

After changing into her comfortable pajamas, Rani worked at her lap top studying maps and directions to Hotevilla and Kykotsmovi Village – Old and New Oraibi- until 11:00. She stood up and stretched. *Time for bed.* A continental breakfast was served from 6-9 pm, but Rani thought having a more substantial meal in the restaurant would make more sense. She planned on getting up at 8:00, having a leisurely shower and breakfast and leaving for Hotevilla about 10:00. That would put her in Hotevilla around 11:00 in time to get settled before the dances began at noon.

Rani had a supply of melons, grapes and some *baklava* she had discovered at a Middle Eastern bakery in Flagstaff in her cooler along with plenty of water; she left her room at 9:00 and headed for the restaurant, wearing the same floral print sun dress that she had worn the day before. She had a bright red shawl that she could use as a covering for her head and shoulders against the intense desert and wore comfortable red Sketchers in preparation for a lot of walking.

A young Navajo woman greeted her as Rani walked into the room. Her black uniform fit snugly about her heavy figure. She was friendly and professional as she asked, "how many?"

"Just one," said Rani.

"Booth or table?"

Rani glanced around the dining room. She saw a two person booth next to a window in the corner. "That booth will suffice," she said.

"Follow me," said the host. "Your server will be here in a minute."

A woman dressed in the same black uniform handed Rani a menu and silverware. She carried a carafe of coffee and a mug. She put the coffee mug on the table and started to pour when Rani held up her hand to signal "stop." "I would prefer some hot tea," she said.

The server set the carafe on the table as she asked, "What kind? We don't have a big selection of teas. I think we have Lipton and maybe some peppermint tea."

"I'll take a pot of peppermint tea," said Rani. "Oh, and I'd like a glass of water with no ice and some lemon please."

The server wrote the order on her pad and asked, "Do you need more time to study the menu?"

"No, I think I'll have the huevos rancheros."

"How do you want your eggs?'

"Poached."

"Hot or mild sauce?"

"Hot and I'll have the corn tortillas please."

"That all?"

"Yes."

"I'll be back with your tea." Rani watched as the young woman walked away. She couldn't help but wonder what her life was like. Was she married? Did she have children? Rani noticed the host seating the young woman she had seen last night in the booth directly across from her. This time, the woman saw Rani and nodded her head with a polite smile and said, "Good morning," as she sat down. Rani returned the smile and greeting.

After ordering, the woman pulled out a bound notebook from a canvas bag and started to read and take notes. *That must be what she was doing last night.* The book seemed to have agricultural drawings and curiosity got the better of Rani. "Is that some type of irrigation system?" she asked nodding toward the open page.

"Not really irrigation. The Hopi don't irrigate their land the way American farmers do. They use a system called dry farming. I'm here studying the technique. There is a site just south of here in the village of Moenkopi."

"Oh, I saw that on the maps I studied last night. I'm going to Hotevilla and Kykotsmovi villages today, but I plan on going there tomorrow morning before I leave for Kayenta Township. By the way, my name is Rani."

"Listie Stratton, nice to meet you." Rani noticed a question mark on Listie's face when she mentioned Kayenta Township. *Or did I?* The server brought Rani's order and sat it on the table, then turned to take Lisite's order.

Rani began eating and after Listie finished ordering, she asked, "Could I join you tomorrow? It would be nice to see the farms with someone. I am a long way from my family because I moved here from New York to take a job in teaching the blind and deaf at Monument Valley High School." Again, Rani noticed the same look when she mentioned her job.

"I would like that. Maybe we could get to know one another a little better. My husband is in Kayenta Township on business at the moment and I think we have some other things in common. I would love to show you the Humetewa Farm."

"Great," said Rani as the server brought Listie's order. The two ate in silence after that. Rani finished before Listie and said, "See you tomorrow," as she stood up and walked toward the lobby to pay her bill. *Wonder what those other things we have in common are,* she thought as she walked to her car. Once inside, Rani activated her GPS.

"Turn left and head southeast toward Arizona Highway 264," said the female voice. Highway 264 would take her directly to Hotevilla so there was no need to keep the voice command activated. Rani liked the silence.

The stillness soothed her tired, jet-lagged body and she breathed it in with gratitude. Rani had a natural affinity for the quiet that resulted from living in a home with a deaf mother where sign language was the major form of communication. Signs allowed the speaker to give the listener a word picture of what the symbol represented. For instance, the word for mother was a gentle caress of one's face, giving the listener a concept of what the word Mother represented.

Rani liked this method of communication. When she and her mother disagreed, as they often had when she was an adolescent, their communication was not constrained by the shackles of yelling or screaming at each other. Finding common ground was easier when the disagreement was not convoluted with impulsive outbursts generated when people spoke in anger. Letting go with a barrage of angry words was not so easy when each word had to be carefully signed or in some cases spelled. The impact of the anger was lost in the silence.

The lack of background noise in Rani's home also created an atmosphere that was more subdued and connected to the inner rather than outer voice. Rani had been much more introspective than her adolescent peers in Albuquerque; she listened more and was less impulsive. Attracted by the quiet of the Native American pueblo people living outside of Albuquerque, Rani had often sought solace there when faced with adolescent coming of age issues in high school.

The quiet voices of the elders who spoke with the wisdom of the ages drew Rani to their villages to hear those inner voices. Rani's peers had sought the stimulation offered by the loud noise, music and entertainment available in a big city. Being inner directed had served Rani well and had helped protect her from some of the typically impulsive behaviors of her adolescent peers.

Rani had graduated with honors from Rio Grande High School in 1993 and had received a scholarship to the University of New Mexico. Completing the four year undergraduate program had posed no challenge to her. That inner strength and wisdom not only helped with her academic success, it also brought solace to her to help heal the trauma of her early childhood. Those qualities also served her through adolescence and every situation since with a poise and grace born of compassion and forgiveness.

When Rani walked into a room, she owned it – not from great sexual beauty, although Rani was indeed beautiful, but from a presence that drew people like a magnet. This quality has been called charisma, but Rani did not nurture it for personal power or gain. On the contrary, she didn't have to nurture it; the charisma came from a confidence born from within and that serene light filled any space she occupied with a soothing calm that discouraged disharmony. People were attracted to her, but Rani had a hard time forming long term relationships, especially with men.

Rani studied the picturesque landscape that surrounded her. With only a narrow, two-lane highway stretching across it, the view was suspended in time almost like a gigantic snapshot flashed upon a huge screen in an IMAX theater. *This was so much better!* The stillness echoed with sounds of the creatures living in and on the earth.

Rani inhaled the scented, fragrant air - smells of the sagebrush and moist, red earth that had been fed by the recent rains. She felt their vapors soothing away any frayed edges of her nerves. The sun's rays in the clear, blue sky used nature's prism to create a still life of brilliant Technicolor displayed in red, green, blue, indigo and violet. Rani understood why artists such as Frederick Remington and Georgia O'Keefe had sojourned to the West

Driving this isolated, two-lane highway that seemed to stretch into the horizon, Rani felt as though she were truly entering another dimension – a parallel universe where time did indeed stand still. God's brushstrokes could still be seen everywhere, although Rani noticed some blemishes – discarded beer cans and plastic bottles along with contemporary gang graffiti on larger stones. Here, however, there were still fewer distractions created by the endless chatter of humans and their machines of progress that stampeded over the land. These machines, however, had already left huge, almost irreversible carbon footprints in the bigger cities such as Phoenix and Flagstaff and were even threatening the Grand Canyon. For now, Rani basked in the beauty, and the forty-eight miles into Hotevilla passed quickly. She felt an exhilarating calm wash over her as she saw the adobe dwellings on the high cliff in the distance. Rani felt as though she were traveling back into time.

Pulling over to the side of the highway, Rani stopped the car to study some of the brochures she had picked up in the motel office. Hotevilla, on the Third Mesa had been settled after the split between the traditionalists and progressives in 1906. Traditionalists, who desired no social or political interaction with the Spanish and American settlers, had settled Hotevilla just outside the ancient village of Old Oraibi, and the progressives had moved to the village of Kykotsmovi.

Hotevilla, like Kykotsmovi, maintained a Kachina cult that still practiced the ancient ceremonies that included Kachina worship. Kachinas were living spirits that appeared from the winter solstice on December 21st until the end of the growing season in mid-July. The rest of the year the spirits resided in the village of Old Oraibi.

The desk clerk at the Navajo Inn had given Rani a brochure describing the purpose of the summer solstice dance that she had come to see today. "Because the Hopi believe Kachinas control some aspect of the natural world, periodic dances called *tivas* are held in the village plazas throughout the year to gain their assistance in blessing the people with rain, healing, etc. Fully masked Kachinas appear from the opening in the center of the plaza. This is called a *kiva* and represents Grandmother Spider's womb from which the people entered into the Third World of Creation after the Second World was destroyed in a great flood. *Kahopi* (non-Hopi) may attend the ceremonies, but picture taking or viewing the subterranean *kiva* is strictly forbidden."

Rani put the brochures in the glove box and pulled out onto the paved highway once again. She crossed the highway onto the dirt road that wound to the top of the Mesa. At the summit, the road disappeared into a flat area where the dust had been compacted enough to form a natural parking lot. Rani found a place to park among the trucks and cars jammed helter-skelter along the edge of the pathway leading to the village plaza. *What an oxymoron*, she thought. *Modern machines in front of ancient adobe houses and dirt roads.* Rani joined the throng of people walking toward the square now filled with chairs.

Women and children made up most of the crowd in the square. The women carried baskets of food – summer squashes, apples, breads and other fruits. They put the food in the baskets in the center of the square and then took their seats. Rani sat down and breathed in the power of the stillness. Not only were all the seats in the plaza filled but the chairs on the roofs of the houses were also occupied. *Mostly men and boys.* Everyone sat in quiet anticipation.

Rani looked at the blaze of color provided by the colorful skirts and dresses on the women. She found it hard to keep her eyes off one older woman seated in front of her.

The woman was ageless. She had the sun dried, lined face like those that Rani had seen in photographs depicting the people of the Southwest. The woman wore a beige, cotton dress, but Rani was enthralled with the shawl that she used to hold back the glare of the sun. The shawl was emerald green with golden thread woven throughout. The woman's stature and manner in which she was treated made her appear stately and well-respected. Rani had read that the Hopi were a matrilineal society that respected elders, so she was not surprised. Without any fanfare, a group of mud caked, bare chested men appeared carrying more baskets of food.

The men started throwing fruits, candies and brightly colored breads from the baskets into the crowd, primarily to children and adults seated in the plaza as well as on the roof. There was no pushing or shoving of each other to get to the tossed food and Rani once again was impressed with the stillness. The men kept dispersing the food, but the baskets seemed to stay filled from the constant renewal of the supply. Rani watched as the men tossed what appeared to be circular "donuts" with a bright green and yellow icing that created a spiral across the top to the children. Eventually, one was tossed to her. The topping reminded Rani of the spiral drawings she had seen carved into the lava rock at Petro glyph National Monument near Albuquerque. The bread was sweet with a moistness that was most pleasant to the taste. A drumming sound announced the arrival of the musicians.

Although fully covered and masked, the musicians appeared to be female and wore bright red robes with black and white appliqués. The masked Kachina dancers came next, entering the circle from the *kiva* in the center of the plaza. Masks with red and black spirals on a white background covered their entire faces and the designs on the mask matched the designs of the long tunics they wore. Their legs were bear with ink stain designs that appeared to identify their clan on their calves. Their knees were covered by turtle shells and bells jingled around their ankles. These provided the background percussion as the dancing began in unison. Throughout the dance the mud caked men periodically sprinkled the dancers with pinches of dirt they held between their thumbs and fingertips.

When the dancing ended, the dancers started passing out larger boxes of fruits and vegetables to the audience – this time to the women in order of age. The woman with the green shawl was served first, then mothers with young children. Rani looked up to see a dancer holding a large; zucchini squash as though making an offering to her. She motioned as if to say "me" and the dancer nodded and handed her the squash. The emotion that ran through her then was one she found difficult to explain. The irony – a group of people American society would deem poverty stricken obviously enjoying an abundant harvest that seemed to have no end and then giving a perfect stranger one of the largest vegetables in the basket! Rani felt a sense of empowerment as she walked to her car that made it difficult for her to be anywhere but present.

Rani had spoken to no one since her arrival, and no one explained the ceremony or what it represented, but Rani needed no words. She felt it. Rani had seen many dances performed by the Navajo at the Indian Pueblo Cultural Center and other Pueblos that dotted the landscape around Interstate 40 from Albuquerque to Gallup, New Mexico. Those dances were performances just like her flamenco dancing. The members of the audience cheered and took pictures and some even joined in the dancing. *This was not a performance,* she thought. *This was sacred. Like one long prayer! I'm where I am supposed to be. Or did I ever leave?* More answers lay in wait for her at her next destination – Prophecy Rock.

CHAPTER

4

Rani picked up the brochure on Prophecy Rock – a petro glyph just a few miles Southeast of Hotevilla. She looked at her watch. It was almost 1:00. She took a slice of cantaloupe and some grapes from the cooler in the car and ate them while studying the brochure. *There are guided tours every thirty minutes. I'll need to get started if I am to make the 1:30 tour,* she thought. Once again, Rani felt a sense of timelessness as she drove along Highway 264 until she saw a massive, red sandstone butte rising above piles of beautiful red and white rocks of all interesting shapes and sizes on her right. Rani noticed what appeared to be a portable structure not unlike the trailers that provided government housing to Indians in the pueblo villages outside Albuquerque. There were cars in the dirt area that evidently served as a parking lot. She saw people gathering around a dark-skinned, heavy man wearing a fleece jacket and black skull cap with blue edging. He wore sunglasses to protect his eyes from the blazing sun. *This must be the tour guide.*

Rani joined the silent crowd as they followed the guide, a Hopi elder, along a dirt trail that wound around the red sandstone rocks. The rocks contained drawings similar to those she had seen outside Albuquerque. Rani was fascinated by the shapes of the rocks; *These could be fictional homes for hobbit like characters or Fred Flintstone,* she thought. The guide stopped in front of a large, sandstone butte that sat atop a pile of rocks. One piece had been sheared by the elements to form a rectangular flat surface containing a series of hieroglyphics that contained The Hopi Prophecy.

The quiet voice of the Hopi Elder filled the stillness above the faint whisper of the wind.

"The first stick figure represents *Maasaw* – or Great Spirit," he said pointing to the first of the hieroglyphics. *Maasaw/Messiah?* "*Maasaw* is the Gatekeeper who greeted our ancestors when they arrived from the Third World of Creation into the Fourth where we now live. *Maasaw* gave instructions to the ancestors to migrate in four directions from the rectangular area here that represents what we believe to be the center of the universe. *Maasaw* gave leaders of each of the four clans a stone tablet that outlined the parameters of their land. He gave these instructions as he handed them the tablet "You must live as caretakers of that land until the time of the final evolution into the Fifth and final world where the destruction of the two hearted people is complete."

Maasaw continued, "The Fire Clan is the keeper of all the sacred tablets and interprets the meanings of each petro glyph. The time of the fulfillment of the prophecy will occur when a leader from the East appears carrying the missing right hand corner of one of the Fire Clan's Stones. This long lost white brother is called *Pahana*."

The tour guide then explained the meaning of the Hopi Prophecy as inscribed on the Rock. "In the Hopi Prophecy when the time of the Convergence approaches, all two-hearted people (evil) will finally disappear ushering in the Fifth World – the final evolution of the Golden Age of Peace and Harmony. Do you see this cross in the circle to the right of *Maasaw?*" he asked pointing to that area on the petro glyph. "When the Spanish arrived with their crosses in the 15th Century, the Hopi believed their leader was the *Pahana*, but their experience with the Spanish proved that was not the case. We are still waiting for the *Pahana*," he said.

"The two parallel lines extending from the center of the universe represent the two life paths," he continued. "The lower path is the path the one-hearted or good people choose. They live in harmony with the earth and are the Elects or Peacemakers who will enter the Fifth World." *Blessed are the Peacemakers, for they shall be called the children of God*, thought Rani. She watched the guide as he ran his hand along the top line extending from the Center of the Universe.

"See this top line? It represents the path chosen by the two-hearted people. These people will create the chaos that will lead to destruction from abuse of the land and its resources. It is the path of science and technology that will eventually lead to the decline of the two-hearted people that will not enter the Fifth World.

See this third figure on the top line? The head is off center representing his/her lack of balance. This figure is in danger of falling before the squiggly line that represents the Convergence. If the two-hearted person can regain the balance, the fall might be prevented before that time. We see that happening today with the white people studying the ancient methods of organic farming and use of traditional herbs for medicine and healing. There are also those who are working to repair the damage done by our carbon footprints and to promote peace instead of militarism.

The circles between the corn stalks on the bottom line represent the three World Wars. The corn stalks between each circle represent a time of false prosperity after each war. The gourd of ash represents destruction from a nuclear explosion. According to our Prophecy, the third world war will be started by countries in Asia and the Middle East. At the end of this war, the two-hearted people will be destroyed and the one-hearted people will enter the Fifth World – the Golden Age of Peace and Harmony."

"Is there any hope for the two-hearted people?" asked Rani.

"I think there is a chance for the two-hearted people to change and begin to live like the one-hearted people and be saved. It is possible for the last figure on the top line to return to balance and harmony. There is always a choice; the choice is where hope lives."

Rani wanted to ask more about the stone tablets given to each of the clan leaders – especially the one given to the Fire Clan. Although she did not believe she would be allowed to see the sacred stones firsthand, she believed she might find some information on the internet and keep that with her when the time came to discuss her tablet with the appropriate elders. *That goes on my list after I get settled. Three o'clock. Time to visit Kykotsmovi Village.* Once again, she pulled another brochure from her packet and sat in the parking lot while she quickly reviewed the location and places to stop, if any.

It was 3:30 when Rani drove into Kykotsmovi Village. She noticed a large sign on the side of the rode welcoming visitors.

Welcome to Kykotsmovi Village
Please Respect our Privacy

Absolutely Not Permitted
Photographing
Sound Recording
Removal of Objects
Sketching

You Are Welcome to Respectfully Observe Certain Ceremonies

Kykotsmovi Village did seem a little more modern than Hotevilla. The brochure had said that the village was the home of the Hopi Tribal Government. There was a large building with a sign in the front that said Hopi Veterans Memorial Hospital. *Strange, I thought the Hopi were peaceful people. Maybe their service was in auxiliary support like that of other conscientious objectors. Something to think about but not now.* Farther along the main road, Rani noticed a cluster of buildings that had what appeared to be *Kykotsmovi* written in Hopi on a long sign above a mall like area that included a pizza place and a general store. Close to the entrance to Highway 264 Rani saw a building with a sign that said Hopi Day School.

Must be an elementary school, thought Rani. There was a young woman about 20 or 25 stooping with a group of elementary aged children. She was apparently instructing them about planting some vegetable starts in rows identified by a twine edge that formed a border for them. Although Rani was curious, she looked at her watch; 4:05 already. She would have to hurry to get to the Inn by 5:00. Rani went directly to the Café upon her arrival at the Inn. *Good.* Listie wasn't there yet. "How many?" asked the same host that had seated her previously.

"There will be another woman," said Rani. "You remember the woman who sat across from me this morning?"

"Oh, yes. Ms. Stratton. She's been here the whole week."

"We were to meet here at 5:00." Rani heard someone walking up behind her.

"Am I late," asked Listie?

"Not really," said Rani. I just arrived myself.

"Follow me," said the host as she led the two to small booth in the corner of the room.

As Rani and Listie were settling into their seats, the same waitress appeared. This time she brought a pot of hot tea for Rani and a carafe of coffee for Listie. "You need more time with the menu?" she asked.

"Any suggestions?" Rani posed this question to Listie.

"I like the sample tray with servings of the different kinds of bread and fresh produce from the gardens."

"I think I will try that, and could you also bring me some water with no ice and lemon if you have it?"

"I'll do the same," said Listie as the server looked in her direction.

"There's so much I want to ask you," said Rani, "although I have a sense that we already know one another." For the first time, Rani felt no need for her protective wall. *Or did it ever exist with Listie?*

"I sense the same thing," said Listie. This time Listie supplemented her words with sign language.

Rani signed back, "You know sign?"

"My daughter Polly is deaf," said Listie. Both my husband and I have learned sign. Was your mother always deaf?"

"For as long as I can remember," said Rani. *Mama (mom may)* lost her hearing when she was a small child. *Madarbozorg* (Grandmother) was walking with *Mama* outside the family home in Avaz in Khuzestan Province when a man stepped on an unexploded bomb left from the Allied Invasion in 1941. The man died, and although *Mama* and *Madarbozorg* survived with only cuts and scratches, the noise of the explosion burst both *Mamas'* eardrums.

"I didn't know the Allies invaded Iran during that war," said Listie.

"Well, they did. Unfortunately, Americans are not highly regarded in Iran for the way they have interfered with our government. Mostly for the control of the oil. But, I am happy to live here. At least here, members of my faith are not beheaded and tortured."

"What is your faith?" asked Listie. I am a follower of *Baha 'a Ilua*, the prophet who started the faith in the middle of the 19th Century in Persia. Our people have been persecuted from the start because of this."

"Interesting," said Listie. I know a lot about persecution. My mother was Native American and our people have not been treated very well in America. Part of why I am here is to work to help save the land in the Hopi Reservation from even more destruction. I am also here to learn more about Hopi farming practices. There is a movement sweeping across the country to return to the Native American philosophy of land stewardship and working in harmony with nature in the way we produce our food."

"Oh, that was part of what the tour guide said at Prophecy Rock."

"You've been there?"

"Just today. Funny thing, I felt so in tune with everything I heard. Just like talking with you now. Was your daughter born deaf?"

"No, she was so healthy, but the American doctors and public officials forced us into getting her vaccinated after she was born. After the MMR vaccination, we noticed a marked change. Polly developed a high fever and had a seizure about a week after the vaccination. After she recovered, we discovered she had lost her hearing. That's another reason my husband and I have worked to change laws that would force parents to vaccinate their children."

"How old is Polly? Asked Rani. "Is she with your husband?"

"Polly is ten. No, she was with us, but she had to go back home to get ready for school. Her grandfather met us here two days ago and picked her up to take her back to Coos Bay, Oregon with him where we live. We moved there in 2001 to live with my dad after my mother died in the crash of United Flight 93 on September 11th. Polly is named for her; her name was Pauline."

Another connection, thought Rani. "What does your father do?" asked Rani.

"He's a retired horticulturalist from Southern Oregon University. He and my mom shared an interest in organic gardening. After they married and settled in Coos Bay, Mom opened a cranberry store called Sweet Treats. Dad couldn't manage both after she died, so he sold the store. I was living in Florence, Oregon when Mom died; my husband, Derrick, is a naturopath and I am a public health nurse. We all missed Mom terribly and needed to be together, so we closed the practice in Florence and opened up a new one in Coos Bay. Dad and I started a medicinal herb garden and I worked with Derrick in the office. In addition, Polly and I continued with the Women of Red Nations."

"What's that?" asked Rani.

"After the American Indian Movement began in the 1970's, this organization was started to unite Indian women all over the country. My mom and I became interested when Winona LaDuke, a member, was Ralph Nader's running mate in the 2000 election. We organize pow-wows; work with elders and youth of our local tribe, do organic gardening, drumming and connect with Native women all over the country to improve the overall quality of life for all indigenous people regardless of tribal affiliations."

Rani had just finished eating and noticed that Listie was just finishing. "It's already 6:00. Should we finish up here and continue with our plans for tomorrow here or go someplace else?" asked Rani.

"I think we could use one of the Conference meeting rooms," said Listie. "That way we can free up the table for other diners. I know the manager, and I'm sure she would let us in one for a couple more hours so we can continue talking in private." The host brought the bill just as Listie finished talking. "Why don't we settle with the server and you can stay in the lobby while I go and get the key?"

"Sounds great," said Rani. "But I need to go to my room and freshen up a bit in the bathroom, so I'll meet you back here about 6:30?"

"Sounds great," said Listie as she started walking toward the lobby.

Some modern facilities such as bathrooms aren't so bad thought Rani as she flushed the commode and washed her face and hands. She then organized the pile of brochures she had hurriedly dropped onto the bed, picked up her purse and a notebook and left to meet Listie. *We certainly have the same internal time clock*, thought Rani as she saw Listie entering the lobby to the restaurant just a few steps in front of her.

"We're in Conference Room A just around the corner there," said Listie pointing her head straight ahead and walking in that direction. Rani quickly locked steps with her.

The conference room was small, with a table and seating for about 10 people. Listie took a seat at the head of the table. "You can sit at this first seat here. I have some printed material you may want to read as we talk about tomorrow." Rani sat down and placed the notebook in front of her. She pulled a pen from her purse and then placed her purse in the seat next to her.

Listie showed her a picture of a well-groomed garden containing bright green rows of corn. "We'll be visiting these gardens tomorrow; these are the gardens of the Humetewa family of the snake clan. *Ankti* (repeat dance) Humetewa will be our guide. The Hopi are a matriarchal society, so the women do more of the planning and administration while the men do more of the actual farming."

"Do you know anything about the name *Ankti?*" asked Rani.

"It means repeat dance," said Listie. "Rain dancing is very important to the people of the Snake Clan, and snake dances to bring rain are done here every two years. Snakes are used because it is believed the snakes carry the prayers underground where the gods live. Climate change has resulted in a series of droughts that have affected the water tables in this area, and there is a desperate need for rain. In addition, fracking is releasing dirty sludge into the already limited supply of water for drinking and other household uses. This is another reason the Hopi believe we are close to the time of Convergence."

"I saw what looked like a group of elementary students working with an older woman showing them how to plant a garden in Kykotsmovi today," said Rani.

"Oh yes, those are programs run by the *Natwani Coalition* in all the schools to teach permaculture and dry farming techniques to the children. The Hopi think working with the young to transfer the ancient methods is the way of not only providing food but also teaching the ancient ways to the future generations," said Listie. "My people, the Mohawk, were part of the Iroquois Confederacy started by a great Peacemaker in the 11th Century; their teaching was much like the Hopi. Our Great Law of Peace stated that 'in our every endeavor, we must consider the impact upon the Seventh Generation.' We have started organic gardens on our lands in upstate New York and our ceremonies and connection to the earth are quite similar to what I have learned in the past week here. One of my distant cousins has a biodynamic garden that uses practices going back to the days of the Confederacy."

"I think this permaculture idea that I see in your book is quite similar to the methods used in my native country of Persia which was built in a desert area much like the American Southwest. I'm looking forward to tomorrow," said Rani as she stifled a yawn and closed the book Listie had given her.

"You've had a busy two days and I think you are ready for bed," said Listie.

"I think so. What time do you want to start tomorrow?"

"The afternoon sun can be intense so we need to get to the garden about 7:00 am; is that too early?"

"No, do you want to meet for a bite to eat about 6:30?"

"No need to do that. My host family will feed us while we are there. We will have breakfast, view the garden and see permaculture in action. We will be finished by lunch time. My husband, Derrick, is driving here from Kayenta Township to pick me up and take me back to our apartment there for another two weeks. Derrick has been working with other doctors to study chronic illnesses related to the dirty air and water in the area. I will help him file his reports after the research is complete to create awareness about the health dangers created by the Peabody Coal Company. We also want to be there when the United Nations Investigators visit the site," said Listie.

"Investigators from the United Nations? I have worked with my mother as a translator for the United Nations since 1993. That is the job I left when I decided to move here to work at Monument Valley High School. When are the investigators going to be there? I know the work of the UN Investigators and I would like to meet them."

"That should be any day now; I'm sure we can arrange for you to be there with us. Derrick and I will need to leave as soon as the investigators leave and we file the health reports. Derrick needs to get his practice going again, and I will need to get my herb garden going; Polly will be back in school as well by then."

"Let me know when the investigators arrive," said Rani. Here's my card with my new address in Kayenta Township and my email and phone number. If you email me, then I will have your information," said Rani.

Listie looked at Rani's card. "You must be our neighbor. Your address is in the same apartment complex as ours. That's no surprise; Kayenta is a small place." Listie put Rani's card in her purse and said, "Let's meet here at 6:30 tomorrow morning; we can walk to the garden from here. Be sure and wear pants and comfortable shoes."

"See you then," said Rani as she picked up her purse and joined Listie on the walk back to their rooms.

"I must write my mother and tell her about this dry farming," said Rani as she and Listie walked toward the bale house owned by the Humetewa family. The house was one of a few post and beam, straw bale, energy efficient homes built with the help of volunteers from the Red Feather Development Group. The lush gardens that surrounded the house contained rows of corn, beans, squash and melons. *Where did the water come from?*

Rani recalled the lecture from *Ankti* earlier in the day. "This area was founded in the 1870's as a summer farming area," said *Ankti*. "The land is irrigated from nearby springs. We dig deep holes to plant the seeds and do not plow the fields in order to keep the moisture in the dirt. We place wind breaks at intervals to retain moisture from the rain and snow. This is our harvest," said *Ankti* pointing to rows of corn, beans and melon. "We own the land, but everyone in the community works the fields and we share our produce."

"I can't wait to tell *Mama* about this," said Rani. "This is so much like what she has told me about ancient Persia and the land she knew when she lived there."

"We had better be on our way," said Listie as she thanked their host. "Derrick will probably be waiting for me at the Inn, and I'm sure you want to be on your way also."

"Thanks again," said Rani and the two walked the short mile to the Legacy Inn. Rani had already checked out and her car was packed. She planned on picking up some fruit and a sandwich before she left for Kayenta Township, so she walked inside the Travel Center with Listie.

"I don't see Derrick's car here yet," said Listie. "I think I'll give him a call." Just as she said that, her phone rang. "It's Derrick," she said.

Rani stopped as she heard Listie say, "What? I think I can get a ride there. Wait a minute."

"Rani, could you possibly give me a ride to meet Derrick at the Tuba City Police Headquarters?'

"Sure, but why?"

"Derrick's being held there for questioning in a murder investigation and I need to meet him there." Listie's eyes moistened and her hands were shaking.

Rani reached out and took Listie's hands into hers as she said, "no problem." Listie's hands relaxed and she smiled wanly as Rani reassured her. "I'll wait here while you check out and get your things. Listie felt a soothing calm wrap around her like a warm blanket on a chilly morning. *I feel so protected! Well, why not? After all, aren't we in the presence of the Kachina spirits?*

CHAPTER

5

Jeanette looked up from the videos she was studying when she heard the activity in the outer room. *Must be Josh Overton, the FBI man. I've heard some rumors, but they don't do him justice!* Jeanette couldn't help but stare at the tall man (about 6'3" at least) with the build of an NFL quarterback. She sheepishly turned her attention back to the videos from the Peabody Coal Company security cameras when she noticed George Yazzie looking in her direction.

Jeanette knew George was interested in her, but she couldn't quite bring herself to think seriously about any of the men who worked at the Tuba City Justice Center. Jeanette had known scores of men like him: she often joined her colleagues for pizza after work at the Pizza Edge in town. She sometimes drove to the Majerle's Sports Grill in Flagstaff on weekends, especially during football and basketball seasons.

Every Friday was the same – beer and pub food with loud talking over the games being shown on one of the large television screens there. She could hardly hear what was being said over the din of loud voices and laughter. She really didn't need to hear. It was all the same banter about the current status of Arizona's ball clubs combined with sexual innuendos in the hope of going back with her to her place at the end of the evening. How Jeanette wished she could find a man with some depth who liked good music, good books and an occasional trip to Flagstaff for a good dinner and movie. *An invitation to go hiking or rafting would be nice.* Jeanette sighed as she rehashed this silent conversation once again.

There was one man who didn't seem to be like the others - Robert Beneè.

Jeanette wanted to know what was going on behind those impenetrable dark eyes. Robert seemed to distance himself from any of the socializing after work and kept conversation limited to the task at hand. *Having someone like Josh Overton here for a while could certainly make things interesting.* Jeanette returned her attention to the videos.

"Any word about those videos?" The voice of Robert Beneè brought her back to the present.

"Just finishing the last one. I think there are some things Mr. Overton will want to see when he finishes with the briefings from the rest of the investigators."

"I'll let him know," said Robert. In five minutes Robert was back with a message. "Josh says to take your lunch break and he will get with you after that to look at the videos."

"Okay," said Jeanette as she turned off the machine and headed to the locker room to get her bag lunch. Curious about the man as well as the case, Jeanette found a seat in the back of the room to listen as Yazzie filled in Overton with the details of the murder while she ate. Overton had a file in front of him as he questioned Yazzie and the others while writing pertinent notes on a timeline on the murder board in front of them.

"Murder victim was a transient named Ole Jack?" he asked.

"That's right," said Yazzie as Josh placed a picture of the deceased on the board.

"Time of death?"

"Dr. Cameron says death occurred sometime between 12:00 and 1:00 am yesterday morning." Overton drew a horizontal line across the board and placed a vertical line near the end and marked 12:00 am, Wednesday, July 22nd. He would back track to fill in any information about the last hours of Ole Jack's life. Overton liked that part of the investigation. Always gave him an adrenaline rush much like the time just before the center hiked him the ball at the start of a play in football.

"Cause of death blunt force trauma to the back of the head?" asked Josh.

"That's right," answered Yazzie. "Evidently caused by that huge black cross you see in that picture there."

"Fingerprints?"

Robert Beneè answered. "We identified one set as belonging to the victim. There's another set that we are running through the data base system to find a match. Might get lucky. Could belong to some of the people we have coming in for questioning this afternoon. One possible match is a Dr. by the name of Derrick Stratton; he has been working in the area with some other doctors looking into breathing and cardiovascular disorders that the doctors think are related to carcinogens in the air around the coal mine." Beneè showed Josh a picture of Derrick Stratton. "This is a picture of Dr. Stratton involved in protest activities at the Navajo Nation's Kayenta site in New Mexico in 2010. See those black crosses in the background?"

"Yeah. Good work," said Josh as he placed Stratton's picture next to the picture of the black cross.

"Any DNA evidence?"

George Yazzie spoke up. "The only traces of DNA we found on the murder weapon belonged to the victim. There was some DNA on a brown feather we found at the scene. We've sent it off to be profiled to see if there is a match to DNA we have in the CODIS (Combined DNA Systems) at the Center for Disease Control."

"We'll need to start collecting DNA from all possible suspects. See if you can get a sample from Dr. Stratton when he comes in for questioning."

"Will do," said Yazzie. "We also swept the pick-up truck. Lots of smudged prints could belong to most anyone, but none of them matched the current suspects. Back of the truck was a mess; filled with cottonwood branches, dirty clothes and food garbage. Not much identifiable DNA.

"Anything else?"

"There are some videos from the security cameras that I think you will want to see," said Yazzie.

"Maybe I should go look at the videos now, before we go any further. Tell Robert to run background checks on Stratton and Munson and bring them to me ASAP. I may need some time to go over the files before I see them." Josh looked at his watch and said, "It's almost 1:00 now. Before I go over the files, I want to go and see those videos. Where's Alice?"

"Been a while since you've been here, Josh. Alice retired last year," said George. "Jeanette took her place," he said as he nodded toward the attractive red head seated near the back of the room."

Josh couldn't help but admire Jeanette's looks but he was a master of political correctness as he walked toward her. "I'm going to get a cup of coffee and I'll meet you in the viewing in about ten minutes? Would you like a cup also?"

"That would be nice," said Jeanette.

Josh noticed a slight flush as he said, "Sugar or cream?"

"Just two Splenda's."

"See you in about ten." Josh knew better than to say anything about her choice of sweetener. Josh was a juice man himself. His physical fitness training from his football years had not been forgotten. FBI agents had to keep themselves in top shape also – one of the requirements of the job, but Josh didn't mind. He enjoyed a burger and Mexican food, and he was a gourmet cook, but his daily fare when he could get it was a Middle Eastern diet supplemented with green juices. Josh always had his green juice available, especially when he was on an assignment. *Not a lot of variety here.* A good brew tasted good when he could get it, but bars and night spots were sparse in this region plagued by alcoholism.

Josh thought about Jeanette as he was preparing the coffee. *Easy conquest,* he thought. In his younger days he would have gone for the chase. His penchant for pursuit and conquest had destroyed his marriage. Josh had been a military brat who never spent more than 4 months in any one school during his formative years. As a result, he never really learned to form long term relationships. Josh was outgoing and made friends easily but long term relationships were not his forte. For Josh in his professional as well as personal life, it was about the pursuit; daily routines became tiresome very quickly. That's why he had become an agent; he enjoyed the danger and adventure while working a case.

Josh was tall and strong and built to be a quarterback. He had played football in high school and attended the Air Force Academy on a football scholarship. Josh loved everything about playing football from the excitement of the game to his celebrity status with desirable females. Josh's father had wanted him to follow in his footsteps and make a career of the air force, but Josh had trouble taking orders. He had opted for a career in criminal justice, working first doing background checks for the Office of Personnel at the Los Alamos National Laboratory in Los Alamos, New Mexico. That's where he had met his wife in 2000.

Emma was beautiful, with blonde hair and an athletic build. Both she and Josh enjoyed rock climbing and snow skiing and marriage seemed the right thing to do. Two years into the marriage, Josh was bored and needed a change of scenery. Emma wanted a baby, so the two compromised. Eli was born in 2003 just after Josh finished his FBI training and the couple moved to Flagstaff, Arizona. *One too many affairs* thought Josh.

Josh enjoyed the status of the FBI agent, the good looking, tough man who brought criminals to justice. Josh's presence in a local community created a stir like that of a rock star coming to town. Affairs were inevitable. For a while, Josh was able to keep his liaisons separate from his home life and Emma was able to deny the truth, although she knew what was happening. *Caroline brought it to an end*, he thought. She just wouldn't follow the rules. *Was it really Caroline or did I want Emma to know?* It didn't matter. The two were ready when the divorce was final in 2005, but Josh felt guilty about Eli. *Why can't I be like Chris?* Chris Parker was Emma's current husband. He and Emma had a daughter Julia and the blended family worked well – the typical all American family, with one exception. *Me*

Twelve year-old Eli seemed happy spending his time with his dad at his grandparents' home in Colorado Springs two weeks in the summer, alternate holidays and occasional three day weekends hiking or skiing with his dad. Josh loved Eli and wasn't jealous of Chris' relationship with his son, but after nine years of divorced life, Josh found himself envying the family lifestyle. The thrill of the chase was losing its charm. Josh put a lid on Jeanette's full coffee cup and thought; *do I even care enough to make an effort?* As he walked into the viewing room, he handed Jeanette her coffee. She had the tapes ready. "Let's see what we have," he said.

"This first video is the night of the murder about midnight. The only things visible are the shadows you see there behind that winch drum on the excavating crane. See how they seem to blink? The light just picked up the shadows; the drum hid the identity of the shadow."

Josh stood watching the video. "There, look at that," he said. "Rewind the video just a bit. See how the blinking stops there? Stop it here. Look at the time stamp." Josh wrote 12:33 in his notes. "That has to be the time of death. Start the video again.'

This time Jeanette stopped the video. She pointed to a triangular shadow at the edge of the drum. "See that?" she said.

"Zoom in on that if you can," said Josh. The two stared silently at the shape for a minute. "What do you make of that?" asked Josh.

"Making it larger has distorted it so much can't really tell," said Jeanette. "But take a look at this video. It's from a week before the murder." Jeanette started the new video. Everything seemed normal for the first few minutes then a giant shadow appeared in the corner of the screen. There was no excavator to conceal the giant bird figure that was responsible for the shadow.

"Stop the video here," said Josh. The figure that stared back appeared to be a giant, golden bald eagle. Josh could tell it wasn't really an eagle but a person dressed as one. The figure preened in front of the camera – obviously wanting to be seen, but all the time the face was concealed under a giant headdress. *Is this what Pete Munson had meant about strange sightings?* Josh turned away from the video and returned to the briefing room. "Where's Yazzie?" he asked.

Just then both George and Robert came into the room with files in their hands.

"He turned and addressed them both. "What do you have for me?" he asked.

"I finished running those prints through the data base and have something you might want to see," said George.

"What is it?" asked Josh.

"We got a match on those prints on the black cross. Belong to Dr. Derrick Stratton of Coos Bay, Oregon."

"Make him the first one to be interviewed," said Josh. "And get a DNA sample from him if he is willing."

"You'll need this also," said Robert handing him two files that contained information on both Dr. Stratton and Pete Munson.

"Thanks," said Josh taking the files. "I need you to do something else George," he said.

"What's that?"

"Run a check on the bald eagle and its relationship to the Kachina cult."

Robert shivered upon hearing this as though a chill had run up his spine. *First time I ever saw any kind of response from Robert,* thought Jeanette. *What does that mean?*

Neither Josh nor George noticed anything as George responded with, "will do."

Josh placed the file on the desk in the interview room and sat down across from Pete Munson.

"Need to ask you some questions, Pete," said Josh.

"Sure, but don't know how I can help. Didn't know anything about this Ole Jack."

"Never met him at all?" asked Josh.

"I do remember seeing him one day at The Blue Coffee. Went there for a birthday celebration for Eric Halverson, the excavator operator. Jack was there; been drinkin' as usual. Started talkin' trash 'bout the mine. Said greedy corporate bastards needed to stop destroying the land. One of the mine bosses, Luther, got pretty riled. Got in Jack's face. Told him to shut up. Lives were better all-around because of the mine. Jack called him a corporate whore. That's when he got hit. Owner came over, broke it up. Told Jack to leave; he'd had enough. 'This is a family operation. Go sleep it off,' he said. Told everyone to sit down, relax and enjoy the party."

"Where is this Luther?"

"Workin'. He works first shift."

"I'll need to question him, probably do that when I go to the mine. Let him know I'm coming tomorrow when he reports for work. He may know something about Ole Jack's red pick-up truck also." Josh wrote himself a note and then said, "So, that's the only time you ever had anything to do with Jack?"

"Yeah, just that one time. You might want to talk to more of the men than just Luther when you come to the mine," he said. "No one really knew Ole Jack, but the men who frequented The Blue Coffee Pot probably know as much as anyone."

"What about these strange sightings you mentioned when you talked to George Yazzie?"

"Oh, yeah, those. Security guy told me something about some strange doin's at night. Noises like eagle or hawk calls. When he went to investigate, saw some Kachina lookin' "spirit" dancing around in front of the building. Disappeared before he had a chance to get close to it."

"What's the security guy's name?"

"Charles Chee."

"I'll need to talk to him also. Now, what about these black crosses?"

"Few years ago a group of doctors started studying the quality of health in areas with active coal mines. Big protest movement. One doctor, Dr. Stratton, from Coos Bay, Oregon joined the Black Cross Alliance. That group went around placing crosses all over the country where Peabody Coal Company was active. Came to the Southwest in 2010 and placed crosses and protested in front of the Navajo Nation's Kayenta Coal operation in New Mexico. Lots of ill will because protests had already been successful closing the Black Mesa mining operation in 2005.

This Dr. Stratton is married to a woman whose ancestors were part of the Coquille Nation on the Oregon Coast and the two returned here this summer. His wife is investigating farming practices in Upper Moenkopi Village, and Dr. Stratton's been working in a clinic with another doctor doing more research about these health issues. People upset and think he might start something to shut down the Kayenta Operation."

"You think he had something to do with the black cross found at the murder scene?" asked Josh.

"Most likely. Nosey fellow and pushy too."

"I'll be talking to him after we finish here," said Josh. "What about the United Nations people?"

"Got word that a group is here to look into the source of some sacred Hopi artifacts that landed in Paris. Tryin' to find out where they came from and how they got to Paris. Chief Ranger Nat'aanii is coming back from New York with two United Nations delegates. They'll be lookin' round the mine site sometime on Friday. We dig up a lot of overburden to get the coal. Think there could be some involvement there and maybe even more artifacts." Pete pulled out a couple of antacids from a tin in his jacket pocket. "Got an ulcer and all this ain't helpin'. Are you finished?"

"That's all for now. I want to come to the site tomorrow and talk to this Luther fella and any other men you think might have knowledge of Ole Jack and what he was doing the day before the murder. I'd like to talk to the people from the UN as well. Something came up on one of the videos from the security cameras and I think they may be interested."

Pete coughed as though disturbed by what he had just heard. "Stay close to home. I'll see ya tomorrow." Pete hurried out and almost ran into Derrick Stratton on the way; the doctor was following Robert Beneè to the interviewing room. Robert handed a file to Josh as he ushered Dr. Stratton in and told him to take a seat.

Derrick Stratton did not look his age. He was obviously close to Josh's age but his red, curly hair and freckles across his nose made him appear younger. *This man may be an activist but he doesn't appear to be a murderer,* thought Josh. Years of interviews had honed Josh's instincts. *Maybe Pete Munson, but not this man.* Once again, however, Josh put on his police investigator's hat that said "everyone's a suspect." Dr. Stratton, you are here for questioning only at the moment. We are at the beginning stages of the investigation into the murder of a transient named Ole Jack at the Kayenta Coal Mining Operation in Kayenta Township. You're here because the murder weapon was a black cross and we found your fingerprints on the cross. We also found some DNA evidence on a brown feather found near the victim. That's why you were asked for a swab of your mouth. Thank you for cooperating."

"No problem," said Derrick.

"Can you tell me where you were between 12 and 1 am on July 22nd?" asked Josh.

"Well, like most people, I was in bed asleep in the apartment I am renting in Kayenta Township."

"Can anyone verify that? I understand you are here with your wife."

"Unfortunately, my wife has been in the Upper Moenkopi Village for a week observing permaculture techniques of the Hopi people who live there."

"That is unfortunate. Did you know Ole Jack?"

"Yes. I met him when he came to the clinic last month complaining of chest congestion."

"Did you treat him?"

"I work with a licensed medical doctor who supports the use of herbs and alternative methods of treating illnesses. Dr. Baker diagnosed the problem as COPD (Chronic Obstructive Pulmonary Disease) and I assisted with providing herbal remedies."

"Did he prescribe anything besides the herbs?"

"Dr. Baker is Dr. Eleanor Baker. No, she always starts with natural remedies and only uses pharmaceuticals if symptoms persist."

"Excuse me. Did Ole Jack get better?"

"Yes, he responded to the herbal treatments, but the overall prognosis was not good. Lots of damage that was probably irreversible. Dr. Baker and I concluded that his illness was due to a history of heavy drinking and smoking exacerbated by chronic exposure to dirty air and water around the mining area. When Ole Jack discovered this, he became angry. I told him he bore some responsibility for the drinking and smoking, but there were numerous people including children who were exhibiting the same symptoms directly related to dirty air and water. I told him we were working to help clean up the air and water and raise awareness to alleviate the suffering. He became very curious and started asking a lot of questions. That's when I told him about the black crosses. Asked if he could have one so I told him to come over to my apartment and I would give him one; I guess he was attempting to plant the cross when he was killed."

"What else do you know?"

"That's about it," said Derrick.

"When's the last time you saw Ole Jack?"

"When he came to my apartment two days ago to get the cross."

"Did he say anything to you about the fight he had with a mine boss at The Blue Coffee Pot?"

"Yeah. When protestors get together they usually share war stories."

"Did Ole Jack indicate he was afraid for any reason?"

"No. Protestors usually have a sense of danger. We both believed that Luther was impulsive – mob anger and alcohol come to mind; Jack said he had been drinking as well. Luther might have killed him in the moment but not likely a cold blooded murderer."

Robert Beneè came into the room. "I sent the bird feather to CODIS (Combined DNA Systems) to run a profile and look for a possible match. Might be a while before the results come back," said Beneè. "Stratton's wife is also here, waiting outside." Josh looked through the open door and saw two women. For a moment he forgot all about the DNA results. *Which one's his wife? Hope it's not the dark skinned woman.*

"We're almost finished. Tell her to sit down. Offer her some tea or coffee and tell her Dr. Stratton will be out shortly."

"Okay," said Robert as he closed the door behind him. Josh felt a surge of excitement he hadn't felt in a long time. *Calm down. You don't even know which one is the wife.*

Once again, Josh gave no indication of any emotion as he said, "you can go home, but stay close. I know you are not local, but you may not leave the area until you are told you are free to go. You are still a person of interest in this case." *Not even interested in the DNA test.* Josh's instincts told him this man was innocent.

"Thank you," said Derrick as he walked into the waiting area. Josh smiled briefly when he saw who rushed to the doctor with a concerned look and embrace. *I can't make a case for him as a murderer. Wonder who that other woman is?* After a few words that looked as though Derrick's wife was introducing him to the dark skinned woman, his wife stayed with her husband while the other woman walked to Robert Beneè. Josh heard her ask if she could have a little more tea. Derrick and his wife walked to an empty corner and began using their hands as though communicating in sign language.

Josh walked up to the dark haired beauty and said, "Josh Overton, I'm the chief investigator in this case. Could I ask how you know Dr. Stratton?"

"I actually just met him. I met his wife Listie when I was visiting the permaculture gardens in Upper Moenkopi. Derrick was supposed to pick her up there because he had the car. When he called, Listie asked me if I could drop her off here before I continued to Kayenta Township."

"Oh," said Josh. *No reason to hold her anymore. That feels a little depressing.* "Is that sign language the two are using?"

"Yes," said Rani.

"Do you know sign?"

"I do."

"What are they saying?"

"Mr. Overton, you are overstepping your bounds. I will not help you eavesdrop on what is obviously a private conversation."

Josh had never felt so awkward with a woman in his life. *You blew it Dude.*

CHAPTER

6

Josh was still kicking himself over his faux pas in Tuba City as he drove along Highway 160 toward the Kayenta Coal Mine. *Stop stewing! You'll probably never see her again. But she did say she was on her way to Kayenta Township. Come on! Get your mind on the job, Dude.* Josh parked the car in the lot that said *Visitor's Only*, grabbed his files and walked toward the mine's office. There was a lot of noise coming from the hilly area that surrounded the mine. Josh looked up and saw a huge excavator's claw digging into the dark soil on the side of the Black Mesa. He stood and watched as the soil was dropped into a large pile below. He noticed a black seam of coal that was revealed once the overburden had been discarded.

"If you stand there, you'll need to wear a hard hat!" said a voice near the entrance to the mine office. It was a security guard. Josh started walking toward the door. He flashed his FBI badge to the guard. Are you Charles Chee by any chance?"

"No, he comes on at 7:00 pm."

"Okay, can you show me where Pete Munson is?"

"He's just inside near the break room. He's expecting you. Go right through this door; you'll see him."

Josh walked in and saw Pete standing in front of the coffee counter of what was obviously a break room. He was ready for Josh.

"It's almost break time," said Pete. "The men you need to question will be in the break room in about 15 minutes. You want a cup of coffee?"

"Sure," said Josh.

"Help yourself. The pot's over on the counter by the door to the break room. Everything you need." Pete then turned as though he were in a rush to get somewhere.

"I'll need you to stay also. I want to talk with you after these interviews."

"Okay, but can I go take care of this one thing and come back? You won't need to talk to me until you finish with the men, right?"

Josh really wanted Pete to be there for the entire session, but didn't think he had the authority to hold him without more than a suspicion that he had not been entirely truthful during the first interview. "Sure," said Josh. "By the way, I'll need to talk to that crane operator also. Was that the man I saw working the crane when I came in?"

"Yeah. He works a little different schedule than these men. Can you wait until after he finishes his shift to talk to him? We're on a schedule here."

"What time does he get off?"

"Four o'clock."

"Well, when I finish with you and these guys, I'll be ready to talk with Mr. Halverson. If I finish early I'll wait for him. Have him come to the break room."

"All right," said Pete. *Was that a disgruntled sigh?*

Overton kept his stoic FBI face in place as he sat down to wait for the men.

Just then, he heard a whistle followed by a group of men dusting off their clothes and taking off their miner's hats as they walked to the coffee counter. He saw Pete Munson hurrying outside from the corner of his eye.

"You the FBI man we need to talk to?" The voice brought his attention back to the current situation.

"That's right," said Josh. "Get your coffee and have a seat and I'll try to make this as quick as possible. One of you named Luther here yet?"

"That'd be me," said a dirty-faced man about 40 years old. Josh thought he might be younger, but the hollow eyes and tight wrinkles around his mouth made him appear tired and angry.

"I'd like to talk to you and all the others about the altercation you had with Ole Jack a few days before the murder."

"You mean fight don't ya," blurted out one of the men.

"Seems there was a lot more yelling than hitting according to Pete Munson," said Josh.

"Ole Jack took a mean upper cut and he laid a good one on Luther before the owner separated them," said the same man.

"None of you wanted to stop the fight?" asked Josh.

"Naw," we would 'a if we thought there was serious danger, but didn't 'pear to be."

"So you think both parties were just letting off a little drunken steam?"

"Yeah," said another man. "Ole Jack wasn't the only one who had been drinking. We're all pretty uptight over these damn, nosey people interfering with our livelihood. Not much work in these parts of the country and minin' is good pay."

"Any one of you upset enough to kill over?" asked Josh.

"Hell, we wouldn't kill Ole Jack. More likely we'd kill the nosey people, but no job's worth goin' to prison or the gas chamber over."

"That about sum it up for you, Luther?"

"Sure does. I ain't no murderer."

"Where were you between 12:00 and 1:00 am this morning?"

"Sittin' in our monthly poker game at Estle's house. His wife spends every Tuesday night with her sick mother, so we all go to Estle's for a poker game."

"Who's Estle?"

"That'd be me and I can vouch for that," said a man sitting at the table next to Luther. Several men shook their heads in agreement.

"Okay," said Josh as he wrote down the alibi in his notes. "What else can any of you tell me about Ole Jack? Anyone see him the night before he was killed?"

"I saw him in that ole pick-up of his about 6:00 pm," said Estle. "He always kept it parked behind the Golden Sands when he was here peddlin' his cottonwood. He'd been here 'bout a week. Heard he was sick and went to see the doctor after he arrived. That was 'bout three days ago. After he got back from the doc's he wasn't feelin' too good. When I saw him at 6:00 he was sound asleep in the back."

"Anyone else see him?"

"Think I saw him later that same evening. He was drivin' in the direction of the mine around 9:00. Wondered where he was off to. Not too much business for cottonwood that time of night." A spurt of light laughter filled the room.

"Well, I guess that's all for now. If you think of anything more, I'll be leaving my card with Pete Munson. I don't think I have to tell you to stay close until the investigation is over." The men finished their coffee, stood up, put on their mining hats and walked away. *Wonder where Pete Munson is?* Josh walked to the door leading to the back. Just as he started to walk outside, he saw Pete Munson engaged in conversation with the crane operator, Eric Halverson. As he walked toward the two, the conversation stopped abruptly. Pete turned and said, "You ready to talk to me now?"

"Sure, what about Halverson?"

"Can't let him go right now. I was just telling him where to take the crane. He needs to finish up a section today."

"All right. Let's go talk. What time is it?"

"'Bout 3:30."

"That should be enough time to finish with you before I talk to Halverson. Let him know to wait in the break room when he finishes his shift."

"Will do," said Munson. "Wait here and then I will take you up to my office where we can talk in private." Josh turned and walked toward the entrance to wait until Munson finished with Eric Halverson.

Nice digs! Thought Josh as Munson directed him to a chair he placed in front of a huge mahogany desk. Josh sat down, put his tablet containing a note pad on his lap and took a pen from the pouch inside the cover. Josh noticed a picture of a woman with a dog and two other pictures. One picture was of a female about 23 receiving what appeared to be a college diploma. The other was of an adolescent in a high school football uniform. The athlete was wearing his football jersey with the school logo on the front. The deep pink letter M was placed on top of the letter V. The letters were inside an elliptical shape that resembled a football.

Josh opened the discussion talking about the pictures. He knew how to establish rapport with those he interviewed. *Talking about family breaks the ice.* "These family members?" asked Josh.

"Yes, that's my wife Darleen with our chocolate lab Daisy. The two are almost inseparable. Nobody else can take care of Daisy if she's the least bit cranky."

"And the young woman?"

"That's my daughter Caroline. Just graduated from Arizona State with a degree in environmental studies. Makes for some interesting conversation around the dinner table. She works for the EPA in Phoenix."

"That degree must have set you back a pretty penny."

"Sure did. My children have to make their own way. Don't have the government handing out money to them left and right."

"Ever cause any family conflict over her job and yours?"

"There's some tension now and then, but we just agree to disagree and try to keep our jobs separate from family life."

Josh changed the subject. "And the boy?"

"That's my son, Jason. Star football player. He's bein' scouted by coaches from schools all over the Southwest. His colleg'll be paid for. Then maybe a career with the NFL. We can dream big."

"What do the letters stand for?" asked Josh still keeping the conversation light as though this were just small talk.

"Monument Valley," where he goes to high school. Name of the team's the Mustangs."

Monument Valley, where have I heard that before? Josh's face once again gave no clue to any thought other than the answer to his question as he said, "nice family," while writing college loans on his pad with the notation – *family debt?* Without missing a beat, he continued as if nothing pertinent to the investigation had been said during the small talk. "After talking with the men who were at the bar the night of the fight, I have just a couple of follow-up questions with you."

"Okay, what do you need to know?"

"You said the get together involved a birthday celebration for the crane operator Eric Halverson. I find it strange that he didn't get involved in the argument between Luther and Ole Jack. You told Ranger Yazzie that Halverson was 'pretty pissed off' over the closing of the other Black Mesa operation in 2005. Seems odd that he wouldn't have been part of the argument."

"Oh, Eric's that way. He has feelings about things but he keeps to himself. Don't want to get involved in it one way or the other. He talks to me 'bout it 'cause I hired him, but he don't go 'round mouthin' off like the rest of the miners."

"That makes sense. But did you two ever discuss what might happen to this operation if these doctors and the Black Cross Alliance start stirring up more trouble here?"

Josh wrote "*squirming a little*" in his notes as Munson answered. It took him a while to frame a response, as though he were trying to remember dialogue from a script in a play. "Well, of course, you know, we may have like discussed these things. Everyone here who, you know, depends on this operation for their livelihood is going to discuss things. But Eric and I don't socialize that much and we have too much to talk about during the work day to take time for theorizing about it."

"Oh," said Josh as he wrote *no socializing yet goes to a birthday celebration. Need to ask the owner about that birthday party.*

"Now about these strange sightings? What exactly do you know about that?"

"Well, about a week ago, the security guard, Charles, came to me after his shift and reported some noises that he went to investigate. Didn't see anything when he went out, but when I had Maria play the video from the security cameras the next day we saw this giant figure that appeared to be a man dressed as an eagle, you know the way those Kachina people dress for their dances?"

"What was the figure doing?"

"Dancing like they do in their ceremonies like it was trying to get the help of the eagle to protect the Mesa against the giant claws of the excavator. Lot 'o nonsense if you ask me."

"Do you have any idea who might have been wearing the costume?"

"Could be any of those Kachina dancers. They keep everything secret and they never appear in public without their masks. That's 'bout all I know. Don't get involved with the local people aside from the mine workers."

"Know anything about the eagle costume?" asked Josh.

Pete took a sip of his coffee before answering. "Well, these people worship nature and use birds in their dances. Don't know anything about any significance. Don't want to either." Pete leaned back in his chair and placed his hands over his head. "Anything else?"

"Yes, where were you between 12 and 1 am on the morning of the murder?"

"In bed, with my wife."

"She can corroborate that if I ask?"

Pete leaned forward to grab his coffee again and said, "Sure."

"Is there a number where she can be reached?" Pete wrote his wife's cell phone number down on some office stationary and handed it to Josh. Josh put the number in his file and said, "I'll have one of the men in the office call and confirm. That's all for now," he said as he stood up to go. Josh looked at his watch. "It's 4:05. Halverson should be ready by now."

"Just go back down to the break room. I'm sure if he isn't already there, he'll be there shortly." Munson shook hands with Josh and opened the door for him. *Hands are a bit wet. Maybe it's the coffee.* Josh pulled out his phone and pulled up Robert Beneè's number. "Robert, I need you to run a background check on two people, Eric Halverson and Luther Samson. Also, call this number. That is Pete Munson's wife. Need you to confirm his alibi for the time of the murder."

"Okay. I have the information on that eagle costume you requested."

"I'll want to look at that first thing tomorrow morning. I'm finishing up with Eric Halverson now and won't be back at the Center until tomorrow. Those UN investigators will be there Friday afternoon, right?" Josh heard a muffled sound as though Robert had covered the phone while speaking to someone in the background.

"Yazzie says they're supposed to be in Tuba City by noon and plan on driving out to the mine site after that."

"Just have everything ready for me when I get there tomorrow morning. I want to review all the information with you and Yazzie before those investigators arrive. I'm going back to the mine this evening to talk with Charles Chee, the security guard. May be that the eagle information is something the U.N. people will want to see. Do we have an address on the owner of The Blue Coffee Pot? It it's not too late I want to talk with him on my way back. After speaking with a lot of the people involved, I really don't think I'll learn much from him, though."

Josh heard some background noise like the shuffling of papers. "Here it is," said Robert. "Turns out he lives just behind the restaurant."

"Great," said Josh.

As he was checking his GPS for the address he heard Robert say, "Anything else?"

"No, I'll see you about 9:00 tomorrow morning. I want to go over everything you and Yazzie have, including alibi confirmations, any backgrounds checks etc., as well as the eagle thing and compare them with my notes from today. See you tomorrow morning."

"I'll tell Yazzie and we'll be ready for you then. Good-bye."

"Bye." Josh turned off his phone and walked toward the break room. There was a stocky, muscular man with dark hair pouring a cup of coffee. *Must be Halverson.*

"You Eric Halverson?" asked Josh as he flashed his FBI badge.

"That's right," said Eric while he stirred some creamer into his coffee.

"Let's go in and sit down so we can have a talk. I'm Josh Overton the lead investigator in the death of a man named Ole Jack on the morning of the 22nd. The body was found under the winch drum of the excavator that I'm told you operate. I need to ask you some questions if you don't mind."

"Shoot," said Halverson. "But don't know if I can be of much help."

"How well did you know Ole Jack?"

"Well, like most of us who live and work around here, couldn't not know Ole Jack. Character was a transient who drove pretty much all over the Hopi Mesas and the Navajo Reservation selling those cottonwood branches. Kept to himself unless he was doing business or eating' at The Blue Coffee Pot. Slept in his truck that he parked behind that restaurant that closed a few years ago. Anyone who seen him couldn't help but notice how much he drank, but he was nice enough."

"Know anything about his connection to the Black Cross Alliance?" Halverson straightened up, took a sip of his coffee before answering.

"Well, I knew some people connected with that group were here stirrin' up some more trouble like they did in New Mexico and the operation further south. But this is the first I've heard about Ole Jack working' with them."

"What about the footage from the security camera videos that captured a huge eagle dancing around your excavator?"

"Well, yes, I heard some talk from Maria and Charles Chee the security guard, but that's all, just rumors and speculations."

Did he almost spill his coffee? "Didn't talk to anyone directly about that?"

"Can't say as I did." Eric drank the rest of his coffee and put the empty cup in front of him.

"What about these United Nations Investigators?"

"Well, yeah, you know, news like that spreads and this is a small community. I know they are coming here to look for information about the return of some sacred Indian artifacts that have ended up in Paris?" Eric said this as though he were asking a question rather than making a statement.

"Yes, that's about the jist of it. Know anything else?"

"No, can I go now?"

"Just need to ask you about the altercation at The Blue Coffee Pot on the day of your birthday party."

"Wasn't really a party. Workmen usually get together for lunch and have cake when one of us has a birthday during the week. Ole Jack was almost always at The Blue Coffee Pot when he was in town. Men knew him and his drinkin' habits. He usually kept to himself and didn't socialize much, but that day, he seemed angry and had to start mouthing off 'bout the mine. Most of us, 'cept Luther just ignored him. I'm afraid Luther had been drinking a little also; he's scared he's going to lose his job. Wife's pregnant again with their fifth child and she doesn't work. Not much work for anyone except what the mine offers and Luther blew up. Never saw Ole Jack after that. This about over?"

"Almost. Where were you between 12 and 1 am yesterday? That's the time of the murder."

"I guess I had just gotten home. I went to Estle's poker party, but I left around 11 because I had work the next day and didn't want to be hung over operating that excavator."

"Anyone corroborate that?"

"Unfortunately, no. I live alone. I have a girlfriend but we only see one another on weekends. Need a good night's sleep, if you know what I mean." Eric actually smiled for the first time. Josh returned his smile as he wrote, *story sounds reasonable* in his notes. "Can I go now?"

"That's all for now, but you know you are a person of interest along with many others in this case, so don't leave the area."

"Not much chance. Work every day and too tired on weekends to drive two hours to find a good time," said Eric as he stood up, threw his empty cup in the trash can by the door and walked out. Josh took a few minutes to organize his file as he looked at his watch, *5:30. Someone mentioned a place called the Pizza Edge. I think I'll go grab a pizza there and come back to speak with Chee.* Josh was getting directions on his phone as he walked toward the door. *Was that Eric Halverson walking upstairs? Wonder where he is going?*

It was 6:15 when Josh pulled into the parking lot of the Peabody Coal Company. He picked up the box with a small pizza; a juice bottle filled with green juice and his notebook, locked his SUV and headed toward the mining office. Josh was filled with a sort of nervous energy that had very little to do with the upcoming interview. *You're acting like a nervous school boy! Get your mind back on the job, Man! You've never let a woman get in the way of your work before.* Josh shook his head to free the image of a beautiful woman smiling discreetly at him behind Derrick Stratton and took a deep breath. As he felt his cool, calm investigator's energy return, Josh saw Charles Chee standing inside the kiosk at the entrance to the coal company.

Now focused on work again, Josh walked toward the outside security kiosk where two men were standing inside engaged in conversation. They both wore gray uniforms with the insignia of Peabody Coal Company on the shoulder. Each wore a thick black belt with an attached holster for a gun. Josh noticed the name Charles Chee on the pocket of a red skinned man about 50 or 55 with straight dark hair and eyes. Josh put his pizza on the window ledge, flashed his badge and looked at Charles Chee.

"You the guard on duty the night of the murder?" He asked.

"Sure am. Told you wanted to see me before I start my shift. Let's go inside and get this over. You can leave now Carl," he said. "I work from the inside after the front gate closes," he said as walked in front of Josh, opened the door and ushered him into the front lobby. "I work inside here," he said leading Josh behind a table with an inner area enclosed by the table and four large television monitors behind.

As Josh took the seat indicated by Chee, he said, "I'm here to question you about two things. First, were you on duty when Ole Jack was murdered?"

"I hear the murder took place about 12:30 am on Wednesday so I would have been on duty."

"Where were you at the time?"

"Well, right here where I'm sitting," he said. "I sit here and watch the television screens that are hooked up to four cameras, three that cover the hallways of each floor and one that feeds from the outside. Unless I see or hear something unusual I don't get up and investigate. This screen here transmits from an outside motion camera that moves back and forth to sweep the area. The other three cover each of the hallways on all three floors. It's important that I keep an eye on all areas, so I don't get up much. I eat my dinner sitting here. Sometimes I go to the bathroom, but that's about it. The night of the murder I didn't see anything unusual on the cameras and didn't hear the noises that I had been hearing for about a week, so I was sitting here probably eating my dinner about that time."

"So, you didn't hear any noises that night?"

"No, but you probably know about a week ago I reported some strange noises that I went to investigate. Sounded like a bird of some kind. When I went outside I didn't see anything, but the next day, we saw this strange figure dancing in front of the cameras. I think the noises were made before the figure started dancing. In the video it looked like the figure was performing for the cameras. It was almost like he wanted to get noticed. I'm sure you've seen the video."

"Yes, I have. I'm here to see if you can give me any more information than we already have."

"Fraid I can't. What I told the bosses is all I know."

"Did you know Ole Jack?"

"Who didn't? I knew who he was when I saw him. Heard the rumors but never spoke to him at all."

"Ever see him at The Blue Coffee Pot?"

"Sometimes I would go there for breakfast after my shift. Too early for him then. I was asleep by the time he would come in to eat. Made it hard to see him there. I did see him drivin' around in his pick-up truck and saw the truck parked behind the Golden Sands but that's about all the contact I ever had with him."

"Did you see Jack's pick-up truck anywhere close to the mine before you started your shift on the night before the murder?"

"Don't recall seeing it. Just the usual things. Saw the SUV that the park rangers drive somewhere around 6:30 that evening, but that's not unusual. They do patrols around the area sometimes at night to make sure there's nothing screwy being done. Sometimes get poachers and graffiti artists and so forth who want to destroy the land."

Josh wrote, *check with rangers about patrol car in the area* in his notebook before closing it and standing up. "I guess that about does it then. We'll be back and forth investigating and if you think of anything, call me at this number," he said, handing Charles his card.

"Okay, I'll follow you out so I can lock the door behind you."

"Thanks," said Josh as he put his trash in the receptacle by the door and walked out in front of the security guard.

"Good luck," said Chee as he closed the door and locked it. Josh was tired. It had been a long day. He looked at his watch. *7:10 still light. Enough time to try to catch that restaurant owner. Another long day.* Josh sighed, unusual for him when working a case. He hardly ever slept or considered the time. This was the kind of thing he relished. He felt a surge of adrenaline. *Good. Thought I was getting too old for this. Needed that surge. Need to stay focused, stay in the case until it is resolved.* In the back of his mind, however, Josh felt a slight urge to get away from the case for a while. *Maybe I can take some time on Saturday to take a hike. Must be lots of good places to hike around here. I'll ask the owner about that. Hear he is Navajo. Wish I had someone to hike with.* He thought of Emma. *Regret for what might have been?* The female he pictured in his mind was not a blonde, however, but the raven haired beauty he had just seen at the Pizza Edge.

CHAPTER

7

How did this happen? wondered Rani as she walked to her car after saying good-bye to Listie and Derrick. *What does all this mean? I feel as though I'm in an episode of the Twilight Zone. Hurled from a quiet little detour before beginning my adjustment to a new situation into a full-fledged mystery involving people I never knew last week. And that Josh Overton! Why can't I forget about him?*

Back on Highway 264 driving toward Kayenta Township, Rani felt her sense of calm returning. Surely, Derrick's role in this murder would be settled quickly and he would be cleared of any involvement. She would be seeing Listie and Derrick one more time before Derrick took Listie to Flagstaff for her flight back to Coos Bay. *Wonder how much longer Derrick will be here?* She knew she would continue the relationship with both even after Derrick returned to Coos Bay. Rani had felt a connection with Listie that would be long term no matter how long the murder investigation lasted. *Probably will be settled by the time I start to school next week. Why does that unsettle me so?*

Rani had to report to work on Monday, July 27th, only four days away. Somewhere at the edge of her conscious mind, there was a feeling emerging and Rani couldn't quite wrap her mind around it. Despite trying to deny it, the feeling involved a handsome FBI agent that she would probably never see again. Lost in confused, silent dialogue, the seventy-five mile drive from Tuba City to Kayenta was over before she knew it. Rani looked at her watch; it was almost 12:30. *Maybe I should get something to eat.* Rani pulled over and checked her phone to find a suitable place to eat. *The Blue Coffee Pot – one review.*

"Good home cooked food, reasonably priced. Very popular with locals. Rani set her GPS and followed the directions to a blue and gray geometric building at the intersection of Highways 160 and 163. The parking lot around the huge sign that said *The Blue Coffee Pot* was indeed full. The bright sun illuminated the rich, red sandstone rock formations that surrounded the back of the building. As usual, Rani created a stir from the diners, mostly male. *Look like utility workers and miners along with Navajo ranchers.* There were also some who looked like tourists finishing up their vacations before heading back home for the start of the school year. A young girl who looked like she might be someone's daughter greeted her with a menu and silverware in her hand. She asked, "How many?"

"Just one," said Rani as she followed the host to a small table next to a window with a great view of the Valley.

"Can I get you something to drink?"

"Water with no ice and some lemon, please," said Rani.

"Sure thing," said the young girl as she turned and walked back to the serving area.

A man returned with her water. He was the owner of the restaurant, probably Navajo. "My name's Oscar Yellowtail. I own this place. Are you traveling through," he asked?

"No, I'm starting a job at Monument Valley High School on Monday. I will be working with the blind and deaf students as well as teaching sign language and doing interpretations for public gatherings. I'm from New York City where I worked for the United Nations. I am fluent in English, Farsi, Spanish, Tewa and most recently have started studying Navajo in connection with my move here."

The owner's face lit up at the mention of United Nations. "You connected with those investigators coming out here on Friday?"

"No, but it seems my arrival has coincided with an unusual amount of activity here. Seems there was a murder at the Coal Company yesterday morning?"

"How'd you know about that?"

"I happened to meet a woman in Upper Moenkopi Village who was studying dry farming techniques. Her husband had some connection to the man that was murdered and she needed a ride to the Justice Center in Tuba City. I took her there since it was on my way here. Maybe you know them Listie and Derrick Stratton?”

“Oh, yeah. Know the man better than the wife. He’s part of that clinic that is doing the health studies related to the air and water, right?”

“That’s what I learned; I left Derrick and Listie in Tuba City. I’m on my way to my apartment now to get settled and then I’ll start school on Monday.”

“Maybe you’ll see my daughter Lillian there. She’s the one who seated you. Works in the restaurant during the summer, but she’s going to be a senior this fall. Wants to get a culinary arts degree and work as a chef. What can I get for you?”

“I think I’ll try the Navajo taco. Looks interesting.”

“It’s one of our most popular dishes along with the blue corn pancakes. How about a short stack?”

“Think I’ll wait on that,” said Rani as she handed him the menu. “I’ll have a little more water if you don’t mind.”

“Lillian, come get the lady more water,” said Oscar as he took the menu and walked away.

Rani was lost in thought studying the dark red, pink and white sandstone formations outside the window of the restaurant. A voice brought her back to the present. “Your order, Miss.” It was Lillian.

“Oh, I was just lost in the view. I can’t get over the colorful landscapes that seem so untouched by modern civilization. It’s like going back in time.”

“I guess you could say that. We native people have a saying, ‘learning how to walk in two worlds.’”

“What does that mean?” asked Rani.

“It is hard to explain in a few words,” said Lillian. “At one time where we live now was one world and it belonged to our people. We have had to learn to live with the loss of our land, language and way of life for over 500 years now. What little land we have left and the oral histories that have survived is all that is left of that world. Assimilation into the European culture has cost us a lot, and we are struggling to hold onto what is left while trying to make our lives better through education and participation in the larger culture. Living with the memories of what was lost and trying to preserve what little is left is like a ghost that haunts us and keeps us trapped between "heaven and hell" so to speak. Walking in two worlds. If you are going to be at the high school, you will learn more about this."

"I look forward to that. I have already started studying Navajo and hope to continue while I am working in the high school. I've also been trying to learn more by getting here a little early in order to visit the Hopi villages. I lived in Albuquerque, New Mexico from the time I was five until I moved to New York in my twenties. After we had to leave Iran, my mother and I came to New Mexico to live with my aunt and her husband. We are all Iranian by birth and the tribal life of the pueblo people living in New Mexico is quite similar to that of Iran."

"I don't know much about Iran except that there is a lot of terrorism there."

"Iran has changed from the ancient Persia that was at the crossroads between Europe and Asia. During its time, the arts flourished and there was religious freedom, but we were ruled by a royal dynasty that controlled the economy as well as the people. In addition to this, after the overthrow of the dynasty we still did not have control of the one industry that has made others quite rich, oil. All the fighting for control of the region by foreigners has led to two puppet governments of two different Shahs supported by the West. These governments were very harsh to the common people and hatred and distrust of the West developed as a result. This led to the Revolution of 1979 that overthrew the second Shah. After the overthrow the moderate Parliament allowed the Ayatollah Khomeini to return from exile back to Iran. Radical extremists took control after the Ayatollah's return and religious freedom along with women's rights disappeared. People of my faith who tried to stay in Iran were persecuted."

"How do you know so much?"

"My uncle is a Professor of Middle Eastern Studies at the University of New Mexico, and my father was killed for not abandoning our faith when I was five. My mother and I were lucky to escape and to find a place so much like our homeland. That's why I had to come here from New York City. This feels like home; I already speak the Tewa language and look forward to learning Navajo and more about the Anasazi people. I want to visit the Navajo National Monument this weekend. Do you have any information about it?"

"There are brochures along the front counter. Make sure you call tomorrow and get your permits in order. Non-natives need a permit before visiting tribal lands, but they're not so hard to get. Brochures give you numbers and everything you will need. Do you need anything else now?"

"Some more water would be nice. Thanks. I'll pick up some brochures on my way out. I'll probably be seeing you at the school?"

"Sure. Enjoy your taco."

"Thanks," said Rani. The taco on Indian fry bread was an interesting mix of Mexican and Native American flavors.

While she ate, Rani observed the diners around her. The diners were also an interesting mix of Mexican, Native American and Anglo. All of the men were wearing jeans and outdoor apparel including cowboy boots and wide brimmed hats.

There were very few females aside from the servers working in the restaurant and some tourists. One family of tourists was seated across from Rani. All of them wore casual outdoor clothing suitable for hiking the rugged terrain. Rani felt a bit overdressed in her cotton sun dress. *Probably suitable for work but not for everyday wear.* Rani was glad her suitcase had a full selection of jeans and hiking apparel and gear. She picked up her ticket and walked to the front desk. After paying Lillian she picked up some brochures. *I'll need to read these this evening.*

Rani's apartment was a two bedroom, furnished unit in a complex designated for employees of the Kayenta Unified School District. Rani had chosen two bedrooms to allow for visits from her mother and step father as well as her aunt and uncle. The rent was an amazing one-hundred forty dollars a month. Even with utilities that was quite affordable on her teacher's salary.

Rani had already shipped linens, dishes, small appliances, and other personal items needed to make the apartment her own space before leaving New York so that they would be there when she arrived. *Unpacking might have to be put on the back burner for a while. Don't know how long this murder thing will last or how much longer Derrick will be in Kayenta.*

Derrick and Listie had rented a two bedroom unit in the same complex for the summer and had been planning on moving out before school started on August 3rd. The deadline was now up in the air because of the murder investigation. It seemed as though the murder had impacted the entire township that now included Rani as well. *Settling into the new situation may take a little longer than I had thought.* That was one good thing about being single; breaks from a routine were easier when there was the only person to consider. *A lot harder for Listie and Derrick. Wonder how long Josh Overton will be here? What was that all about?* Rani almost drove past the entrance to the apartment complex. *Pay attention!*

The building was typical Southwestern adobe style architecture with a brown exterior and red tiled roof. Rani parked the car in the visitor's lot and walked toward the building with a sign that said *Office* in the small yard. She walked inside to a lobby with two comfortable leather chairs separated by a glass table with Southwestern travel magazines in between. Behind that was the manager's desk and work area. A young Navajo woman greeted Rani; she had been expecting her. "I'm Charlotte Begay," she said. "Are you Mehrrani? I've been expecting you."

"Yes, I am, but I prefer Rani if you don't mind."

"Sure, you can call me Charlotte. First things first. Bill, the maintenance man, took some packages up to your apartment earlier today; he left them just inside the front door. You will be in apartment 211 on the second floor. There's only a freight elevator so I hope you don't mind the stairs."

"Not at all," said Rani.

"Here are your keys. You have two keys to the apartment that unlock the dead bolt as well as the door knob on both the front and back doors. I'll take you to the apartment after we finish here and we can walk through it together. Your security deposit covers any damages beyond normal wear and tear to the apartment as well as the furniture provided. Your lease is for one year, renewable at the end of the year. If you leave before the end of the lease, you lose the security deposit. If there are no damages and the apartment is clean and tidy, your security deposit will be sent to your forwarding address within 30 days. We require a thirty day notice before you move." Charlotte was explaining this while showing Rani pages of the lease to initial and sign.

As Rani was writing the check, she said, "I have already made arrangements with the utility company." She handed Charlotte the check.

"Yes, your utilities were turned on today; here are your other keys for your mailbox and the laundry room that is located on your floor. Each floor has its own washer and dryer." Charlotte gave Rani a copy of the lease with the rest of her keys.

After signing the lease and placing the keys on her key ring, she asked, "Anything else?"

"No," said Charlotte as she put the original of the lease in a file folder. "Let's go see your new home." Rani followed Charlotte up the stairs. While they were walking Charlotte pointed to the mailboxes, the laundry room and a computer room located on the second floor. This is the room with a computer for your use. We also have Wi-Fi in the individual rooms if you have your own computer, and there is a satellite dish for your television. You requested these services, so there is an extra monthly charge which you noticed in your lease. As you know, the utilities are paid separately, but laundry room services are included in the rent."

"Correct," said Rani.

Rani unlocked the door which opened directly into the living and dining area of the apartment. There was a tile floor at the entrance leading to a carpeted, L shaped area furnished with a sofa, end tables and coffee table. There was a round dining table with four chairs. The half wall behind the dining table provided a view of the kitchen and there was an arched doorway at the end of the wall leading into the kitchen itself. The galley type kitchen included a sink and dishwasher along the wall to the left; the window above the sink looked out onto a concrete walkway that wrapped around the building. A bar with two bar stools filled the half wall facing the dining area. On the opposite wall was a door that led to the patio. Next to that was a stove and refrigerator.

"I'll show you the bedrooms and bath rooms," said Charlotte. "You have two bedrooms, so there is a guest bath with a commode, bathtub and sink on your left off the hallway. The guest bedroom is here. Charlotte opened the door to a small room with a double bed and night stand and a small closet with louvered doors on the wall opposite the foot of the bed; there was a window on the wall facing the doorway.

"Here is the master bedroom," she said as she opened the door to a larger room with a queen sized bed and two night stands and a double closet on the opposite wall. A door to the right of the bed opened into a master bathroom with a shower, commode and sink. A bathroom window with frosted glass was open to reveal the back of the apartment complex. Charlotte turned and started walking back to the front of the apartment. "Let me know if there are any concerns after you have had a chance to settle in. The office is open 9 to 5 Monday through Friday. We are closed for lunch from 12-1. Any more questions?"

"None that I can think of now. Your office number is on the lease, right?"

"Yes, but this magnet on the refrigerator has all the emergency numbers you might need. I'll leave you to get settled; call me if you need anything."

"I will," said Rani as she said good bye and closed the door. Rani took off her shoes, sat down and stretched out on the couch thinking about how to proceed. She looked at her phone. *Three o'clock already! Which one of these boxes has the dishes in them? Bill has been quite efficient. This box on the kitchen counter must have the dishes.* Rani opened it, found a set of glasses rinsed them and put them to drain on the counter. She went downstairs to her car and returned with her cooler and other food items that she stored in the refrigerator. *Enough fruit and yogurt to last until I go to the store.* Rani made a mental note to ask Listie about places to shop for food.

After drinking some water she went back downstairs to her car and brought up her suitcases.

Rani was hanging up her last piece of clothing and putting her empty suitcases away when she heard the doorbell. It was Listie and Derrick. "Come in," she said. "How are you? Sit down. I'm a little short on refreshments at the moment. In fact I was going to ask you about grocery shopping here, but I do have water and some glasses."

"No thanks," said Listie as Derrick shook his head, no. "We're a little shaken up by this whole thing and so is the family. We called my dad and Derrick's family. They're very concerned. I told my dad I was flying home Saturday and that I expected Derrick would be back within the next two weeks. The investigation should be over by then. Derrick might have to come back for a trial, but we're confident there won't be any charges against him. I have to get home and get my herb garden harvested and get the clinic in order. We have an assistant who's been taking care of sales for us, but Derrick's patients are anxious for him to return. Polly will be back in school next week, also. Do you need any help with anything?"

"You're leaving on Saturday; you need time to take care of your own packing. I've unpacked my clothes and toiletries. All I really need is to unpack my dishes and bed linens. I do need to go to the grocery store though."

"Right," said Listie. "The most convenient store is Bashas' Grocery at the intersection of Highway 160 and 163 about three miles away. It's a locally owned store but well stocked with basic staples. The only ethnic selections are Mexican and Native American, not much like New York. My uncle and his wife live in Syracuse, New York, so I've been there a lot. You won't find such large selections here."

"I guess I will have to cook more. Actually, the basic vegetables and fruits are very much like what we had in Iran which is also a desert. Fortunately, I have shipped most of the cooking spices that are important in Persian dishes – dill, saffron and turmeric. I'm sure I can find fresh cilantro here. I think I can manage with those basics." As she was talking, Rani was making a mental note to find her Persian cook book her mother had given her for Christmas a few years ago when Rani had been in one of her relationships that had seemed promising for a short time. *Nate Harrison. Wonder what he's doing?* "How late is this store open?"

"This is Thursday, so it's open 'til 9:00." Listie looked at Derrick. "Do we have anything to eat at home?" Listie and Rani laughed. "For a naturopath he doesn't do so well when left to his own devices," said Listie.

"Well, at least I know how to juice," said Derrick. "I could use some fresh ingredients for the juicer."

"What if I went to the store with Listie and picked up some things for dinner as well as a few items for you while I'm gone?"

"Okay," said Derrick. I need to go to the clinic anyway and check in with Eleanor."

"I want to say good-bye to her also," said Listie. "Maybe I'll go with you instead. We can stop at the Pizza Edge for dinner on the way."

"I'd like to meet Dr. Parker also," said Rani. Mind if I tag along? I don't mind pizza myself and I can go to the grocery tomorrow. Don't feel much like cooking anything tonight anyway. I want to relax and read these brochures on the Navajo Monument since I want to go for a hike there this weekend. Besides, I have enough fruit and yogurt to sustain me until I get to the store tomorrow. Would I be imposing if I tagged along?"

"Not at all, we'd love to have you," said Derrick and Listie together.

"We can give you some pointers about permits on the drive, also," said Derrick. "What time is it?"

"It's 5:30," said Listie. "Maybe we should get the pizza to go and share it with Eleanor when we get to the clinic."

"Won't Dr. Parker be gone by the time we get there?" asked Rani.

"Oh, the office will be closed, but the clinic is just three rooms in front of Dr. Parker's house. She lives in the back," said Derrick.

"Oh," said Rani as she picked up her phone and purse. "I'm riding with you, right?"

"Sure," said Listie. "Let's go, I'm hungry."

The drive to the Pizza Edge was a short, ten minute ride on Highway 163. Long enough for Listie to give Rani the information she needed to get a permit to visit the Navajo Monument.

"Navajo National Monument is easy to find from here. You are centrally located. All you do is take SR 564 to the North off Highway 160. It is nine miles to the visitor's center that has everything you will need. There are guided tours every day to the Betatakin Cliff Dwelling and you don't need a permit for those. One leaves at 8:15 and the other at 11:00. The tours by the park rangers are available on a first come first served basis, so I would suggest getting there early. It is, however, the end of July and there aren't many people making the tours; it's very hot and most vacationers have left because school is starting."

"Yes, I know about that," said Rani.

"I would suggest you do the guided tour this time but be sure to get your permits, especially for overnight camping. Betatakin is one of the three ancient dwellings of the Anasazi that have been abandoned since the 13th Century. You will probably want to see them all eventually. The ruins themselves are unstable so they are closed to the public, but you can hike the Sandal Trail to the overlook of the Betatakin ruins that is atop the 560 foot Betatakin Canyon. That's an easy one day trip, but there are other trails and a lot to see. There is overnight camping, but there are only two campsites and I wouldn't recommend camping alone. Oh, we're here," said Listie. "Wish I was going to be here a little longer. Maybe you can find someone to camp with after you've been here for a while."

"Look," said Derrick as he pulled into a parking space in front of the restaurant. "Isn't that Josh Overton?"

Rani sat up and looked and flushed as she felt her heart rate quicken. "I think it is," said Listie. "Should we say something?"

"Yes," said Derrick. "It's not like we have anything to hide." He stepped from the open jeep just as Overton stepped off the sidewalk and walked toward his dark SUV. "Mr. Overton?"

Josh turned and said, "Yes," and smiled as he saw Rani stepping from the jeep. Josh sat his pizza on top of the SUV and walked toward Rani. "You need any help?" he asked. Rani turned an even deeper red as she took Josh's outstretched hand and stepped onto the sidewalk. "I hope this makes up for my *faux pax* yesterday," he said.

"Certainly," said Rani.

Everyone stood quietly, surrounded by an awkward silence until Derrick said, "We were just getting some pizza before going to see Dr. Parker. Maybe you would like to go with us?"

"Wish I could but I am on my way to the coal company to do some more interviews. We've had quite a few leads that have put your connection to Ole Jack on the back burner. Sorry to keep you hanging, but you are still a person of interest and need to stay in the area." Although Josh was talking to Derrick he was looking over Derrick's head in Rani's direction.

"I have extended my stay at the apartment complex until further notice," said Derrick. I'll be letting Dr. Parker know also that you may be visiting the clinic sometime. I am taking my wife Listie," Derrick nodded in Listie's direction and for the first time, Josh looked away from Rani, "to Flagstaff Saturday catch a plane back to Coos Bay."

"Sounds good," said Josh, "but I do have to make this appointment. "Keep in touch," he said once again directing his gaze over Derrick's head as he walked away.

"Well, that was interesting," said Listie as she smiled at Rani.

"Aren't we going to the clinic? Pizza's getting cold," said Rani. For the first time since this whole thing started, Derrick and Listie laughed and Rani just turned a darker red to match the red sandstone in the distance.

CHAPTER

8

Rani sat quietly in the back of Derrick's jeep as the three headed toward the health clinic that was in Tsegi, Arizona off Highway 160. The clinic was just 9 miles south of the Kayenta mine. Derrick and Listie's' voices were a mild hum against the voices in Rani's head. *Why am I so shaken? What is it about this man that bothers me so? I know almost nothing about him and yet I want to learn everything I can. We certainly made eye contact and neither of us seemed to want it to end.* Rani's conversation with herself was interrupted by Derrick's voice. "Here we are."

The health clinic/slash residence was a mobile home with an extension in the front. *That must be where the clinic is.* Although the sign on the door said, "closed," Derrick knocked on the door. Within a few seconds the door opened to reveal a woman with shoulder length, platinum hair who looked more like a hippie than a physician. Eleanor Parker smiled broadly and said, "Come in," as she directed them through a door that led to her living quarters.

"This is Rani," said Derrick as though Eleanor already knew who she was. Before Rani could say anything, Eleanor hugged her along with Derrick and Listie.

"Have a seat," she said taking the pizza to the kitchen area and pulling out plates from the cabinet. "Can I get you something to drink?" Water with lemon seemed to be the consensus. As Eleanor prepared the drinks, the three filled their plates and stood at the bar separating the kitchen from the living room to eat.

Rani studied Eleanor as Derrick and Listie chatted. The word *crone* came to her mind. Before the Middle Ages, a crone referred to a female sage and healer, an expert in the use of herbs and oils.

During the Dark Ages, after the Catholic church came to power, these women were considered heretics and witches. In colonial America, women who practiced the art were often tried as witches and hanged.

In the 21st Century respect for the intuitive healers and mid-wives was making a comeback. Rani understood why Dr. Parker consulted with Derrick in her practice. After filling up on pizza, Derrick and Eleanor went into the living room to discuss Ole Jack and prepare for any questions Josh Overton might have should he come to the clinic. "Come with me and I'll show you the clinic while Eleanor and Derrick talk," said Listie.

The clinic had an outer office that served as a waiting room, nurse's station and place for patient files. There were two computers on the L-shaped desk that formed a partition between the waiting area and nurses' station. "There are two treatment rooms that are identical," said Listie as she opened the door to the first one. Listie walked into the room that held all the instruments needed for an initial examination – scales, blood pressure monitor, etc. There were eye charts and a food pyramid on the wall. Before Rani could say anything, Listie said, "So what's with you and Mr. Overton?"

Rani flushed and said, "Nothing, we don't even know each other."

"It appears that both of you would like to change that." Listie had a big grin and her eyes sparkled.

Married women always want to live vicariously through their single friends, thought Rani. "I do have a mild curiosity, and he does seem to go out of his way to talk to me. I've never known anyone like him. Aren't they the type who run away from women after the adventure ends?"

"That's the general thinking, I guess, but are you interested in anything more yourself?"

Rani had never been this open with anyone except her mother, but this felt quite normal. This sudden intimacy with someone who was almost a complete stranger was certainly different. Until now, Rani's mother and Aunt Sizdah had been her only confidants, but this intimacy with someone her own age felt quite nice. "I left New York because I wanted a change of scenery, to be away from my mom and perhaps find someone who could inspire me to break down this wall of resistance I seem to have when it comes to men. I haven't allowed myself to love a man because I'm afraid of losing him."

"Oh, your father," said Listie. Rani shook her head "yes" and felt her eyes moisten. "You know your mother lost a great love, but she seems to have found another. I lost my mother too soon. I think that if we stay away from relationships from fear of losing someone, we never experience the joy the relationship brings. Just being in love with someone seems to bring out the best in me. If you find someone who brings joy into your life, I say go for it! I would never want to lose Derrick or Polly, but if I did, I would always remember the great joy they brought into my life while they were here. That's how I remember my mom."

Rani grinned. "I do want to get to know this man. He intrigues me, and he's certainly easy on the eyes."

"Just relax and see where it goes. I sense Mr. Overton is feeling the same way."

"Hey, what happened? Did you two get lost?" Derrick stood in the doorway. Eleanor and I are finished and it's 9:00. We need to head back."

"Give me a hug, Listie," said Eleanor. "I guess this is good-bye for now. I'll probably be seeing you again, Rani, but I'm a hugger. I hope you don't mind."

"Not at all," said Rani. "I enjoyed meeting you and hope to see you again. I will be here at least for the current school year, maybe longer. Who knows?"

"I hope you make it longer," said Eleanor. Good-bye all. Be safe. I love you."

Rani was quiet on the way home. Although she had found a friend in Listie, she still relished the quiet and didn't engage in small talk very well. Derrick parked the jeep in his parking spot and Rani said good night as she walked toward her apartment. "I want to see you before you leave, Listie," she said. "Maybe we can get together tomorrow evening for a light dinner. You can come over to my place. I'll unpack my Persian cook book and maybe I can find all the ingredients to make a simple meal for us. How about 6:00? I don't drink, but is there anything you like?

"We actually don't drink either," said Listie. Lemonade or tea is nice."

"I make a mean carrot juice float," said Rani.

Listie twisted her face to form a question mark. "Carrot juice and ice cream? Sounds interesting. Looking forward to trying it. Sure it won't be too inconvenient?"

"I'll have the whole day to go shopping and unpack the basics. Plenty of time to get ready for hiking on Saturday also. All my outdoor gear is in the same place. I'll just fix some lentil soup and a Persian salad. No problem, I'll see you two around 6:00?"

"Sure thing," said Derrick. "I could go for some home cooking, and don't forget the carrot juice float. Good night." The two walked toward their apartment and Rani went upstairs toward her new home.

Rani checked her phone for messages after she entered the apartment. She saw a text from her mother and looked at her watch. *Almost 9:30 here-12:30 in New York. Communication with Mama sure has been simplified with texting!* Rani read the text and decided to answer.

Are you settled yet? How was your sightseeing trip? – Mama

I am in the apartment and received all my boxes. I haven't had time to do a lot of unpacking yet – just necessities. Lots to tell. Let's talk when Craig is there to help interpret. For now, I visited Hotevilla, Kykotsmovi Village and the Upper Moenkopi dry farming area. I met a woman who is so great! Seems like I've always known her. We have so much in common. Her name is Listie Stratton and she has a daughter who is deaf named Polly. She and her husband Derrick know sign. That's just a start. The couple is staying temporarily in the same apartment complex but they are from Coos Bay, Oregon. More later. The biggest news is that because I know them I have been caught up in a murder investigation. An old transient was found bludgeoned to death in front of the Kayenta Coal Mine. Derrick was brought in for questioning because he helped treat the man at the health clinic where he is working for the summer. I'm going to the Navajo National Monument on Saturday and hope to have everything in order in the apartment by Monday when I start work. How are you and Craig?

Rani was heading toward the bedroom when she heard the alert. *Must have been waiting up to hear from me. Oh, well. I guess I'm the same way.*

We're doing well. We want to come see you sometime in September. BTW I received a call from Nate Harrison. He wanted to know if you still had the same phone number. Seems he is a member of a delegation that will be visiting the Hopi Reservation this week and he wanted to give you a call. I think the group is adding the Kayenta Mining Operation to their list of site visits. I told him your number was the same and to give you a call.

Thanks for the heads up. I may not be able to do anything but talk on the phone, but if he is here long enough we could get together for dinner.

Still not interested, huh?

No, Mama. Rani thought better of even mentioning anything about Josh Overton.

No. But I am trying to stay open to the possibility of finding someone who can help me understand true intimacy and trust in a relationship. I'm having Derrick and Listie for dinner tomorrow evening. I want to put that Persian cook book to use, plus there are no Middle Eastern restaurants here. If Craig is available to interpret, maybe you could call me sometime Friday evening say 8:00 East Coast time?

I'm sure we can do that. Talk to you soon. Love.

Love to you and Craig.

Rani put her phone on *Do Not Disturb*, changed into pajamas and fell asleep almost as soon as her head hit the pillow.

*   *   *

Josh pulled into the parking lot of the Tuba City Justice Center at exactly 9:00 am. Thursday had been an extremely busy day which wasn't unusual when he was working a case. As expected, Oscar Yellowtail had not been able to tell Josh much more about the altercation between Ole Jack and Luther than he already knew. One new piece of information, however, involved Yellowtail's noticing Ole Jack talking with Robert Beneè outside the restaurant about a week before the murder. Josh had made a mental note to ask Robert about that when he checked the information about the patrol car sighted on 163 the night before the murder.

As usual, Josh had not slept much, but the reason had little to do with the case. Josh didn't spend the night pouring over his notes and trying to find connections between any of the persons of interest he had spoken with that day. He tried, but all he could think about was the dark haired beauty that had flushed and smiled discreetly at him when he offered his hand to her. How he wanted to find the answer to the enigma that was Rani hidden behind those dark eyes! When he found the answer would that be the end of it? Would the spell be broken?

What was it about this woman that beguiled him so? This was more than his usual pursuit and conquest. What came to mind was Don Quixote's search for his *dulcinea* - a sweetheart that inspired the knight errant in his battles against the windmills of evil in the world. *Whoa, fellow. That's way out there. You have real criminals to find and bring to justice. Get your head out of the clouds.* Josh shook his head and was all business by the time he reached his desk inside the Justice Center. George Yazzie and Robert Beneè were waiting for him.

"I checked out the alibis on Munson and Halverson," said Yazzie. "Munson's wife said Pete went out about 9:00 the night before the murder and came home around 11:30. Says he was there the rest of the night. Their dog woke her up around 1:00 am and she let him out. Pete was asleep next to her at that time. Halverson was at the poker party until about 10:00 when he left. No one saw him after that, so he has no alibi for the time of the murder. Luther Samson was at the poker party until 2:00 am."

"Good work, Yazzie. What about that eagle costume, Beneè?"

"As it happens, I have been researching this costume myself. I hadn't mentioned this yet, waiting for the right time. About a week ago, Ole Jack stopped me outside The Blue Coffee Pot to tell me about an eagle's costume he saw hidden behind one of the sandstone buttes a few miles south of the Kayenta Mine. He told me where he had seen it so I went to investigate the night Ole Jack was murdered. I went after dark because I figured if this was connected to the case of the stolen artifacts, it would be better then."

"What time were you there?"

"About nine or so."

"Did you find anything?"

"No, I guess I searched around the immediate area for about an hour or so and then left. When I heard about the figure that was spotted on the security cameras, I knew it must be the same. I did the investigation as you asked and looked at the video on the cameras. The figure is wearing a costume that appears to be made entirely of eagle feathers. The interesting thing is that this costume would have to have been made before 1918. The Migratory Bird Act of 1918 and the Bald and Golden Eagle Act of 1940 made it illegal to use golden eagle, red-tailed hawk, kestrel, cactus, wren, northern flicker, dove or ladder-backed woodpecker feathers for any costume, religious or otherwise. This costume appears to be made entirely of golden eagle feathers. I'm sure it must relate somehow to the stolen artifacts that have been sold in Paris," said Robert.

"Sounds very likely," said Overton. We'll need to give a copy of that report to Chief Nat'aanii and the investigators when they arrive. They may want to search the area around the coal mine themselves." *Well, that explains the meeting and patrol car, thought Josh* as he crossed through the note to question Beneè on the subject. "That may provide a motive for the murder. Ole Jack may have found the costume another way, and he may have known more than he told you, Robert. Suppose he saw the people who buried the costume and decided to blackmail them?"

"That's a possibility, I suppose," said Robert.

Josh thought about Pete Munson's financial difficulties. He did have an alibi for the exact time of the murder, but he was away from home for some time earlier that evening. Halverson's activities after he left the poker game were also unaccounted for, including the actual time of the murder. "Yazzie, I'm going to need to get you to run financials on both Pete Munson and Eric Halverson. Let me know what comes up."

"Will do," said George.

"Robert, do you know exactly where Ole Jack said he found the costume?"

"Yes, but I searched the area the night before the murder and didn't find anything."

"We'll need to alert the investigators so they can do a more thorough search. It also will not be dark this afternoon. Pull up a map of the area and highlight the place you believe Ole Jack found the costume."

"Will do," said Robert.

"Oh, Robert, you seem to know a lot about the area. You know anything about the Navajo National Monument?" Robert appeared to be startled by the question.

"Why do you ask?" he said.

"I need to get outdoors and do some hiking, but I don't have a lot of time. My ex-wife and I used to do a lot of rock climbing and hiking in Arizona. I heard there were several trails of different lengths there."

"Before I joined the police force, I was a trail guide there. If you are short on time I would recommend hiking to the Betatakin Cliff Dwelling. You don't have to get a permit for this hike and the guide is free. There are two daily tours, 8:15 and 11:00 am.

"Should I just show up at 8:00 ready to hike?"

"There are only 20 spots so you should get there at least an hour ahead of time. I don't think you will have much trouble this time of year. It's so hot, not many people want to make such a strenuous hike, and people with school aged children have already gone home. The trail is okay going down, but it is very steep, so climbing back up requires that a person be in good physical condition. Make sure you stay with the guide and don't stray away. I know you are an experienced hiker, but there are restrictions about how close you can get to the ruins and they are very fragile. We used to be able to go inside the dwellings but it is too dangerous now. They can only be viewed from a distance."

Josh had a feeling that Robert had more than a casual interest in his staying close to the trail. *Why would he have to tell me that? I'm sure the guide is perfectly capable of explaining that. Oh well, I did ask his advice. Can't always control how much advice is given once the question is asked.* "Thanks for the info. I think I'll take a few hours tomorrow morning for the hike."

"Those financials you wanted came back," said George Yazzie as he handed Josh a folder. "Think you'll find some interesting information there."

"Thanks," said Josh. He placed the folder on his desk and said, "I'm going to get a cup of coffee. I'll look at them when I get back."

"Mind if I take a look while you're getting coffee?" asked Robert. "Sure, have a look," said Josh.

Josh ran into Jeanette who was just finishing pouring a cup of coffee. "I overheard your conversation with Robert about the Navajo National Monument. I haven't been there yet myself. It sounds interesting."

"Do you like to hike?" asked Josh.

"I enjoy being outdoors, but the heat bothers me a lot here. I wouldn't mind hiking if I had someone to go with me."

"Maybe you should start with the guided tour hike Robert recommended. Robert's also very knowledgeable about the area. Maybe you could go with him sometime."

"I'd like that, but Robert seems to be quite a loner, not interested in company."

"Well, be sure and check out that guided tour when you get the chance." Josh filled his cup and walked back to his desk. In the past, Josh might have taken Jeanette's hint about going with him, but as attractive as she was, he just wasn't interested. *I think I'll give Eli a call this evening. Maybe I can schedule a back country trip for us at the Monument after this case is over.* Josh picked up the financial file and began to read. *Yazzie was right!*

Pete Munson had a retirement program with Peabody Coal Company and had been making annual purchases of the Company's stocks that were matched by the Company. During the last few years, Munson had been making large withdrawals from the account that Josh assumed went to pay for his daughter's college expenses. Mrs. Munson did not work so Munson had to be under stress about their future retirement. In addition, Pete's health didn't look too good. There were large hospital bills from last year due to Pete's massive heart attack. Then, Josh saw it!

Beginning in March of 2013 and again in February of 2015, there were two deposits made into Munson's account of $25,000 each from an east coast company named Energy Development West. Those amounts and dates coincided exactly with deposits made into Eric Halverson's account from the same company.

Six months ago, Munson had opened up a trust fund in his son's name with a deposit of $50,000. *I need to find out about this right away!* Josh closed the files and looked at his watch. *11:00. If I leave now I can get to the mine around noon and talk with Munson about this before the UN people arrive. Could probably catch Halverson on his lunch break.*

"Robert, since you know where Ole Jack found the eagle costume you're going to have to take care of the United Nations people. Yazzie, I'm going to need for you to find out all you can about an east coast company headquartered in Atlantic City, New Jersey. The name is Energy Development West. I'm going to the mine to talk with Munson and Halverson about these financial reports. I'll meet you at the mine.

"Won't be able to talk with either of them, Boss," said Yazzie.

"Why, not?"

"We just got a 911 call from Pete Munson's wife. Appears he may have committed suicide."

"What about Halverson?"

"Didn't show up for work this morning. When Maria called his residence, there was no answer. He seems to have disappeared."

CHAPTER

9

George Yazzie was supervising the team of forensics investigators gathering evidence from the crime scene at Pete Munson's home and social workers were upstairs talking with Mrs. Munson and her son Jason. The daughter Caroline was on her way from Phoenix after receiving a phone call no one wants to get. Josh did not want to talk to any of them until the investigation of the crime scene was finished and the family had had time to absorb the shock. Everything indicated it was, indeed, suicide. Pete had left a note taking responsibility for this death. Unfortunately, his wife had found him hanging from a light fixture chain in his study when she had gotten up that morning. Jason had found his mother crumpled up in a ball upon hearing her frantic screams. The boy had called 911.

Josh was reading the note. Not much there but it did seem to be written by Munson.

Darleen and Kids,

I've made a mess of things. My health is terrible and I don't want to put you through a scandalous inquiry about my actions over the last year. Believe me, this is the easiest way for all of us. Darleen, you've always been the strong one in the family and I know you will get through this. I love you all.

The note was unsigned, written on a piece of scratch paper as though it was written hurriedly to be put on the refrigerator before rushing out – *called away on an emergency don't know when I'll be home* – except everyone knew Munson wasn't coming back. Josh handed the paper to Yazzie who put it in a plastic bag and labeled it.

"I'm going to go through the computer," said Josh. "When you guys finish here, you need to go to Eric Halverson's place and find out where he is. Not only do we need him we will need his computer files as well. I will check out the company's computer in Munson's office when I go to the mine this afternoon. Make sure you dust the whole area for fingerprints," he said as he walked toward the dark cherry desk that held the family computer. "Does anyone know the password?"

"We asked Mrs. Munson before she went upstairs with the social worker," said Yazzie. "Password's Daisy, like the dog."

Josh turned on the computer and typed in the password. He pulled out a flash drive and downloaded everything from the past year – emails and Munson's personal and financial records. He hated doing this but he downloaded Darlene Munson's personal records as well. After the downloads were complete, he handed the drive to Yazzie and said, "Put this with the box containing all of Munson's office files. When you get to the Center, take the box to Jeanette. Tell her to go through the files as well as the flash drive and record any suspicious activity. I expect you to follow up on her report. In the meantime help Robert in locating Halverson and getting any information on that energy company," he said. "I'm going on a hike Saturday morning, but I will want a briefing from you, Beneè and Jeanette when I come headquarters on Saturday afternoon. I'm going upstairs now."

Darlene Munson was an attractive, middle-aged woman. She had the slender, toned body of someone who paid attention to her diet and was either very active or followed a regular work-out regimen. Despite the situation, she appeared poised and calm, but her swollen, red eyes betrayed that. She sat cradling her son Jason who looked like a lost little boy in his mother's arms. "May I interrupt to ask a few questions?" Josh was addressing the social worker who sat across from mother and son.

Karen stood up and said, "I think we've finished here for now. I want to give you my card, Mrs. Munson. Call and schedule another appointment with us when your daughter arrives so I can talk with the whole family. I am so sorry for your loss."

"Thank you," said Mrs. Munson as she stood to take Karen's card and show her the way out. Jason just sat quietly on the couch. "How can I help you, Mr. Overton?" she asked when she returned to the couch.

"Do you know anything about your husband's involvement in any illegal activities recently?"

Darlene's face flushed with anger. "Certainly not! We were having financial difficulties what with college and Pete's health, but he certainly wasn't desperate enough to break the law — was he?" The last question was almost like a plea to Josh to tell her that her husband hadn't resorted to breaking the law. Once again, the floodgate holding back tears opened and she stammered, "Pete was a g-g-good man." Josh reached to take her hand tightly wrapped around a knotted handkerchief. "He was working so hard. Lately, he was spending more time at work – taking on more responsibility since his heart attack – almost like he had to prove he could still do the job."

"You're sure it was just work that was taking so much of his time?"

"If you mean, was he having an affair, certainly not!" The swell of anger stopped the flow of tears.

"Sorry, Mrs. Munson. I don't think there was another woman, but we do have reason to suspect your husband may have been involved with an employee named Eric Halverson in some illegal activity. Did you know Mr. Halverson?"

"I know Mr. Halverson came to work for Pete in 2005. Transferred from the Black Mesa Coal Mine that was closing down; nobody liked that. Pete used to talk about what a great crane operator Eric was. I think Mr. Halverson was originally from Kentucky; that's where he started working in the coal mines. Pete would talk to me about the rotten deal coal miners in Kentucky had when those "tree hugging" environmentalists started making it difficult for the mining companies to continue to operate. Mr. Halverson told Pete that too many federal regulations shut down the mines, said the same thing happened with his job south of here. That's why he came to Kayenta. Both he and Pete were concerned about what was happening here with all those federal investigators. Lots of stress for Pete."

"Did you ever talk to Mr. Halverson directly?" asked Josh.

"The only time I ever saw Mr. Halverson was at the usual social gatherings for the company. Pete and I didn't associate much with the employees. Our lives centered around the kids and their activities. Pete was a wonderful father." Once again, the tears started and Darlene let go of Josh's hand to dab her eyes and wipe her nose.

"I'm sure he was, Mrs. Munson, said Josh as he gently stroked her shoulder and stood to go. "I won't take any more of your time now, but if you can think of anything out of the ordinary about your husband's activities in the past year, here's my card. Thank you again for your time and I am also sorry for your loss." *Really don't think this family knows anything.*

Josh shook his head thinking about the young boy who had just lost his father in such a tragic way. *I really have to call Eli soon! Almost one o'clock. I should eat something before going to the mine. I'll stop at The Blue Coffee Pot and get one of those Navajo tacos to go.* Josh felt that refreshing rush of adrenalin kick in from the excitement of a case that was getting more and more complex and challenging. This time, however, he wasn't so sure he didn't want to be doing something else.

*   *   *

Josh saw her the minute he walked into the restaurant. Rani was sitting at a small table near the back engaged in conversation with a nice looking man about his age. That excited rush of the last half-hour dissipated quickly and Josh started to resent his job and everything that prevented him from getting to know Rani. In addition, he was startled to realize that maybe Rani was involved with someone! "May I help you?"

"Oh, yes." It took Josh a few seconds to realize why he was here. "I'd like to order the Navajo taco to go."

"Certainly, will that be all?" asked the young woman as she wrote up a ticket.

"That's it," said Josh. "I have my own drink in the car. How much?" Josh paid the host and stood waiting for his order with his eyes peeled toward the back of the room. When he saw the two stand up, he averted his eyes and started looking at the brochures on the front display. He heard the footsteps walking toward the register, but kept his eyes on the brochure he had picked up.

His heart skipped a beat when he heard his name. "Mr. Overton," isn't it?

"Oh, hello, Ms.?" Josh flushed. "I forgot your last name. All I remember is Rani. You can call me Josh if it's all right to call you Rani."

"My last name is Bijan, but you may certainly call me Rani." There was that awkward silence again until the man with Rani spoke up.

"Josh Overton. I believe I know you. In fact, I heard your name at the Tuba Justice Center; my name is Nate Harrison. I'm with the United Nations delegation looking into the return of some sacred artifacts belonging to the Hopi Nation that were sold illegally in Paris."

"That's right!" exclaimed Josh. "You were supposed to be at the Justice Center at 2:00 and then come out to the mine."

"We caught an earlier flight when the Chief heard about the murder. I asked the Chief if I could rent a car and meet him and my boss at the mine. Rani is an old friend from New York and I wanted to connect with her while I am here."

"That's great! I guess I'll see you later at the mine," said Josh. "I just stopped in for a taco to go. I don't know all you have heard, but there have been more developments in the murder case since I met Rani. I see my taco's ready. Nice seeing you again, Rani. I'll see you later, Harrison."

Rani watched Josh walk out the door. She was aware that Nate was saying something, but it took her a few seconds to get grounded. "Is this where you are going tomorrow?" Rani looked at the brochure Nate was holding, one for the Navajo National Monument.

"Yes," she said. Rani was trying to be polite and focus on Nate, but her mind was clearly somewhere else.

"What if I make plans to stay over for a week? I have some vacation time. Maybe you could show me around; I've never been to

Arizona before."

"School starts on Monday, Nate. The only time I will have after that is on the weekends. Besides, I told you at lunch not to get your hopes up about us. I just don't feel that way about you. I wish I did; you're a great catch for someone but for me, you will always be a dear friend. Your life is in New York and for some reason; I feel this is where I am meant to be."

Nate writhed at hearing the words every man hated – dear friend. He sensed something different in Rani during that brief encounter with Overton, and replied, "with someone like that?" Nate nodded toward the door. "Men like that are not prone to settling down, Rani."

"I hardly know him Nate. Please don't go there. Anyway, you know my difficulty with relationships. I don't know if there is anyone who can penetrate this wall. I moved out here to try and get to know myself a little better and finally figure this whole thing out. For the first time I feel like I have a female friend. She's the reason I met Mr. Overton. Her name is Listie Stratton and from the moment we met we both felt like sisters; she is an only child, also. Her mother died on United Flight 93 on 911.

Unlike me, Listie has been able to marry and even has a child that is deaf. I think I can learn a lot from her about overcoming fear and having the courage to love. I don't want to end up alone when *Mama* and Aunt Sizdah are gone, but I also want to know I am really in love before I commit to someone. I have to find out how that love feels. I don't know that yet."

"Maybe if you would give me a chance, I could help you find out."

"I don't know how that feels yet, but I do know that when I find someone who makes me want to open up and take a chance, I will recognize it. And as much as I like and respect you, you are not the one, Nate."

Nate opened the door of the restaurant to allow Rani to walk outside. Once outside, Rani put her hand on Nate's shoulder and he brushed it aside. "I have to go," he said. Rani watched as he drove away in his rented car toward the Kayenta Mine. She wished she was going with him, but for another reason entirely.

Josh felt his phone vibrate just as he pulled into the parking lot of the Kayenta Coal Mine. It was a text from Robert Beneè who had gone to search Halverson's apartment.

Apartment empty. Manager let us in. Didn't know Halverson had left. All of Halverson's personal belongings including computer are gone. I'm going back to the Justice Center and check with Jeanette on what she has found out. Let me know the next step.

Josh quickly replied:

Stay at the Justice Center and keep looking for information about that energy company. Yazzie should be back there by now to help. Put out an APB on Halverson and watch for any credit card payments for gasoline, motels, etc. I'm coming back after finishing with the Chief and the United Nations people to go over everything this evening. I'm going on a hike tomorrow morning and will check in after that.

*   *   *

"This carrot juice float is very good!" said Derrick. He seemed pleasantly surprised. "Is there a secret ingredient?"

"I don't know about a secret ingredient, but I do use ginger. Ginger is a root and root beer is made from a root, so maybe that's the same idea."

"Here's to carrot juice floats and new friendships," said Listie raising her glass to the other two. She looked at her watch. "I have an early flight tomorrow and you have to leave early for the Monument, so we better go. Do you need any help cleaning up?"

"There's not much to do, but if you could put those dishes in the dishwasher for me that would be a big help. Rani reached out to hug Listie at the door. "It seems strange; I just met you two, but I feel as though we have known one another for years. I'll miss you."

"We'll miss you. First chance you get, you will have to come to Coos Bay. Bring your Mom and Craig along with you. We will be going to Syracuse during the Christmas break. Maybe we could meet you in New York then also."

"That would be terrific, but for now, I want to immerse myself in the area and find out what is here for me. My Mom and Craig called earlier this evening; they are thinking about making a trip out here near the end of September. They want me to have time to get settled here before discussing any plans to go back to New York. Right now, I'm just taking everything one step at a time. Meeting you and Derrick, however, has certainly been an important step."

"And maybe someone else?" smiled Listie.

"I'm here to break down a lot of walls and find answers that still linger concerning my father," said Rani. "I am open to whatever direction that takes me."

"Focus on the joy and the journey and, as they say, lighten up," said Derrick. "Hug for me?"

"For sure," said Rani. "Talk to you soon."

Lighten up. I do need to be less serious, that's for sure, thought Rani. Everything was ready for the hike tomorrow. *Boy, I do need to lighten up. It's hard not to be serious about hiking in extreme temperatures, though. Maybe I'll show up at 8:00 instead of an hour early. If I don't make the first hike there's always 11:00. Lighten up.* Rani smiled as she heard her telephone ring. She really missed her mother.

Rani drove into the parking lot of the visitor's center at 7:50 despite her promise to get there at 8:00. She parked next to a black SUV that looked very much like Josh Overton's vehicle. *Wishful thinking.* She grabbed her bag with water and protein bars and put on a wide brimmed hat and walked to the front entrance. The door opened automatically or so she thought. She looked up and there stood Josh holding the door for her. Rani smiled and said, "Good morning."

"This is certainly a good morning now," said Josh returning her smile. "Are you here for the hike?"

"I hope to go on the 8:00 hike if there's room," said Rani.

"Plenty of room. There are only eight of us. You will be number nine after you sign in."

Rani walked to the front desk and signed in. "I have these request forms for an overnight permit," she said to the desk clerk. "How long will it take before I get one?" she asked. "I'd like to do some back country camping while we still have longer days. These additional permit forms are for my mother and her husband. They won't be here for a while, but I would like to have them ready for them."

Josh was listening intently. *All the more reason to get my permits and call Eli*, he thought.

"It takes five to seven business days to process. You should have them in less than two weeks. Is this your correct mailing address?"

"Yes," said Rani.

The clerk who was helping her said, "You'll need to go now. Your group is leaving."

"Thanks," said Rani and walked toward the group. Josh was lagging behind, waiting for her. She smiled and stood next to him while listening to the guide's instructions.

"My name is Shilah Begay; I am Navajo and live in Navajo County. I will take you on the hike to the edge of the Betatakin Cliff dwellers' ruins. The Betatakin were one group of the ancient Anasazi who lived here from about 1100 A.D. until their disappearance in 1280 A.D. I will tell you more about them during the hike. The hike is a five mile round trip and the trail is steep and rocky; we will travel 2,221 feet to the bottom of the cliff, so the climb back up will be strenuous. I hope you brought plenty of water and if anyone is unsure of your ability to make the hike, you will need to leave now." He paused then started walking. "Follow me," he said. "And do not stray from the trail. When we get to the bottom, there are some portable outhouses concealed by those trees over there."

The group was quiet and serious as they walked down the rocky cliff and listened to the guide. "The name Betatakin means *Place of the Corn Tassel*." The guide's voice drifted in and out of Rani's consciousness as she carefully negotiated the rocky trail that led to the canyon floor. *Should have brought a walking stick,* she thought. But Josh's hand was always available whenever she felt shaky. There was a clump of juniper trees and desert grasses at the bottom of the cliff. The guide pointed to the mud brick structures carved into a ledge surrounding the red, sandstone buttes in the distance.

"The Anasazi built their homes in the cliffs and used the flat lands for growing corn. Living high in the cliffs provided protection for sleeping and safety from the nomadic, warlike tribes of the plains Indians. The ruins are unstable so you can no longer go through them, and picture taking is also prohibited. See that alcove over there beneath the homes? That is a cave where you can see ancient drawings."

The group walked into the alcove beneath the cliff homes to see the petro glyphs. Rani gasped when she saw one of the pictures. Josh looked at her with a questioning gaze, but she said nothing. She moved closer; Josh was watching her intently. The face painted into the sandstone was very much like that painted on the stone that her father had left for her. As she examined the sandstone rocks, Rani also discovered that the texture and color were exactly like the stone in the cotton, drawstring bag at home. Rani knew the answer to her questions about this stone lay here in these ancient ruins, perhaps with the clan elders who told the stories of the Hopi Prophecy. *There must be a way to see the ancient tablets kept by the Fire Clan,* thought Rani.

"Do you need to use the restroom?" Josh's voice brought Rani back to the present. "We're getting ready to go back up," said Josh.

"Yes, thanks," said Rani.

The outhouses were indeed well hidden by the thick growth of trees. *Strange,* thought Josh. *That open area behind the outhouses looks as though the land has been recently disturbed, like someone digging. Perhaps an animal.* "How're you doing, Rani?" he asked when the group returned to the visitor's center.

"That was just hard enough. I'm going to have to build up my stamina if I expect to do some back country hiking. What about you?"

"You know agents have to stay in top condition in order to keep our jobs, so that wasn't too difficult for me. If you would like, after this case is finished I can put together a workout regimen for you and you can use the gym at the Justice Center."

"I really don't want to wait until the case if finished. I'm going to purchase a bike and start riding it to work and in the evenings for conditioning."

"That sounds good. Maybe I could join you sometime? I have to get to the Justice Center after lunch, but that hike made me hungry. Would you care to join me in the restaurant here for lunch?"

"That would be nice," said Rani as she handed him a card with her contact information. Their hands touched briefly and both felt the electricity. Once again, silence.

Josh smiled and let go of her hand to point the way to the restaurant and gift shop. "Lunch awaits," he smiled. Josh noticed Robert Beneè sitting at a table next to the one where he and Rani were seated. Robert stood up to acknowledge Rani and smiled briefly at Josh.

Josh was still basking in the glow of lunch with Rani when he walked into the Justice Center at 1:00. He hated that every time he was with her, he had to rush to another appointment, but Josh knew it would take more than a long lunch to get to know this woman. Rani was complex and quiet but Josh did not sense aloofness; she was someone he wanted to know on a deeper level than common interests or even sexual attraction.

Rani needed to be wooed, not in the romantic sense, although romance was part of it. Josh was interested in cultivating an intimate relationship that would stay joyful and exciting long after the initial rush of adrenaline and sex hormones; he was so over that. Somehow he wanted a connection deeper than ego centered desires and fantasies that always fell apart after a few weeks or months; he wasn't quite sure if he knew how, but he knew patience and respect were vital keys. Josh wanted to find a relationship like Emma and Craig's – one that would fulfill the words of that poet – "come grow old with me, the best is yet to be." *Focus, man.*

During the lunch, Josh had learned that Rani was born in Iran and practiced the Baha'i faith. In fact, her father's murder because of that was what had brought her and her mother to the United States. Josh felt that he had been given a thread that he would need to pull to start unraveling the mystery that was Rani. Deciding against that at this time, he skillfully brought the conversation back to the present. "By the way," he said. "What was it about that cave drawing that held your attention?" Rani had taken quite a while to frame a response. It was almost as if she were engaged in a silent conversation about whether to answer the question or not.

Rani had wiped her hands with her napkin and spoken carefully and cautiously. "When I was seventeen my mother showed me a stone that she said had been sewn into the hem of a doll's dress. The doll was a gift on my fifth birthday; that was the day my father was killed. My father had shown *Mama* the stone the day after he visited the House of *Bab* that had been destroyed by revolutionaries." Seeing the look of confusion on Josh's face, she explained, "*Bab* was the founder of the Baha'i faith who was exiled and killed in the late 19th Century. Anyway, my father told *Mama* he thought the stone had some significance and she was to keep it safe until the time came to bring it back to Iran. When I told *Mama* I was moving to Arizona, she gave me the stone. She said she felt somehow the stone was connected to the *Hopi* people. The picture drawn on the cave is exactly like the picture on the stone."

Josh exhaled and said "Whew! You know what I think?"

"What?" asked Rani.

"I think Chief Nat'aanii needs to see that stone."

"You don't believe he will think I stole it, do you?" she asked.

"I never thought about that. I know you didn't pick it up on the hike because you were never out of my sight except to go to the bathroom and you saw the drawing before you went in there."

Rani had flushed and said, "really?"

"Really," smiled Josh. But I do think the Chief needs to see it and the sooner the better. I'll mention it to him and set up a time for you to bring it in next week. Maybe we could go out for dinner after that."

"That sounds good, but dinner places are limited here. Maybe I could fix something at my place. You have my card. I'm free almost every day after 3:00 at present. Let me know. How's the murder investigation going and what about Derrick Stratton? I'm sure he's anxious to get home."

Josh didn't discuss the details of the case except to say that the case was moving in an entirely different direction from a connection with Derrick Stratton and the Black Cross. Since the news of

Munson's suicide and the search for Halverson was already in the news, Josh told Rani what Jeanette had told the press, that all efforts were focused at this time on locating Eric Halverson who had disappeared and was apparently headed for Greenville, Kentucky. Rani was happy to hear suspicion was now directed away from her friends. Lunch ended too soon for both of them.

Josh had walked Rani to her car and said, "I wish we had more time." His voice was subdued, the message clear.

Rani had touched his shoulder, looked into his eyes and said, "I want to get to know you better as well. Please call me when you get an opportunity." No more words had been necessary. Josh closed her car door and walked away but he could feel her gaze watching him. She smiled and waved good-bye as she had waited for him to back out of the parking space and head toward the Justice Center.

Josh's reverie came to an end as he pulled into the parking lot of the Justice Center. He saw Yazzie and Beneè in the computer room with Jeanette. "Got any more news on Halverson or that energy company?" he asked as he walked into the room.

"Strange, the only thing we could find was a bank withdrawal for $100 at an ATM at a Valero Service Station in Gallup, New Mexico on Friday morning. Navajo Police also found an abandoned car registered to Halverson in the parking lot this morning. Nothing after that," said Yazzie. "Someone must have picked him up there. There aren't any reports of stolen cars anywhere in the vicinity, so I'm figuring he must be on his way back east somewhere with the person who picked him up.

Halverson's from Greenville, county seat of Muhlenberg County in Kentucky; family worked in the coal mines there. That's where he got his start until all that business about clean air and strip mining closed a lot of the mines. I think we should alert state troopers along Interstate 40 and federal marshals in western Kentucky to be on the lookout for him. Halverson's parents still live in Greenville; might get lucky and find him there."

"Sounds good," said Josh. "You go and make the alerts to the state troopers. I'll take care of the federal marshals. Yazzie handed

Jeanette the files that contained all the reports and left. What about that energy company?" asked Josh.

Jeanette read from the file Robert had given her before he left for the mine. "The wire transfer into both the Munson and Halverson accounts came from an off shore account in the Cayman Islands. The name on the account was that of Energy Development West out of Atlantic City, New Jersey. We're still running financial checks to connect a name in the United States to the company – no luck so far. The Chief's guess is that this company is a money laundering operation for illegal mob activities including the sale of those stolen artifacts," said Jeanette.

"How do you know this?" asked Josh.

"Just got a text from Robert, who is still at the mine," said Jeanette. "Text also says Chief Nat'aanii will be taking over that part of the investigation and working with Interpol. Says for us to concentrate on finding Halverson and extraditing him back here in connection with the murder of Ole Jack first and then find out if and how his murder is connected to the larger concern. The Chief is also interested in locating Halverson's computer because there was nothing on the downloads from Munson's home computer or the computer at the mine other than the bank deposit. The Chief figures everything was kept on a thumb drive that originated on Halverson's computer."

"Good work," said Josh. "You might as well leave for the day. I'm going to call the office in Flagstaff now and start the ball rolling on getting federal marshals to Halverson's family home in Greenville. I'm leaving after that. Unless something unusual happens with Halverson, there's no need to stay any longer; I'll see you on Monday."

"Right," said Jeanette. "See you then." Josh waited until he got back to his rented suite to call Flagstaff. After making the call for federal marshals in Kentucky, Josh decided to call Eli. He hoped he could catch the family at home.

"Hi, Dad," said Eli. "We won our game today."

"Oh, that's great!" Josh had been so caught up in the murder and Rani he had forgotten Eli's soccer team was nearing the end of the season. The win today would put them in the finals being held next week. "How did you play?"

"I blocked three goals; that's why we won," said Eli. Josh could hear his son's pleasure coming through. "I wish you could have been there, but I know it's hard for you to get away when working a case."

"I'm glad you understand, Son. I went on a short hike to the Navajo National Monument this morning before work. I applied for some permits so that I can take you on an overnight hiking trip to the back country there just as soon as I finish this case. When would be a good time for you? I know I missed this week end with you, but if the permits come through by the time of your next week end visit, how about then? I could come for the tournament and then take you back with me afterward." Josh could hear Eli talking to his mom.

"Mom says the finals are on Friday. Maybe you could come to the game that Friday and I could go back with you then?"

"That sounds like a plan, Son. I'll call you later and check in with you to confirm, okay?"

"Sure," said Eli. Love you and stay safe."

"You, too, Son." Eli always said that, but today the phrase took on a new significance. Josh heard the concern this time.

CHAPTER

10

Josh's phone vibrated, waking him from a sound sleep. Startled, he grabbed the gun he kept loaded next to his bed when working an active case. *Don't usually sleep this well when on a case. Good thing I didn't shoot someone!* Now oriented to his surroundings, he picked up his phone, 3:00 am. There was an alert from the Justice Center. *Federal Marshals located Eric Halverson at a Motel 6 in Caseyville just outside of East St. Louis, IL. SWAT teams on the way to the motel now. Watch for updates.* Josh got up and dressed and headed for the Justice Center. He had to push his way through a throng of media reporters outside the entrance responding with "no comment," to their shouted questions.

Once inside, Josh met with the Chief to get an update. Phones and computer screens were broadcasting live footage of the SWAT movements in East St. Louis. Josh walked out into the briefing room. The case had become more complex in terms of jurisdiction. Josh was still in charge of the murder investigation and Halverson certainly was a person of interest. Chief Nat'aanii was handling the investigation into the stolen artifacts, along with the United Nations. For the time being, until Halverson was apprehended and extradited to Arizona, Josh was still in charge of the murder investigation.

The Chief, however, decided how communications with the media would work. "Jeanette, you will deal with the press when the time comes to answer their questions. You will have to be debriefed first. Josh will be in communication with law enforcement in Illinois and the rest of the country. Let's sit tight until we have Halverson in custody somewhere. The Chief of Police in East St. Louis is on a private line giving constant updates to Mr. Overton. We can't control what information is going out to the people of the local area, but we will try to keep as much order as we can here while updating the public in order to maintain safety."

All the staff had their eyes peeled on the camera relaying footage from outside the Motel 6 parking lot in Caseyville. Two squad cars were parked near the front of unit 36 located in the back of the motel on the 3rd floor of the complex. SWAT team units exited the back of two black SUV's and slowly approached the stairway with rifles at the ready. Each person wore a helmet and bullet proof vest. A local police officer with a bull horn announced their arrival. "Eric Halverson, we have the unit surrounded. Come out with your hands up!"

Hearing no response, one of the dark suited Federal Marshals asked to anyone who might have the answer, "are you sure he's in there?" The quiet was overpowering. Motel guests peeked from their doors or windows, too afraid to step outside. "Where's the manager?" he asked.

"He's inside the office," said the officer with the bull horn. "We talked with him before we called you. Manager confirmed the man calling himself Joseph Anderson with a driver's license to match, checked into the motel yesterday evening for one night only. The manager called our office after he saw a news report with Halverson's picture in the broadcast. Said Halverson wasn't driving a car. Someone in a dark, four door sedan dropped him off. He didn't pay much attention to the car at the time. No one saw the car return last night or this morning and no one reported seeing Halverson leave the unit after his arrival."

"Tell him to come out or we are coming in," said the Federal Marshall. Once again, the bull horn blared instructions into the hot summer air. The Federal Marshall gave the signal to go in.

As the team approached the door to unit 36, the man in front noticed a Do Not Disturb sign on the door. "Federal Marshalls, open up!" he exclaimed. The next sound was the breaking of the door locks from the dead bolt in the middle to the safety chain at the top. A sweep of the unit indicated it was empty. The casing of the bathroom window had been removed leaving an opening large enough to accommodate a man the size of Halverson. The bathroom window opened to the concrete walkway near the stairs next to the office. "Must have left that way and walked to a meeting place near the Interstate undetected," said the officer. Remains in the bathroom sink and garbage indicated Halverson had altered his appearance by dying his hair and adding false facial hair. There were also several receipts from the nearby Wal-Mart.

After seeing that yellow tape marking the crime scene had been put up, the Federal Marshall said, "you guys can leave." He contacted the Justice Center to report to Overton and order a forensics unit to come and collect evidence as well as go through all the trash. The Federal Marshall reported all he had seen and heard during the raid in Caseyville.

Josh said, "Make sure the forensics team gets the credit card receipt from the manager while they are there. Looks like our man has had some help getting fake identities. It appears Halverson is on the run with a fake identity and changed appearance. My guess is he is on his way to Kentucky in a car with a stolen license plate. He probably has had a good start. May already be over the Kentucky state line. Let's concentrate on working with the state officials in western Kentucky anywhere close to the Green River or Mammoth Cave area. Lots of hideouts in the area for a man who has connections plus money from someone who has lots of motivation to help him elude authority."

"Will do," said the Marshall as he hung up the phone.

Before Josh could say anything, Chief Nat'aanii, who had heard the conversation, spoke up. "Overton, there's an office for the Peabody Coal Operation in St. Louis, Missouri, isn't there?"

"Are you thinking what I'm thinking – that maybe Halverson stopped in East St. Louis to pass off the information that was on his computer?"

"Could be possible. Halverson had time to clean his computer and download everything to a thumb drive. What if he managed to get rid of that in St. Louis? Without that information, we have little to use in any extradition case. The evidence we have connecting Halverson to the murder of Ole Jack is purely circumstantial."

George Yazzie came into the room with an initial report from forensics. "The team found Halverson's lap top in the dumpster behind the Motel 6. Hard drive has been ripped out and crushed but left there. Don't know if anything can be retrieved. The unit found a receipt from a Wal-Mart dated yesterday afternoon in the dumpster near the computer. Items purchased included two flash drives, a Halloween make-up kit and hair dye. Color is dark brown. They are taking all the evidence to the Criminal Investigative Police Division located in East St. Louis."

"Jeanette, get a picture of Halverson and create a computer image of him with facial hair and darker hair color. Print that out and send it to state officials in Kentucky to be on the lookout for anyone fitting that description driving on or near the Western Kentucky Parkway. Yazzie, send out a bulletin to state troopers in Kentucky to watch for a driver who matches Halverson's description. If they see someone have them run the license plate number of the vehicle he is driving and get information on the vehicle and its owner. Send the picture to all the local police stations near tourist sites in the area. I think I need to make a trip to St. Louis," said Josh.

"How soon do you want to leave?" asked Jeanette.

"As soon as possible," said Josh. "Is there a local airport nearby to catch a flight to Flagstaff? It's only 7:00 am here; that would be 9:00 in St. Louis. Find a flight that leaves around noon or so. That's 2:00 in St. Louis. Schedule me a room downtown near the Peabody Headquarters so I can walk there on Monday morning. I can stop by the motel and talk with the manager on the drive from the airport; where is the airport in relation to downtown St. Louis?" he asked.

"St. Louis Regional Airport is northwest of downtown St. Louis," said Jeanette.

"Good. Then I can also look at the evidence that is being taken to the Criminal Investigative Police Division in East St. Louis on my way into downtown St. Louis," said Josh.

"I'll make the flight arrangements," said Jeanette.

"Great, I'm going back to the apartment and pack an overnight bag. Where can I pick up the plane to go to Flagstaff?"

Jeanette gave directions to the small airport near the mine and proceeded to arrange Josh's flight to St. Louis. Chief Nat'aanii went to his office to talk with Robert Beneè and the two United Nations delegates, Nate Harrison and Sarah Brown Crow. Sarah was a member of the Lakota tribe that had representation in the United Nations. It was time to discuss what they had discovered at the Kayenta Mine on Friday and decide how to proceed given the strange turn of events. There was not a lot to report.

Robert had shown the security videos of the costumed eagle dancer to Chief Nat'aanii, Nate and Sarah. "Those eagle feathers look like the real thing," said the Chief. "Tell me about your meeting with Ole Jack, Beneè."

"Not long after we heard about the Kachina dancer on the video, Jack stopped me outside The Blue Coffee Pot when I went there for lunch," said Robert. "Told me he had found something buried in one of the overburden piles next to a sandstone butte on the Black Mesa near the mine. Said it appeared to look like the eagle costume everyone had been talking about. I asked him if he had told anyone else and he said no. Said he thought I should know first because I would know what to do with it; wanted me to meet him after dark that night at the area where he found it."

"When was that?" asked the Chief.

"Last Monday. I met him in the area behind the mine near a large, sandstone butte and followed Jack to the place where he said he found the costume. When we got there, there was no sign of anything."

"Why didn't you say something about this sooner?" asked Sarah Brown Crow.

"Well, if you knew Ole Jack the way everyone here knew him, you wouldn't have taken him seriously, either. As soon as it appeared Jack's murder might be related to the costume, I did speak up. You were with us on Friday; we searched the entire area and came up empty handed. I don't think Ole Jack ever saw that costume."

"Then why was he murdered? The shadow on the video appeared to be that of someone dressed in that costume," said Nate Harrison.

"Maybe he stumbled on the person wearing the costume when he was digging the hole for the Black Cross and recognized him."

"That's possible," said the Chief. "It's also possible Halverson had the costume with him when he left and, like the flash drive, he's already unloaded the evidence. There's still a possibility that Munson's wife knows about that costume. I don't like doing this, but get a search warrant and go back to Munson's house and see what you can find."

"Will do," said Robert.

After Robert left, the Chief turned to Nate Harrison and said, "There's not much more we can do from here until Overton gets back from St. Louis. Tomorrow morning, I would like for you and Ms. Crow to contact the authorities in Paris and find out if anything resembling this eagle costume has shown up in Paris. After that, get Jeanette to compile a list of the major freight companies in Flagstaff and Phoenix and check their manifests for shipments to the East Coast within the last week, especially any paid for by this Energy West Co. In fact, check all the manifests for the past year. Some of the stolen artifacts that were sold in Paris might have been shipped from Arizona."

"What do we do after that, Chief?" asked Sarah Brown Crow.

"We'll compare notes after Overton returns from St. Louis. Hopefully, Halverson will be located by that time also. For now, go back to your hotel and get some rest. Your flights back to New York are scheduled for Tuesday morning. We may have some leads by then that will give us more information on locating a name behind this Energy West Company. I think the center of this illegal operation has now shifted to the East Coast and I'm pretty sure the eagle costume is no longer here."

Nate looked at his watch – 11:00. He was tired. He had been up since 3:00 and was also still rather jet lagged. "Want to ride back with me to the hotel in the rental car?" he asked Sarah.

"Sure," she replied. Chief Nat'aanii leaned back in his chair with his hands on his head. *What is going on? He wondered.*

*   *   *

Josh picked up the rental car waiting for him at the St. Louis Regional Airport and was now driving along I-255 toward Caseyville and East St. Louis. Jeanette had been efficient. It was 2:00 CDT, so he had plenty of time to go by the Motel 6 and talk to the manager himself and have a look at the crime scene. From there, he would pick up I-64 and drive to the Criminal Investigative Police Division located in East St. Louis to check on the status of the evidence collected at the motel earlier that morning before driving on into downtown St. Louis and settling in his room at the Hampton Inn which was a short walk to the Peabody Coal Headquarters.

Josh parked his rental car in the visitors parking lot located in front of the Illinois Division of Investigation located in East St. Louis. The hotel manager had not been able to offer anything new, but he did tell Josh how to get to the Wal-Mart where Halverson had bought the items listed on the receipts in the trash. Josh had decided to go by there and ask to see video from the security cameras for the date listed on the receipt.

Cameras picked up a man matching Halverson's description walking into the store and paying for some purchases at a self-check-out. Cameras at the exit door captured Halverson walking out and being picked up by someone in a dark blue, four door Honda Accord. Unfortunately, neither the driver's face nor the license number of the car could be distinguished from the picture. Josh called state troopers' offices in Illinois and western Kentucky to confirm the color and make of the car in which Halverson was last seen. He also told the troopers that Halverson might very well be a passenger and that the driver was probably a white male.

Josh showed his badge and identified himself to the security guard posted at the entrance before handing him his gun and walking through the metal detectors. As he was placing his gun back in his shoulder holster, he asked," has the evidence from the raid on the room in the Motel 6 in Caseyville come through yet?"

"Don't know," said the guard. "You'll need to go to the 3rd floor. Elevators are right there."

"I prefer the stairs," said Josh.

"Right next to the elevators, Sir," said the guard.

"Thanks," said Josh as he headed in the direction pointed out by the guard and then followed the signs. There was a window like that in a movie theater with an attendant located next to the door of the stairway. Josh once again showed his badge as he asked, "Where is the information desk for the crime unit?"

"See the door down there at the end of the hall?" asked the female guard. When Josh nodded yes, she said, "It's just inside that door."

"Thanks," said Josh as he walked down the hall. He was oblivious to the appreciative grin from the guard who evidently enjoyed the view from his backside. For the third time, Josh identified himself to the officer seated at the information desk inside the crime unit. "Where can I get information on the evidence collected at the Motel 6 in Caseyville this morning?" he asked.

"Don't know if anything's been done with it yet. It is Sunday, but you can check with Officer O'Connell over there."

Hearing his name, a tall, muscular officer with thick red hair and an unusual handlebar mustache came over to speak with Josh. "What can I do for you?" he asked.

"Name's Josh Overton; I'm with the FBI and we are working on the murder that took place on the Navajo Reservation in Arizona. The prime suspect was located at the Motel 6 in Caseyville, but he got away. Your investigators picked up some evidence that we need to help with the investigation and I came to see if you have found out anything yet."

"We just received the bags of evidence, and officers won't be here to work on it until tomorrow morning. I don't think there's anything we can do for you today. We sent over a report on the details of the physical items found at the motel to the Tuba City Justice Center. Once everything is officially labeled we will fax a report of our initial findings and then forward the physical evidence to the officials at the Tuba City Justice Center."

"Thanks," said Josh. "I'm staying at the Hampton Inn in downtown St. Louis near the Arch. I'll be following up on some leads at the Peabody Coal Headquarters tomorrow and hope to return to Tuba

City tomorrow night. Here's my contact information let me know if anything comes up tomorrow that you think I might want to see before I leave here."

"I think you probably have all the information already, but I will be sure and pass your message along," said Officer O'Connell.

"Thanks," said Josh as he turned toward the door. Josh noticed the female attendant looking at him on the way out. He nodded as he walked past. *Wonder what Rani is doing tonight. Hope she isn't with that Harrison fellow.* For the first time in his life Josh realized he was experiencing jealousy. *So that's what it feels like.* He shook his head and walked to his car without a second glance at the attractive female behind him.

*   *   *

Josh arrived at the Hampton Inn at 6:00. The high rise, red brick building was on Main St. just minutes from the Gateway Arch and Peabody Coal Headquarters. He was feeling tired. It was only 4:00 in Arizona but he had been up since 3:00 am. He was also feeling hungry. After he checked in, he took his bag up to his room on the 4th floor and then came back downstairs to eat at the Tigin Irish Pub and Restaurant located within the hotel building. *A lot different than the Southwest.* Josh remembered how unusual Jeanette's looks were in Tuba City. *She certainly would feel at home here.*

Josh finished his pub hamburger and fries and local microbrew and headed for his room. After emailing the information from his visits to the motel and Criminal Investigative Unit to Chief Nat'aanii, he double checked the location of the Peabody Headquarters. *Easy walk tomorrow.* Josh fell asleep as soon as his head hit the pillow without any thought to the attractive female guard. This was not his usual behavior. Before, he would have spent the evening in the Pub, too adrenalin charged to sleep well and maybe have found a nice diversion for the evening. If he had slept, it might have been somewhere other than his hotel room.

*   *   *

An alert from Josh's phone waked him at 8:00 am. It was a text from George Yazzie.

Josh wrote – *Copy that. On my way to Peabody now.*

Josh found a juice bar at a coffee shop down the street from Peabody Headquarters. After finishing his juice and roll, he carried his coffee with him to the blue and gray skyscraper that held the Peabody Energy logo on one of the two towers. He walked into the lobby and up to the information desk where he showed his badge.

"Name's Josh Overton, FBI agent investigating the murder of a man on the grounds of the Kayenta Coal Mining operation in Arizona. I'm following up on some leads involving this person." Josh showed the receptionist the altered picture of Halverson.

The slightly plump lady dressed like a mid-western housewife ready for church stared intently at the drawing before answering, "Don't recall seeing anyone like that during my shift," she said. "Let me see if I can find someone to help you." Josh heard her speak to someone she called Mr. Cameron. "There's a man here who says he's an FBI agent looking for someone connected to a murder in Arizona. He has a picture and wants to know if anyone has seen him here. Okay, I'll tell him. Mr. Cameron will be down shortly. He says to wait over there." The receptionist pointed to a line of chairs against the wall. Josh walked over and finished drinking his coffee while looking at pictures lining the wall above the chairs.

Josh looked at one after another – each depicting volunteers involved in projects that included service and community charities. He was looking at the one showing the restoration of the St. Louis Opera House when he heard someone behind him. He turned and grabbed the outstretched hand of a man in his mid-forties. Like the receptionist, the man was dressed in conservative mid-western attire, suit coat and tie. *Corporate middle management* thought Josh. *Good family man with a home in the suburbs.* "Mr. Overton?" he said. "Kenneth Burke, in charge of public communications. Phyllis says you want our help in locating a fugitive from justice?"

"Well, not exactly. It seems we have found the man, but now we would like to know what connection, if any, this man has with your company."

"What makes you think there might be a connection?" asked Burke.

Josh could tell this man knew nothing and would probably get more information from him than he gave. Only way to find out was to answer Burke's questions because if someone up the ladder knew anything, Josh was sure that his information would travel fast the minute he left. "The man we are seeking works for the Peabody Coal Company at the Kayenta Mine in Arizona. He worked for Peter Munson. I'm sure you have already heard of the suicide of Peter Munson, a manager of that mine."

Burke cleared his throat with a nod of assent.

"Eric Halverson was a crane operator there with a long history of employment with Peabody Energy. Both men have been connected to a case involving the illegal sale of stolen artifacts from the Hopi Reservation. A transient by the name of Ole Jack was murdered last Wednesday by what appeared to be someone dressed in a quite valuable eagle costume made before 1908. During the investigation we found huge deposits made into both men's accounts."

"Did they come from here?" asked an obviously shaken Burke.

"No, they came from an account held in the Cayman Islands by a seemingly bogus company named Energy Development West with a PO Box in Atlantic City, New Jersey."

"Well, why are you here and not in Atlantic City?"

"We are following all leads at the moment that might have any slight connection to the money trail while continuing to go through the men's personal as well as company computers." *You don't need to know we lost the computer files.*

"Well, until you come up with something more concrete, I'm afraid we can't help you"

"Don't suppose you would surrender video footage of the last week from the cameras in the building?" Josh knew the answer but he wanted to see the expression on Burke's face when he spoke. *Nothing.*

"Not without a warrant. Will that be all?"

"All for now, here's my card," said Josh as he turned to walk away. A man dressed in jeans and a cotton shirt walked past him toward the exit. *Looks out of place here,* thought Josh. Josh watched the man as he crossed the street and headed toward a dark blue Honda Accord. He started the car and drove away.

CHAPTER

11

Josh managed to get the first three letters of the license plate. Missouri tags - He looked at his watch, 11:00 am. *Flight's at 6:00 p.m. The Criminal Investigative Police Unit is on the way to the airport.* Josh decided to call and see what could be done with the license plate number. After giving the information to a detective there, Josh went back into Peabody Headquarters and spoke to the receptionist. "There was a man who left at the same time as I did," said Josh. "He was wearing a cotton shirt and jeans, walked past me while I was talking with Mr. Burke. Do all visitors have to sign in before going upstairs?"

"No, but they do have to check in with me and tell me where they are going."

"Do you remember that man and the person he was going to see?" The receptionist seemed hesitant to give out any information. Josh showed her his badge again. "This man is a person of interest in a federal murder investigation."

The receptionist looked at something on her screen. "Man signed in at 9:15 and went upstairs to the 6th floor. That's where the office that oversees the Kayenta Mining Operations is. Ms. Virginia Carroll is the supervisor you will need to see," she said while dialing a number. "Ms. Carroll will see you," she said after hanging up the phone. "Take the elevators over there to the 6th floor. Office is in front of you once you step out of the elevator."

"Thanks," said Josh as he walked toward the elevator. Josh's phone was ringing just as the elevator doors opened; it was the Criminal Investigation Unit.

"Is this Mr. Overton?"

"Yes, it is," said Josh.

"My name's Detective Brandt. We ran the numbers on that Missouri plate with the car's description. Couldn't find a car with the first three letters you gave that matches a dark blue Honda, but we came up with a car registered to a James Ferguson with the same first three letters on the plates. Reported the plates stolen a month ago when he applied for new plates. That's all the information we could find."

"Call the man and check to see if he remembers anything that might help us identify who stole them. In the meantime, I'm following some more leads at the Peabody Coal Headquarters. I'll be leaving for Arizona at 6:00 p.m. this evening; keep me posted at this number if you find out anything. In addition, alert your patrol units about a car with this license number. The person driving would be a white male around 40, about 6 feet tall with sandy blond hair. He's a person of interest in locating Eric Halverson who is connected with a murder investigation in Arizona."

"Will do. But you'll probably have more luck waiting until you talk with Halverson."

"Probably," said Josh as he hung up the phone and walked into the office marked *Virginia Carroll*. There was a desk in the center of the reception area. *All these receptionists look the same,* thought Josh noticing the middle aged, conservatively dressed woman who smiled at him as he walked toward her.

"May I help you?" she asked.

Josh showed her his badge and said, "I'm here to see Ms. Carroll about a man who was here this morning who is a person of interest in a murder case in Arizona."

"Oh, yes, Mr. Overton, isn't it? Ms. Carroll is ready for you. Go on in."

Ready for me? Thought Josh. A striking woman with dark hair and unusually creamy white skin greeted him as he walked through the door to the inner office. *Looks like Lilith from the television show Cheers.* Her solemn countenance and tight lipped greeting made her seem even more like Lilith. Josh was smiling inside but, as usual, his face gave no clue as to what he was thinking. "Josh Overton, FBI," he said. I'm here -"

"I know why you are here, Mr. Overton. Have a seat. The man you are interested in is named Brad Kellogg. He's a safety investigator who enforces OSHA standards at our mining operations out west; Kayenta Coal Mine is in his territory. Brad was supposed to do an inspection of the mining site last Friday, but when he arrived he found Mr. Munson had committed suicide so he drove back here. He came in this morning to report this. That's really all I know."

"What about the stolen license plates on his car? Does he live in St. Louis?"

"I don't know anything about his car. He has a car that he uses for his business trips. The company pays him a stipend for using his own car. I don't know anything about stolen plates. I'm sure we have a record of the car's plates. I'll have Paulette pull up his last travel voucher for you."

"Does he live in St. Louis?"

"He has an apartment here, but he travels a lot. He should be home because he just returned early from the trip to Kayenta. Our safety inspections will be delayed until these recent events are settled. No use muddying the waters at this time." Ms. Carroll walked to the door and spoke to the receptionist. "Paulette, get me Brad Kellogg's home address and phone number as well as a copy of his last travel voucher."

"Yes, Ms. Carroll."

"Do you know anything about Pete Munson's involvement in stolen artifacts from the Hopi Reservation?" Josh noticed a tinge of color in Ms. Carroll's translucent face.

"Of course not. Peabody Coal is only interested in minerals and mining – not the possessions of the people living around our mines."

At that moment, Paulette walked in with a folder that she handed to Ms. Carroll. "Here's the information you requested," she said.

Without looking at it, Ms. Carroll handed the folder to Josh. "I think we're finished here," she said. "It's almost noon and I have a luncheon meeting."

Josh took the folder and left and walked the half mile back to his hotel at a brisk pace. He had checked out and put his luggage in the rented car in the parking garage before he had left that morning. Since it was after 12:00, he stopped in the hotel restaurant to have lunch. After ordering a pasta salad and garlic bread, he called the Criminal Investigative Unit. "I have an address for Brad Kellogg; that's the name of the man we are looking for in connection with Eric Halverson. He lives in Hampton Garden Apartments, 5927 Susan Place in North Hampton. I've called the phone number listed in his employment file and get no answer. Send a unit to the apartment complex and I'll meet you in one hour." Josh disconnected just as his lunch arrived; he programmed his phone with the address of the Hampton Garden Apartments while eating. It was 1:30 when he paid his bill and headed for his rental car. He sent a quick text to the Justice Center before leaving the building.

Halverson on his way to Tuba City with Federal Marshall. Have a public defender talk with him before doing any interviews and check on the possibility of getting a DNA sample. Halverson should be there by the time I get there tomorrow morning. I should be there by 9:00 am. Have Yazzie handle the interview if Halverson is ready before I get there.

Josh walked outside into the hazy, humid mid-western summer air. *Be glad to get back to dryer air,* he thought. *He couldn't help thinking about Rani also as he walked into the underground parking garage next to the Hampton Inn.* The garage seemed unusually quiet for a busy Monday afternoon. It was, however, almost 2:00. *Maybe employees take an earlier lunch in the Midwest,* he thought. Josh pulled his keys from his pocket to unlock the rental when he heard footsteps close behind him. Before he could turn around, he felt someone grab him and place something over his mouth. There was no time to think or respond.

*   *   *

Members of the SWAT team arrived at Brad Kellogg's apartment unit in North Hampton at 2:00. Seeing no sign of Josh Overton, they called the number he had left at headquarters. The call went directly to voice mail, so they called headquarters and asked for instructions. Detective Summerville took the call. "No sign of Overton here at the complex. We called him and got no answer. Has he been in touch with you?"

"No," said the detective. Last we heard he was on his way to the complex after eating lunch. He was staying at the Hampton Inn. I suggest you go ahead and pick up Kellogg while I try to locate Overton."

"Will do," said Officer Villatoro, the female leader of the three person team. As they approached the front door of the red brick unit, the officer noticed a dark blue Honda Accord. She motioned toward it and said, "What's that license number, Rick?"

Officer Clay walked behind the car and wrote down the number. "MKV 423, Missouri plates," he said.

"Call that in to headquarters. I think that is the car Overton called about," said Villatoro. "Come inside as soon as you do that," she said as she and her partner opened the front door. Kellogg's apartment was the first door on the right. Taking positions on either side of the door, Villatoro knocked and said, "police officers, open up!" Hearing no sound, she knocked again and repeated the same phrase. Officer Clay was now with the other two. Nodding toward Villatoro, Clay broke the door open and the three rushed in with guns ready.

The living and dining area of the small one bedroom apartment were empty. Clay walked toward the kitchen and the other two walked down the hall. Villatoro stopped at the bathroom to look in. Officer Blanton walked toward the bedroom and opened the door. "I think I found Kellogg," he said. The others rushed toward the bedroom to find a man slumped over the queen sized bed, a blank stare on his face turned toward the foot of the bed. It looked as though he had been strangled from behind.

"Call headquarters and get the medical examiner and a forensics unit out here," said Villatoro. "I'm going to talk with the manager and you two see if anyone in the vicinity heard or saw anything. And see what you can find in that Honda out there."

"Okay," said both officers in unison.

*   *   *

Josh was hiking with Rani when he noticed a Kachina in an eagle's costume dancing in the alcove leading to the ruins of the Betatakin Cliffs. He was trying to get Rani's attention but she was busy looking at some petro glyphs on one of the sandstone buttes. "Who are you?" he asked, but the dancer turned away and ran out of sight.

A voice in the distance said, "where is the costume? How much do you know about us?"

Josh could hear himself speaking, "I don't know. Let me go and I'll find out." Josh was in a fog, a nightmare and he was struggling to wake up. He wanted to get up, but something was holding him down.

Josh thought he heard, "He doesn't know anything, let's get out of here." More muffled voices, sounds of things being shifted and moved and then a door opening and closing. He opened his eyes but it was still dark. Josh realized he was blindfolded; he could feel the rope around his chest holding him to a chair; his feet and hands were bound. He listened intently for any sound. "Is anyone here?" he asked. Silence. He started to yell. Nothing. *I need to get out of this chair and get this blindfold off,* he thought.

Josh pushed the chair across what sounded like a wooden floor until he came to what felt like a table. He put his head down and pushed the side of his face against the corner of the table until he felt the bandana across his eyes start to loosen. He kept working until it came off. He was still woozy from the drugs and it took his eyes time to adjust to the light; it was daytime but the room was dark.

The table and two chairs including his were the only furniture in the room that looked like the kitchen of an abandoned house. There were some machines set up on the counter that looked like copy machines and those used in the creation of credit cards and identification. *Probably wiped clean of fingerprints.* There was a computer next to the machines. Josh tried to turn the computer on but there was no electricity. *Probably wiped clean as well, but as soon as I know where I am, I will have to get a forensics unit here. Need to call the Justice Center as soon as I get to a phone.* Josh continued his assessment of the building.

The windows were boarded up but there was enough light to see empty packing crates and shipping materials on the floor. Josh dragged his chair over to an open, plastic bag filled with food garbage and rags. He gingerly sifted through the top and found a glass bottle. He maneuvered the bottle from the garbage onto the floor and then hit the middle with the heels of his shoes until it shattered. Josh found the chunk he wanted and began rubbing it against the rope holding his hands together. After freeing his hands, Josh untied his feet and stood up and almost fell. *Where am I? How did I get here and what did they give me?*

After regaining his balance, Josh looked around; he saw some stairs off the center of the kitchen. He went up the stairs and saw what appeared to be a hallway with doors opening on either side. *Some kind of dormitory,* he thought. He looked inside one of the rooms; the windows were broken so he could look outside. He saw a huge, backyard with a wrought iron fence around it. There appeared to be vacant lots with lots of thick underbrush surrounding the building. Josh walked back downstairs.

I must still be in East St. Louis, he thought. He walked across the room and opened the door to reveal another large room. *Some kind of meeting room?* There was an arched doorway that led to the front entrance to the building, and there was another stairway on his right. *Must lead to the upstairs bedrooms.* The front room was smaller than the middle room. Josh walked through the hallway and noticed a closet and a room on his left. Bathroom fixtures in dire need of repair told Josh all he needed to know. This was apparently an abandoned building that had been used for some type of illegal operation. Josh walked outside.

The abandoned building was red brick and looked much like early twentieth Century architecture for institutional type houses. There were three floors with windows going all around the building. Those on the first two were securely fastened. The third floor windows were open and most of them were broken. Josh stood on the small front stoop and looked up and down the street. This had once been a thriving street, but now most of the buildings were abandoned or non-existent. *That explains the return to nature,* he thought.

Josh searched his pockets. He had no phone, gun or FBI badge, but he still had his car keys and wallet with all his money and identification. *There has to be a convenience store somewhere.* Josh looked at his watch. It was 11:00 am, but he had no idea what day of the week it was. At least one day had passed, of that he was sure. He had certainly missed the return flight to Arizona. If he was in East St. Louis, walking west would probably the best. If he still had his car keys that meant his car might still be in the parking garage where he had been abducted. Josh started walking west and eventually reached an intersection that was marked. He was on a street called Collingsville Ave. at the intersection of Broadway.

There were a few cars parked alongside this street that must have led to a thriving commercial district at one time. There were deserted buildings that had, at one point, housed offices and upscale apartments. The one which he had just left was near the fringe of the district and was probably some type of church or treatment facility for the underprivileged. Looking down Collingsville Ave., he noticed a neon sign on the front of a building that said *Checks cashed here. Pay bills.* There was a Western Union logo below that. Seeing an electrical sign that said OPEN, Josh walked inside the door.

There was a Middle Eastern man sitting behind a counter with a Plexiglas window surrounding it. Josh spoke to the man through a slit above a sliding drawer. After putting his driver's license in the drawer, Josh said, "My name's Josh Overton. I'm an FBI agent from Arizona here on a murder investigation. I was staying at the Hampton Inn when I was mugged in the parking garage there. I woke up in an abandoned building down the street. I lost my phone and have no idea where I am or what day it is; I was kidnapped on Sunday afternoon. Could you help me?"

"You're in the downtown district of East St. Louis on Collingsville Ave. It's Tuesday, July 28. Not much here except abandoned buildings. Really is not a safe neighborhood, and I don't know much about St. Louis or where the Hampton Inn is."

"Do you have a telephone I could use? I have the number of the hotel in my wallet." The manager pulled the receiver from a telephone and passed it through the drawer to Josh.

The counter attendant began dialing as Josh read the number to him. "Hampton Inn, may I help you?" came a female voice at the other end of the line.

Josh explained his situation as well as he could and told he desk clerk where he was. "Could you tell me how to get back to St. Louis from here?" he asked.

"Give me your address again and I'll call a cab to come pick you up. Do you have any money?"

"As a matter of fact, I do," said Josh. "I have everything except my phone and my FBI badge."

"Good. I'll call the cab as soon as we hang up. Wait outside the Western Union Office. Should be there in about half an hour."

"Thanks," said Josh. He returned the receiver to the clerk and started to walk outside.

"Best you wait inside," he said with a knowing look.

Josh nodded his head and went over to the window to wait. After about thirty minutes a green Prius pulled over in front of the building; Josh walked outside and sat in the front seat next to the driver. "Goin' to the Hampton Inn?" the driver asked.

Josh nodded yes and in about 15 minutes he walked from the cab to the parking garage next to the Hampton Inn. His car was where he had left it and he found his suitcase in the trunk. Someone had obviously handled his lap top and deleted all his files; his flash drive with the backup was also missing. *Nice of them not to destroy government property,* he thought. It seemed his kidnappers had been in too much of a hurry to check the contents of his suitcase, so he found all the hard copies of the files given to him in St. Louis. Josh felt lost without his phone, however. *How did we ever live before the smart phone*, he thought. Josh took his suitcase from the trunk and rolled it behind him as he walked into the Inn. He knew he would be staying over in St. Louis but for how long? *Wonder if I'll be back in time to take Eli on that hike – and maybe Rani?*

CHAPTER

12

Rani sat on the couch in the front room of her apartment. She was holding the sandstone petro glyph looking at it intently. Her thoughts strayed to the drawing she had seen inside the alcove at the Betatakin Ruins. *This is the same drawing!* After the hiking trip with Josh, Rani had been busy getting ready to start school. The first two days had been a whirlwind with orientation meetings and getting things ready for the students. This afternoon was the first time she had had to think about the drawing or the stone. Since Derrick was still in town, he had been keeping her up to date on the progress of Ole Jack's murder investigation. It wasn't hard to follow though. Pete Munson's suicide, the man hunt and international intrigue had monopolized the news from Phoenix to Flagstaff.

Nate Harrison had called Rani on Sunday evening letting her know he was leaving for New York. It seemed as though the investigation into the missing artifacts was now an international criminal investigation into a possible mob connection on the East Coast and money laundering. Any items recovered by Interpol would be turned over to the United Nations Indigenous Peoples Council for repatriation. Chief Nat'aanii would oversee this when all the items that had been illegally sold had been recovered. For now, the Chief was staying in Tuba City and would be working with the FBI on the murder investigation, but no one was excluding the possible connection of Ole Jack's murder to the stolen artifacts.

The last thing Rani had heard from Derrick was that Eric Halverson had been arrested in Kentucky and was being brought back to Tuba City for questioning. Rani had asked Derrick about Josh, and her knees had buckled when she heard Josh had not been on the return flight from St. Louis and no one at the Center knew where he was. Derrick had noticed her distress. "He's all right; I'm sure. I don't know the man very well, but I think he knows how to take care of himself."

Rani's stomach was in knots and she really didn't know what to say. She hardly knew Josh, but she knew her feelings were already strong. Maybe this was a signal for her to forget about this man. If she were going to let any man into her life, maybe she needed someone like Nate whose activities were far less dangerous. Sometimes, however, love is not rational. Hearing that she might never see Josh again only made her desire for him stronger. Rani felt her hands tense around the stone. *Careful, girl.* As she put the stone back into the drawstring bag, she heard her doorbell. She laid the bag on the dining room table before opening the door; it was Derrick.

"Thought you would like to know they've heard from Josh at the Justice Center. Don't know details; the department is being very careful about releasing information. There were also police officers at Pete Munson's home this afternoon – had a search warrant to look for any more relevant information to the case that might have been missed beforehand."

Rani breathed a sigh of relief. Derrick noticed. "Your interest in this case is getting a little personal, isn't it?

"I have to admit I am having feelings that I have never experienced before, but I feel awkward talking about this with you. Have you heard from Listie?"

"Yes. Everything in Coos Bay is back to normal. Polly starts school on August 12th. I think now that Eric Halverson is in custody, I won't need to stay here much longer. Listie misses you also and she wants you to meet Polly so the two of them are coming in on Friday. We wanted to do an overnight camping trip at the Navajo National Monument over the weekend. Would you like to go with us if I make the reservations? I'd like to see the drawing you are talking about, and maybe we could take the stone to Old Oraibi Village before Listie and I start back to Coos Bay."

"That would be great," said Rani as she picked up the bag and showed the contents to Derrick who seemed fascinated with it. Derrick put the stone in the bag and placed it on the dining room table.

"Okay to put this back on the table?" said Derrick.

Rani jumped as her thoughts about inviting Josh and his son were interrupted. She shook her head and said, "Sure. How about a carrot juice float?"

"I was hoping you would ask," smiled Derrick.

*   *   *

Josh's stay in St. Louis had been extended until Friday due to the new developments. Chief Nat'aanii had spoken with the East St. Louis Police Commissioner and she had sent a forensics team to investigate the building where Josh had been kept. Josh found out that the building was an historic one that had been the National Catholic Community House until the decline of that part of the city in the 60's. Everyone involved in the case was certain that the building had been used for illegal operations that most likely included the shipping of stolen artifacts from there to some still unknown center on the East Coast. The police commissioner had kindly issued Josh a replacement weapon; a new badge was being sent from Washington to Tuba City.

Josh had had time to go over the file on Brad Kellogg including a forensics report from the apartment search and the coroners' report. There was DNA evidence on the wire used to strangle Kellogg. It appeared Kellogg had put up enough of a fight to cause the wire to cut through the surgical gloves the assassin wore providing some much needed DNA evidence.

Investigators had pieced together Kellogg's involvement in the stolen artifacts. They believed Brad had been the courier for the stolen artifacts and the connection to Energy Development West. Josh needed to return to Peabody Headquarters in order to find out if the Coal Company's involvement ended at Brad or someone higher up the corporate ladder, *perhaps Virginia Carroll?* Some entity with deep pockets was paying for this operation and that was not Brad

Kellogg. In addition, Brad's death was definitely the work of a professional, someone not connected to the Company at all but most likely hired by someone there. Josh's first order of business after settling back into the Inn and contacting Chief Nat'aanii had been to get a new phone. He then called Eli to let him know he was all right. The relief in his son's voice was obvious. *Time to retire?*

"I'm returning to Tuba City very early Friday morning. I have to go to the Justice Center and tie up a lot of loose ends before I can leave. What time is your soccer game?"

"It's at 4:00. I sure hope you can make it."

"I should be able to leave Tuba City after lunch so that I can be there in plenty of time for the game. Make sure you have everything you need for our camping trip. I have made reservations for a camping spot for us. There are only two spots available so I'm glad I was able to get one. If something happens I will call you."

Josh heard the concern in his son's voice when he said, "I just hope if something happens you will be able to call me. I love you Dad."

Ouch. "I love you too, Son. You just worry about your game."

"Okay, good bye."

"Bye, Son."

Josh didn't think he should call Rani and invite her along on the camping trip. He felt like some time with his son alone was the thing to do. After hanging up, Josh spent the rest of Tuesday and Wednesday talking with the Criminal Investigative Unit and going over the forensics evidence from the Catholic Center as well as the evidence from Brad Kellogg's apartment and car. Brad's computer had been cleaned and the hard drive crushed like the others. A report of Brad's financial records did show, however, that he had received monthly deposits into his account from the Energy Development West Company in New Jersey.

After a visit to the Catholic Center, Josh learned the forensics team had found some fingerprints that matched Brad Kellogg's. The others were unidentifiable, and the garbage produced no useful DNA. Josh planned on doing more research of the Peabody Coal Company after dinner in the hope that something might show up within the leadership of the Company to connect someone to Brad Kellogg. Brad Kellogg reported to Virginia Carroll. *Who was Carroll's boss?*

Josh called Tuba City that evening and spoke with Chief Nat'aanii about the results of the search of Pete Munson's home. He also wanted to ask about the possibility of running financials on Virginia Carroll and her boss, Stewart Campbell. Nat'aanii connected him to George Yazzie for information on the results of the search at Munson's home. Nat'aanii also told Yazzie to run financials on the two Peabody Corporate Personnel.

"Hey Man, glad you are okay," said Yazzie. "Chief says you want the results of the second search of Munson's home."

"That's right. Anything turn up?" asked Josh.

"Mrs. Munson was most cooperative. Still grief stricken and concerned about her husband's reputation, but she did hand over something she had found when going through Pete's closet after the funeral."

"What was it?"

"Well, she was going through Munson's things to sort, package and distribute among relatives and friends or to give to Goodwill when she found a box labeled, *gym shoes.* Mrs. Munson thought that quite odd because Munson had joined the gym after his heart attack, but to her knowledge he had not gone back after the initial orientation. When she opened the box, there was indeed a pair of men's gym shoes inside, but when she took them out to look at them, the cardboard bottom came loose. Underneath that was a small envelope with a key inside that said – *gym locker.* She turned that over to us before we started the search. This was the only thing that came from the search. Beneè will be going to the gym tomorrow with another search warrant for the locker contents. I'll have him run the financials ordered early tomorrow morning. They should be available by 9:00 am in time for you before you go back to Peabody Headquarters. When will you be coming back to Tuba City?"

"I have a 5:00 a.m. flight to Flagstaff on Friday. It actually is scheduled to arrive there at 4 a.m. MST. Funny huh? I plan on renting a car and coming straight to the Justice Center. Should be there by 6 am. Anyone talked with Halverson yet?"

"We were going to get him a public defender, but when Halverson got here, a lawyer from St. Louis showed up. Said he was on staff for Kayenta Company employees and wanted to hold off any interviews until he talked with Halverson and until you could be located."

"Interesting," said Josh. "Anything else I need to know before I leave St. Louis?"

"Not now," said Yazzie. "We should have the financials you requested by tomorrow morning as well as the results of the search of the gym locker. If anything turns up there that would keep you in St. Louis longer, I'll let you know by tomorrow morning."

"Sounds good," said Josh. "Good bye."

*　　*　　*

Josh's phone buzzed while he was eating breakfast. It was a text from Beneè.

> *Sent you an email with the results of the gym locker search. Also, ran those financials on Carroll and Campbell. Two federal marshals will meet you in the lobby of Peabody Headquarters at 11:00 a.m. today. After you see Campbell's financials, you will understand. Chief says to study the report on the contents of Munson's locker. Hand over copies of all these files to the federal marshals. Chief says the agents will fly back to Flagstaff with you after taking Campbell into custody in St. Louis. They will want to be part of Halverson's interrogation. From that point forward, the Chief will handle the stolen artifacts. Your job will be to solve Ole Jack's murder. Whether or not the two are related is still up in the air. Plan on briefing at Justice Center as soon as you get back to Tuba City on Friday.*

Josh replied, *Will do.* He then finished his breakfast and went upstairs to his room. He turned on his lap top and opened his email from Beneè. There were two attachments; he opened the financials on Stewart Campbell. There were no files for Virginia Carroll. Evidently, she was in the clear. As expected, Campbell's financials showed two large deposits made into his account about the same time as the large deposits had appeared in Munson and Halverson's account. Josh made a note to ask Halverson about this. The search of the gym locker was a gold mine of information.

Munson had kept a thumb drive that contained all the information on the illegal operation being carried out at Peabody Coal Company. The black market operation had been going on for three years. Brad Kellogg was the connection between Munson and Halverson and Stewart Campbell. There were descriptions of two ancient artifacts that had been delivered by Kellogg and the black market value of each. These two matched the description of two artifacts recently sold at the Paris auction and recovered. One was a blue turquoise full face Kachina mask with dark brown crow feathers spreading from each side around the ears.

There was a beige upside down triangle in the center with slits for eyes. The tip of the triangle ended at a beige rectangular base with an opening for the mouth. Delivery date was listed as March, 2013. This date coincided with the deposits made into Munson, Halverson and Kellogg's accounts.

In June of 2014, there was a picture of an animal mask made from a squash gourd with the elongated tip painted like the nose of some kind of ant eater. This was delivered in February, 2015 and that date matched the date of the second deposit into the three men's accounts. The last entry described two *to be delivered items.* The date was listed as July 30, 2015 with a COD order for $25,000 each to be deposited into the three accounts. There were two images — one was described as a 17th Century full bodied eagle's costume. The other was a stone pestle for grinding corn with no date.

Josh marked the picture of the eagle's costume to be compared to the video from the Kayenta security cameras. Interpol and the Paris police would most likely find the stone pestle in the auction house if it had not already been sold. Josh suspected Halverson could provide information as to the whereabouts of the eagle costume.

Josh downloaded all the information onto a thumb drive and took it down to the large computers in the lobby in order to print out copies to take with him to Peabody Headquarters the next day. As he was going into the computer room off the side of the lobby, he noticed a man in business attire carrying a briefcase walking toward the front desk. Josh quickly checked his pockets – phone and gun were there. Something in Josh's gut told him to stay out of sight until the man got on the elevator.

Josh saw the elevator stop on his floor. He quickly printed out two copies of the file and walked over to the front desk and asked for a mailing envelope and some stamps. He mailed one copy to the Tuba Justice Center and then asked if he could leave the second copy of the file in the downstairs safe. The attendant didn't ask any questions, took the file and gave Josh the envelope and stamp. Josh went in the back with him and addressed the envelope to the Tuba City Justice Center. He then put the thumb drive and the second copy of the file in the envelope, sealed it and handed it to the attendant to be put in the office safe. He told the desk clerk he was going to the bar. "Let me know when you see the man in the suit leave," he said.

Although shaken by the recent events, the clerk nodded his assent. Josh had been at the bar for about 30 minutes when the desk clerk came in to tell him the businessman had left the building. Josh paid his tab and went upstairs to his room. He pulled his gun from his shoulder holster and entered cautiously. After making sure no one was in the room or bathroom, Josh assessed his belongings. Just as he suspected his suitcase had been rifled and the files he had obtained on Kellogg from Virginia Carroll were missing. His computer had once again been wiped clean.

Josh packed his belongings and went downstairs; picked up the file he had left at the desk and checked out of the hotel. He asked the front desk clerk to have the parking valet bring his car around to the front. He then drove to a small motel off I-40 with his eyes constantly checking his rear view mirror. Assured he had not been followed, Josh pulled off at the first exit he saw that had motels close to the Interstate. He checked in and spent most of the night sleeping in a chair with his phone and gun at his side.

Josh called the Justice Center from the motel office lobby while he was eating his complimentary breakfast. He spoke with Robert Beneè and told him of the previous night's incident. "I mailed a package with the contents of the two emails you sent plus another thumb drive to the Justice Center. I kept a copy to give to the Federal Marshalls today. The file I had on Stewart Campbell was taken from my room at the Hampton and my lap top was cleaned out again. I'll get another company file on Campbell today. Also, have a sketch artist at the Center tomorrow. I'd like to get a drawing of the man I saw in the hotel last night and start it circulating. That man may be our hit man and I certainly don't want to be next on his list. Make sure Halverson and his attorney are at the Justice Center by 6:00 a.m. tomorrow. I have plans to go to my son's soccer game in Flagstaff at 4:00 tomorrow afternoon and it is important that I make that if at all possible."

"Will do, Boss," said Beneè.

Josh saw the Federal Marshalls as soon as he walked into the lobby of Peabody Headquarters. As he handed one of them the file from Munson's thumb drive, he said, "You been briefed about the situation to date?"

"Yes," said the balding agent who resembled Tommie Lee Jones. Name's Gus Hardwick and this is my partner, Ken Perkins." Josh handed Hardwick the file with the thumb drive that implicated Stewart Campbell. "I think this man will need to be interrogated before we leave for Flagstaff," said Hardwick.

Josh shook both men's hands before walking toward the information desk. He noticed Ken Perkins was a lot younger than Hardwick and a very nice looking, tall, dark man. *Played basketball at one time?* Thought Josh.

"We're here to see Virginia Carroll," said Josh to the same woman he had spoken to a few days earlier – so much had happened since then.

"Yes, Ms. Carroll and Mr. Carter are expecting you. You know the way, right?" Josh nodded and walked toward the main elevator. Virginia Carroll's door was open and both she and the man in her office walked toward the door to greet Josh and the two Federal Marshalls.

"This is the head of Community Relations, my boss, John Carter," she said. Josh shook the extended hand and looked at John Carter as Ms. Carroll finished the introductions. *I've seen this man before. Where?*

The Opera House! His picture's on the wall downstairs. "I noticed your picture on the wall downstairs," said Josh. "I haven't had a chance to visit the restored Opera House but I was a "guest" at the historic Catholic Community Center for a while," he smiled.

"Oh, yes, that was unfortunate," said Carter. "We want you to know our office will cooperate in any way we can to find out if anyone else here at Peabody Headquarters besides Stewart Campbell was involved in this awful mess."

"Where is Mr. Campbell?" asked Hardwick. "We'd like to speak with him about some information we found in Pete Munson's records."

Virginia Carroll looked at Carter who spoke up hesitantly. "It seems Stewart Campbell has disappeared."

"That's interesting. Perkins contact the St. Louis Police Commissioner and put out a bulletin on this Campbell. Get a unit to go to his residence and gather all the information possible. You will need to stay here in St. Louis and follow up on this instead of coming with me to Flagstaff," said Hardwick.

"Yes, Sir," said Perkins as Hardwick handed him the file on Campbell.

Marshall Hardwick then asked Carter, "Do you know anything about a company called Energy Development West that has a post office address in New Jersey?" Both Ms. Carroll and Carter thought for a minute and shook their heads no.

"Do you know anyone who was a friend of Stewart Campbell that might help us, a girlfriend, buddy or close relative?"

"Campbell was on the road a lot so he didn't socialize much with the people here. As far as a girlfriend, don't know about that. Local police ran a check after they found he was missing from his apartment. No one there seemed to know much about him either. Campbell moved here from Muhlenberg County in Kentucky when the coal mines there started shutting down," said Virginia Carroll.

"That would explain how Campbell knew Halverson," said Josh. "We'll have to ask him about that tomorrow."

As Hardwick shook his head in agreement, Virginia Carroll said, "Is there anything else we can help you with?"

"Think that's about all for now," said Josh. "We're heading back to Flagstaff tomorrow morning and I'll be staying there. After Hardwick hears from Halverson, he'll return to St. Louis to follow up on the Catholic Center investigation and the connection with the New Jersey Company. Hopefully, some information will turn up on Campbell by then. Since Halverson, Munson and Campbell were all employees of Peabody Coal; further investigation for other connections within the Company is still a possibility."

"Here's my card," said Ms. Carroll as she handed one to Hardwick and Perkins. "Feel free to contact me if we can be of further help."

"We will," said Hardwick. "What do you make of those two?" asked Hardwick after the three men were outside the building.

"My instincts tell me they don't know anything," said Josh. "I think if there is a bigger connection within Peabody it's probably somewhere in the Kentucky operations since both Campbell and Halverson have connections there. You'll have to handle that part of the interrogation with Halverson tomorrow. Once I get back to Tuba City I will be trying to see how all this connects to Ole Jack's murder. Somehow, I don't think Old Jack's murder is directly related," said Josh.

"Jack's murder seems to be more of a spontaneous nature since the murder weapon belonged to him. A professional would have had his weapon with him. This appears to be someone running scared, maybe being blackmailed. I haven't ruled out Halverson; however, I think he might also be a target." Josh's usual stoic demeanor changed a bit as he said, "I think I might have been a target last night if I had returned to my hotel room right away. I'll be glad to get back to Tuba City, interview Halverson and then take a couple of days to be with my son."

"Hope you can do that," said Hardwick. "I have a family myself, but Perkins here is still single. Our line of work doesn't exactly fit the suburban family life style, does it?"

"No," said Josh as he thought about Emma and Chris. *Time to think about a career change?*

*　　*　　*

Rani had stayed late at school to attend a Navajo class where she ran into Lillian. Rani had seen her around school and found out that Lillian was the President of her senior class; Lillian was becoming a trusted ally. Lillian told Rani she would help her with her Navajo if Rani would help her with sign language. Rani had consented with enthusiasm. Although Lillian was Navajo, she knew many Hopi students who came from Hopi villages that bordered the Navajo Reservation. On the way home from school, Rani had thought about the clay tablet. She reminded herself that she wanted to pack it with her overnight backpack.

As Rani was walking from her car toward the steps to her apartment, Charlotte called to her from the manager's office. Rani stopped and walked toward her. "What is it?" she asked.

"I was returning from lunch this afternoon when I saw someone coming from the direction of your apartment, a man that I haven't seen before. I asked him if I could help him. Said he was interested in renting an apartment and when he saw I was out to lunch, he decided to look around until I came back. He asked if we had any vacancies and took the information I gave him when I told him one would be coming up soon. You know, Derrick and Listie's apartment. I just felt it was rather odd what with the murder and everything. You have any reason to think Derrick might be in some kind of trouble?"

"Not that I know, but I'll talk to him about it when I see him. Listie and Polly will be here this weekend and Derrick thinks he'll be able to return to Coos Bay with them next week. Eric Halverson is in custody now, and the FBI agent Josh Overton is returning from St. Louis to interrogate him. Derrick is hopeful that will take any connection with him to Ole Jack off the table."

"Hope that's the case," said Charlotte. "See ya."

"Thanks." Rani had an eerie feeling that sent chills through her when she unlocked the door of her apartment. The dead bolt was unlocked but the doorknob was locked. *Did I forget to lock that this morning? I have been distracted lately.* She cautiously peered around the front room and into the kitchen. Everything appeared as she had left it. She went into the guest bath and bedroom and looked around and then into her bathroom and bedroom. The windows in both rooms were open and the sit in screens were still in place. The door to her bedroom closet was slightly ajar. When she opened the door, she had a suspicion that the contents had been disturbed. For some reason, Rani thought about the sandstone tablet.

Rani opened the drawer of her dresser where she kept the tablet. The contents of that drawer had also been disturbed *The tablet was missing!* She went to the dining table where she had dropped her purse and phone to call Derrick. Then she remembered; she had left the bag with the stone inside on the dining table yesterday. *I'm getting a little less organized. Don't know if that's a good or bad thing*, she thought as she picked up a pile of school papers scattered around the table. There, beneath one pile was the cotton bag, undisturbed. *Must have been all in my mind.* Rani picked up her phone and texted Derrick. *Are we set for the overnight camping trip tomorrow?*

Yes, I'm at the Flagstaff airport right now. Will talk to you later this evening when we get back to Kayenta.

Rani took the cotton bag and put it in the overnight camping bag and finished preparations for the trip before having a light dinner. She sat down to read more about the hiking trails at the Navajo Monument while waiting for Derrick and Listie.

CHAPTER

13

The plane from St. Louis to Flagstaff landed just 15 minutes late. Neither Josh nor Hardwick had checked their luggage so they headed for the car rental office located next to the long term parking. Josh had flown from Tuba City to Flagstaff and his car was still at the private airport in Tuba City. Hardwick rented an SUV and the two made the drive to Tuba City in an hour and 15 minutes. There was hardly any traffic on the road. After picking up his car at the airport, Josh arrived at the Justice Center at 5:50 am. George Yazzie took Josh and Hardwick to the interrogation room where Halverson and his attorney were waiting.

George Yazzie placed a video recorder on the table and advised Halverson that everything was going to be recorded. After advising Halverson of his rights, Yazzie gave the date of the interrogation and the names and relationship to the interrogation of all present parties. Josh Overton then proceeded with the questioning.

Josh again asked Halverson if he had been advised of his Miranda rights and asked," Do you understand these rights?"

Halverson looked at his attorney who nodded consent, "I do," he said.

"You are being questioned in connection with two separate felonies. The first is the murder of a man by the name of Ole Jack near the entrance to the Kayenta Coal Mine on the Hopi and Navajo Reservations in Northeast Arizona on July 22nd of this year. The murder is under the jurisdiction of the federal government. As an agent with the Federal Bureau of Investigation, I am in charge of the investigation and I will be asking questions in regard to that murder. When I am finished with my questions, Federal Marshall Gus

Hardwick will continue with questions concerning your involvement in an international theft of sacred artifacts and the murder of one Brad Kellogg." Upon hearing this, Halverson gasped. His attorney placed a warning hand on Halverson's shoulder.

Josh continued, "We'd like to know how long you have been employed by any mining facility of the Peabody Coal Company."

"I went to work first for the Peabody Coal Mining Operation in Kentucky when I was eighteen. Good job. Good pay, but those federal investigators and tree hugging environmentalists started nosing in on the company and jobs became scarce. Moved west in 2003 and worked for the Black Mesa plant until those damned Indians started complaining about 'their land' and shut down the plant." Eric's attorney again placed a hand on his shoulder and whispered something in Eric's ear.

Eric nodded in agreement and continued. This time he was more subdued and stopped the editorializing. I came to the Kayenta operation in December, 2005. From that date until now I was a crane operator and reported to Pete Munson who was the facility manager. I also joined the coal miner's union here. Luther was the union plant steward."

Josh wrote that in his notebook. This was information that had not come to surface in the previous investigations. "What did you or other union members think about the Black Cross Alliance?"

"Naturally, we didn't like all the trouble it was making." Once again Eric's attorney put his hand on Halverson's shoulder. Eric stopped as though that was enough information, no need to elaborate.

At this point the attorney interjected, "This is just an investigation into whether or not this man had something to do with a murder. It's not a court room interrogation; I think the last answer to your question about the Black Cross Alliance should suffice for now."

"Because Ole Jack was placing a Black Cross in front of the Peabody Coal Company and the cross was used as a murder weapon, I think the question is justified," said Josh.

"My client can answer but only for himself, not the other members of the union," said the attorney. He nodded toward Halverson as consent to answer.

"I didn't like those Black Cross people. They caused a lot of trouble, but I didn't know anything about Ole Jack's connection to them until after the murder, and I wasn't involved with Luther's quarrel with Ole Jack."

"But you did know there was some ill will; you had to notice."

"Yeah, but I cared about more important people than that crazy old man," said Halverson.

"Can we move on with this?" asked the attorney.

Changing the subject, Josh asked, "where were you between 11:45 and 12:00 a.m. on the night of July 22?"

"As I told you before, I was at home asleep. I had no one with me since I live alone. I had been to an all-night poker party until about 10:00 then I went home and went to bed because I had to be at work the next morning."

"Did you go straight home from the poker party?"

Josh's instincts picked up on a slight hesitation before Halverson answered, yes. *Hmm. Hard to read that. Sometimes a definite answer can be indication of a lie. I'll want to go back and watch this video later. Hard to read all the body language and focus on the interview.* "I have some more questions regarding evidence from the murder scene but since there were no fingerprints or other forensic evidence to connect you to those, I am going to turn the questioning over to Mr. Hardwick." Josh looked at his watch. 7:30.

Eric's attorney interrupted, "could we have some time for a coffee break and time for me to confer with my client about the questioning?"

"I think we need a break also," said Josh. "Let's meet back here about 9:30. Gus and I just arrived from St. Louis and I think we need some time to look at some things as well as get some coffee and maybe breakfast ourselves."

"That sounds good," said Hardwick. I'd like some time to confer with Chief Nat'aanii myself."

"Follow me," said George." Josh really wanted to text Rani to see if she would be available for the overnight camping trip with Eli, but he thought better of it. This case needed his full focus at present. Even taking time to be with Eli was stretching things – something Josh had never done before.

The first thing Josh did was meet with a sketch artist who put together a composite of the man Josh saw in the lobby of the Hampton Inn in St. Louis. "Get that out to every police department from here to St. Louis and the East Coast," said Josh. "This man is a person of interest in the murder of Brad Kellogg." Josh then walked down to the basement to have a look at the evidence retrieved at Pete Munson's house and gym locker. On the way, he grabbed a "health bar" from a vending machine and took a cup of coffee from the table near the break room.

The contents stored in the evidence room didn't offer any more help than the summary email Josh had received in St. Louis. Josh walked back upstairs and sat at his desk in the briefing room; Robert Beneè dropped a file on his desk. "Sent Halverson's DNA to CODIS," he said. "Results may take a while." Josh was almost certain neither Halverson nor Munson had murdered Ole Jack, and the DNA tests would prove that. That left the most logical suspect – the one whose fingerprints were on the murder weapon – Derrick Stratton. Although Stratton's prints were on the Black Cross they were smeared with Ole Jack's, indicating Ole Jack had held the cross after Stratton which matched Stratton's testimony. DNA tests hadn't come back yet. The evidence was too indefinite to bring Stratton in for questioning again. Josh had talked with everyone involved except Dr. Parker, and none of the witnesses offered any suggestion of any connection between Stratton and Ole Jack except the visit to the clinic the week before the murder. Josh made a note to visit the clinic on Monday.

I just don't think Stratton did this – but who? Who else had a connection to Ole Jack? Robert Beneè had actually met with Ole Jack about the eagle costume. But nothing was found. Was Ole Jack blackmailing someone and if so, who was it? Munson committed suicide. If he had done it, wouldn't he have at least admitted to it? Josh found Stratton's number in his phone and hit dial. He wanted to go to the clinic on Monday and talk to Stratton again as well as Dr.

Parker. No answer. Josh left a message for him to call as soon as possible. *Almost 9:30 better get back to the interrogation room.*

Gus and George were in the interrogation room when Josh entered. "How'd it go with Nat'aanii?" he asked.

"The Chief doesn't have any more information than we have at this point. The authorities in St. Louis are investigating the operation at the Catholic Church. An informant from the drug community has come forward and identified two people involved in a money laundering scam. All he knew about was the drug connection, but he said it could be possible that the group was handling the artifact scam as well," said Yazzie.

"That gives me some new information for my questions with Halverson. Speak of the devil…" Robert Beneè escorted Halverson and his attorney into the room.

George Yazzie turned on the recorder again. "It's 9:30 am on Friday, July 31st. This is a continuation of the interrogation of Eric Halverson by Federal Marshall Gus Hardwick and FBI agent Josh Overton concerning the illegal sale of Hopi Indian Artifacts in Paris, France and the murder of one Brad Kellogg."

Hardwick started with "You have been advised of your due process rights and have legal counsel available?" asked Hardwick. "You also submitted a DNA swab for testing with the profile of DNA found at both murder scenes – Ole Jack and Brad Kellogg?"

Halverson answered with a "yes" and a nod of his head.

"It will be a while before the results come back from CODIS" said Hardwick. "We do, however, have quite a bit of evidence to connect you with the stolen artifacts case. Recent evidence recovered from a thumb drive on one Pete Munson's computer has indicated your participation in a ring that precipitated the transfer of several Hopi artifacts that ended up being sold at a Paris auction in 2014."

Hardwick placed copies of emails recovered from Munson's computer and pictures of the artifacts. "The dates on the invoices from the computer coincide with large bank deposits made into your account at the same time. We have enough to implicate you in this sale. Unfortunately, Pete Munson and Brad Kellogg are dead. We know you were the last person seen in the company of Kellogg, and Stewart Campbell is still missing and may already be dead. We can offer you immunity if you give us the information we need to find the persons in charge of this who may have ordered the murder of Kellogg and possibly Campbell and who may be looking for you."

At this point Halverson's attorney said, "I am representing Halverson on behalf of The Peabody Coal Company. We are interested in our company's involvement in any of the felonies being questioned here and if Stewart Campbell is located, I will represent him for the company as well. I have advised my client in regard to his options and the ramifications of a plea bargain. Mr. Halverson is willing to give you the information he has that will help you in your investigation. Since much of it would be self-incrimination, my client would definitely require immunity. In addition, Mr. Halverson is in fear of reprisals from the organization he believes is responsible for Brad Kellogg's death and maybe Stewart Campbell's as well. He therefore, requests being put into the witness protection program."

Josh Overton spoke, "Immunity for the illegal sales of artifacts and that part of the investigation is possible, but no immunity for the possible murder of Stewart Campbell nor the murders of Ole Jack and Brad Kellogg. Mr. Halverson has not been ruled out as a suspect and cannot be granted immunity in those cases. We can, however, keep Halverson, with his permission, in protective custody until these cases are settled and if he is cleared of any involvement in capital one murders, he can go directly from the trial into the witness protection program."

Halverson's attorney looked at Halverson who nodded approval and said, "since I know I didn't murder anyone, I will cooperate."

Josh looked at George Yazzie and said, "go get a picture of the composite from the sketch artist. Also, bring in a stenographer, we need to get this down in the form of his statement," said Hardwick. Josh looked at his watch. 10:00. *Should be finished with this by noon. Funny, this is the first time I ever thought about time during the middle of an investigation.*

George followed the stenographer into the interview room and handed Josh the composite drawing. While the stenographer was setting up, Josh showed the drawing to *Halverson*. "Have you ever seen this man?" he asked.

Halverson took the drawing; his hands were shaking. "The only person I saw between the time I left Kayenta and arrived in Kentucky was Brad. He kept me pretty isolated because he knew I was on the run. Don't recall seeing anyone looking like this anywhere in Kentucky, but that doesn't mean he might not have been far behind the authorities." Halverson's anxiety was quite apparent; he was starting to sweat and the water glass he picked up almost slipped from his wet hands. Hardwick gave Halverson some time to settle down and then started the video recorder.

After all the legal matters concerning immunity were put into place, Eric Halverson began his statement. "My name is Eric Halverson and I first met Brad Kellogg when we both worked for the Peabody Coal Operation in Kentucky. We both lost our jobs about the same time. Brad moved to St. Louis to work for Peabody's Director of OSHA Standards, Stewart Campbell, as a field operations coordinator for the mines in the Northwest. I went first to work for the Black Mesa operation that was shut down in 2005. Then, I moved to the Kayenta Mine and have worked as a crane operator since then. I became re-acquainted with Brad when he started coming to the mine to do inspections."

"When all these Black Cross people, environmentalists and Hopi's started creating trouble, jobs at the Kayenta site also were in jeopardy. Everyone who worked for the mine was feeling the pressure. All of us were thinking about what we would do if the mine shut down. On a trip to the mine in 2012 Brad started talking about another way to make money rather than dig coal. Brad's boss Stewart Campbell had told him there were people digging around these ancient sites that were uncovering some valuable artifacts of interest to a mafia run group out of New Jersey. The mob was interested in purchasing some of the black market artifacts and then selling them at the Paris auctions. The money from that sale was put into an off-shore account belonging to a company called Energy Development West. Brad wanted to know if I had seen or heard of any artifacts being dug around the coal mine."

"Do you know the names of the mafia families involved?" asked Hardwick.

"I wasn't supposed to know, but Pete found out the name and told me. It was the Giovanni Family in Trenton, New Jersey." Hardwick wrote that down on a sheet of paper that he handed to George Yazzie who nodded his understanding and took the paper and left the interview. "Go on," said Hardwick.

"I didn't ever think I would find anything at the time, but about a year later, I was working the crane at the northeast site of the mine when I dug up something that looked like an ancient mask of some kind. Pete Munson happened to be there and recognized what it was. First, Pete said we needed to turn the mask over to the Hopi Tribal Council, but I knew Pete was having some financial difficulties. I told him what Brad Kellogg had told me. The three of us had a meeting and Pete contacted Stewart Campbell and told him what we had found. From that point on, Munson handled the arrangements with Campbell. The mask was turned over and money was deposited into my account."

"Who took the mask?" asked Hardwick.

"Brad Kellogg, he was the courier who took the mask to St. Louis. There was an operation somewhere in St. Louis that took care of the shipment to New Jersey and then on to Paris. Brad Kellogg would have had that information; I guess that's why they killed him."

"Do you know who killed Kellogg?"

"No, I just think it was a mafia hit because Brad knew too much. That's why I want witness protection."

"When was the next sale?" asked Hardwick.

"In January of 2015, I found another artifact that looked something like a gourd painted to look like an animal. Told Munson about it and once again, the sale was made and Kellogg did the transfer. Then, near the late spring of the year, we found two more artifacts – a stone pestle and that eagle's costume connected to Ole Jack's murder. Munson put the stone pestle in his safe deposit box for safe keeping."

Josh said, "Turn off the recorder." He turned to Hardwick and said, "I went down to the evidence room during the break and there was no stone pestle in the box, nor was there mention of any."

"Who opened that locker?" asked Hardwick.

Josh looked at the text messages from St. Louis. "Looks like that was Robert Beneè," said Josh.

"Go get him and bring him in here," said Hardwick to George Yazzie. After Yazzie left, Hardwick turned the recorder back on and told Halverson to continue.

"We buried the eagle's costume near the site where we found it until Munson could arrange for the transfer, but before we could do that, someone found the costume and started blackmailing us."

"Ole Jack?" asked Hardwick.

"Don't really know," said Halverson. "Munson called me in after he saw the first videos from the security camera. Munson said someone had called him and asked him if he had seen the video. The person wanted to meet with us on the Black Mesa where we had hidden the costume. We went there around 10:00 on the night of Ole Jack's murder to meet the person. That's why I left the poker party early."

"Who was it?" asked Hardwick.

"Can't say. The person was fully covered from head to toe like one of the Kachina spirits in the eagle costume. He told us that we were to get $10,000 together and meet him by Friday at the same place to get the costume."

"What time did you leave?" asked Josh.

"Must have been about 10:30. We were in a hurry to get away."

"Did you see Ole Jack or anyone else at the time?"

"No, but neither of us were anxious to stay there, 'Fraid we might get caught by security."

"Did you go back?"

"We went back on Friday, but the man obviously was scared off by Ole Jack's murder because no one showed up. That was when I decided I needed to get away. Pete told me I should contact Kellogg and let him know what had happened. I contacted Brad and he told me what to do and made all the arrangements for me. Pete didn't want to leave, so Kellogg told him he stayed at his own risk but that he needed to destroy all the evidence on his computer. I think you know the rest."

Just as Halverson finished, Yazzie returned with Beneè. "Robert, we need to question you about the contents of Munson's gym locker. You were the one who opened it and collected the contents?"

"That's right," said Beneè. "Officer Duffy went with me and we transferred the evidence from the safe deposit box to one of the Justice Center's evidence boxes and then catalogued the contents. I brought the file sheet with me. You can see both signatures at the top."

Hardwick turned the recorder back on and again asked Halverson, "Did you actually see what Munson did with the pestle?"

"No, I only know what he told me."

"That's all," said Hardwick. "We're finished with Halverson for now, but we'll keep him in protective custody until further notice." Hardwick turned to Halverson's attorney and said, "I guess you'll need to go back to St. Louis and follow-up on Stewart Campbell. I'll need to call Perkins and find out where he is on the investigation in St. Louis. I'll be heading back there myself, but before I leave, I'll go check in with Nat'aanii about the interrogation. Where does that leave you Overton?"

Josh looked at his watch and said, "It's almost noon. I'm going to check to see if there is any information on that composite drawing, and then talk with Nat'aanii myself. Maybe Munson's wife knows more than she told us. Maybe Munson gave her the pestle and told her to try and sell it if anything happened to him. I'll need to go back to the Munson house on Monday. I also need to follow up on Derrick Stratton on Monday unless something new turns up over the weekend, but I think we all need to take the weekend off and get started again on Monday. It's noon, and I need to be in Flagstaff by 4:00, so you guys take a break and I'll see you Monday."

Josh reported to Nat'aanii who agreed not much more could be done in Tuba City until Monday. He then checked with Jeanette on the status of the composite drawing and what part she had in retrieving the contents of Munson's safe deposit box. Josh found Jeanette in the break room having lunch.

"I'm going to be leaving for Flagstaff to pick up my son for the weekend," he said. "Before I go I wanted to check on a couple of things. Do you mind?"

"Not if I don't have to interrupt my lunch," she said. "Shoot."

"First, has there been any activity on that composite drawing yet?"

"There wasn't anything when I left for lunch just now. What else?"

"You helped Beneè retrieve the contents of Munson's safe deposit box?"

"Yes, why? Is there a problem?"

"Well, according to Eric Halverson, he and Pete Munson had found a stone pestle along with that eagle's costume in one of the overburden digs at the mine. Munson told Halverson he was going to put the pestle in his safe deposit box until time to transfer the eagle costume to the east coast buyers. Did you see anything like that in the box when you and Beneè catalogued the contents?"

Jeanette thought for a minute while she finished her sandwich. She wiped her mouth and said, "Robert and I went into the vault room with the bank teller. We gave him Munson's keys and he opened the box and pulled it from the wall. I was holding the papers, so he handed the box to Robert. We followed the teller out of the vault room and he took us to a viewing room for privacy. Robert put the box on a table and opened it while I shut the door and organized the papers. Everything we put on the report is what we found in the box."

"Well, I guess I'll need to go back to Mrs. Munson's place on Monday. See you then," he said as he stood to go.

"Have a nice trip," said Jeanette.

"Thanks, looking forward to some time with my son." *That's not like me at all,* he thought. *Leaving a case for a weekend when things are just starting to get interesting?* Josh smiled and walked to his car.

CHAPTER

14

It was 2:30 when Josh arrived at the outskirts of Flagstaff. Feeling hungry, he stopped at a coffee house with Wi-Fi that served organic coffees, juices and sandwiches. He ordered a chicken salad sandwich and a green juice and sat down at a table by the window. Josh felt the urge to check his messages, but thought *no news is good news.* Back on the road at 3:00, he arrived at the soccer field at 3:30. He saw Chris and Emma sitting on the bleachers behind the fence near the dugout for Eli's team. Eli was already on the field but he saw his dad and smiled and waved as Josh made his way toward Emma. Chris stood up and shook Josh's hand; Josh hugged Emma and patted Julie on the head before he sat down.

"Eli all ready to go?" he asked.

"Couldn't be more excited," said Emma. "How's your case going?"

"Outside of what you probably have read in the news, you know I can't tell you more, but we have some substantial leads that seem to be getting us closer to some answers."

"It's not like you to take time off like this in the middle of an investigation," said Emma.

"Nothing we have at the moment seemed so important that I couldn't take two days off. I wanted to see Eli's last game and take advantage of hiking with him at the Navajo National Monument. The Monument is located close to the Justice Center, and I know someone who could help out with Josh if there was an emergency."

"Know someone?" smiled Emma.

"It's not what you think. She's a lady I met on a hiking trip to the Monument and we had lunch. She's a teacher and I know I could call on her to help with Eli if such a need arose."

"Interesting," said Emma. "Eli has been extra baggage in the past when you had a woman around."

"Well, maybe I'm realizing how quickly he's growing up - oh, look the game is starting," said Josh, relieved to end this conversation.

Eli walked toward his family holding onto the MVP trophy he had just received. He held it up and posed first by himself while Josh and Emma took pictures. He then posed with Emma, Julie and Chris while Josh took a picture and then Emma returned the favor. "Think you might try for a college scholarship in soccer?" asked Josh as he rubbed his son's hair.

"That's still a little way off, Josh," said Emma before Eli could answer. "We'll have to see how he does in high school." Josh understood the "we" meant Emma and Chris. Josh felt a tug of sadness but realized that his absenteeism during Eli's formative years had meant that Chris had taken on a lot of the traditional father roles. *My choice,* he thought. Besides, Josh knew that Chris was far more capable of handling those decisions than he was. *I've had it pretty easy*, he thought looking at Eli. *Great kid, well-adjusted and happy. What more could I ask for?* Josh looked at Eli standing with his "real" family and saying good bye for the weekend. *Maybe being on the other side of this picture?*

"You hungry?" asked Josh as he drove toward his apartment in Kayenta on Highway 163. He was approaching the intersection of Highway 160 where the local supermarket and the Pizza Edge were located. He needed to stop at the supermarket to get supplies for the camping trip and thought he could pick up some pizza for Eli if he was hungry.

Eli spotted the pizza sign and smiled. "When haven't I been hungry for pizza?" Josh stopped and bought some pizza for Eli (and maybe a piece for himself if he was lucky) then drove to Basha's to pick up some food for camping. "Do I have to go in?" asked Eli as he chewed ravenously on a large piece of pizza.

"No, enjoy your pizza. It'll take me a little while."

"That's okay, I have my phone," he said. Eli was always prepared to entertain himself. *I really am lucky.*

Josh noticed a man talking to Eli when he approached his car. He breathed a sigh of relief when he saw that the man standing there was Robert Beneè. Robert walked around to the driver's side of the car and said, "hi, there. I was stopping for groceries when I saw your car parked here; I saw the boy and figured he was your son. We were just getting to know one another. Says you guys plan on hiking the Monument this weekend and staying overnight. That mean you're going to hike some of the back country?"

"Sure does," said Josh. "We're looking forward to it."

"Think you might need a guide? I used to do those tours and have a lot of information about the history of the area and some of the pitfalls."

"I think I want to do this alone," said Josh. "Just the two of us with some quality time together. I'm an experienced hiker and so is Eli's mom. He's been on a lot of back country hikes and knows how to handle himself. Thanks for the offer, though. By the way, have you any news from the Justice Center?"

"Not really. No word on that sketch drawing. Chief told us to take the weekend off after he heard from Hardwick in St. Louis. Still no luck locating Stewart Campbell; looks like the connection in St. Louis ended with him. There's been no activity on Campbell's phone since Brad Kellogg's murder. Kellogg's phone records show a phone call made to him from a phone registered to Campbell the day before we found Kellogg's body. The Chief seems to think Campbell's probably using a burner phone if he is still alive. Hardwick and Perkins will be leaving for Atlantic City on Sunday to assist in the questioning of the mafia leaders Halverson identified as connected to the trafficking of stolen Indian artifacts. Well, enjoy your weekend and I guess I'll see you on Monday. Be careful on that hike," said Robert as he walked toward the store and entered just before the "closed" sign came on. Something about Robert's demeanor didn't sit quite right with Josh.

You know better than to treat everyone like a suspect in an investigation. Josh started the car and as he backed out Eli said, "Something strange about that man."

"Could be because he is Navajo. Despite the best of circumstances the Navajo and Hopi are at best quite reserved with the Anglo population," said Josh.

"Guess so. You want this last piece of pizza?"

Josh looked at his son and smiled, "Glad you saved a piece for me." The two laughed as they headed toward home.

Josh and Eli arrived at the Visitor's Center at 7:00 a.m. on Saturday morning. Excited to go camping, Eli had been wide awake and ready since 6:00 that morning. Despite the fact that Josh and Emma had not been able to make their marriage work, Josh was grateful that Emma was as much of an outdoors person as he was and had instilled that common love in Eli. Once again, Josh felt a little pang that he had not been able to be a full time dad. Seeing how much Eli had grown this past year made Josh even more aware that times like these were going to be even fewer and farther between than they had been. He sighed as he pulled the camping equipment from the car; Eli was already preparing the tent.

The campsite was rough. There was a flat area for the tent and a fire pit with a grill. There was room for his SUV between their site and the only other campsite available. *Wonder who's using it?* There was one portable bathroom in the distance. Josh was just finishing the tent when he saw a four-wheel drive truck with a camper top pull up to the site next to his. It took just a minute to recognize Derrick Stratton. As Josh walked toward him, he saw Derrick's wife (what was her name?) exit the passenger side. It was then that he saw her; she noticed him immediately. Rani climbed out of the back seat behind the driver's side, and a girl about the age of Eli came around from the passenger side.

From that point on, no one but Rani existed. Josh walked toward her smiling broadly and said, "Fancy meeting you here!"

"I knew you had mentioned camping soon the last time we spoke, but I had no idea you would be free now considering the situation with the murder case," said Rani.

"Yes, it is on-going." Suddenly, Josh thought about Derrick Stratton. He turned to address Derrick. "Did you get my text message?"

"Yes, I did, but I was in Flagstaff when I received it, so I didn't get it until last evening. Didn't want to disturb you over the weekend, so I thought I would return the text on Monday. I'll be free any time you want to come to the clinic and speak with both Dr. Parker and me. I'm sorry you think there is a need to investigate us further; I had hoped you would be finished by now so that I could drive back to Oregon with Listie and Polly at the end of next week."

"That might still be possible. As you know we found Eric Halverson whose testimony has taken the investigation well beyond the scope of Kayenta. There are still some puzzling questions about the extent of Ole Jack's involvement in this. That's why we need to question you again with Dr. Parker in order to exclude you as suspects. Some people are still working on the case this weekend, so who knows what may happen by Monday morning." Josh turned back to Rani who was busy taking supplies from the truck to the campsite. Rani walked over when she made eye contact with Josh.

"This must be Eli," she said.

Eli walked toward her and shook Rani's hand, but he was looking at the cute girl with a mass of thick, curly red hair helping Rani and her mother. "Who's that?" he asked.

"Polly is Derrick and Listie's daughter." Eli noticed that Rani tapped Polly's shoulder and then began to "talk" to the girl in what Eli knew must be sign language. "Polly, this is Eli, Mr. Overton's son," said Rani while signing for Polly.

Polly smiled and signed as Rani spoke, "Nice to meet you."

"Does she have any hearing at all?" asked Eli. Eli noticed that Listie was signing while Eli spoke.

"No," said Rani. "Sign language is her main method of communication, although she can communicate by writing and texting over the phone. Neither Derrick nor Listie is deaf; Polly lost her hearing after a reaction to the measles' inoculation she received as an infant. Derrick and Listie sign and so do I; I know sign language because my mother is deaf. In fact, I am teaching sign language and working with the deaf and blind students at Monument Valley High School."

"Cool," said Eli before thinking. "I'm sorry. I didn't mean . . ."

"We know," said Listie. I'm glad Polly has someone her age here. Let's get this show on the road!" Listie grinned broadly at Rani who turned a bright shade of red, unusual for her olive complexion.

Rani and Listie, with help from Polly, prepared a lumberjack breakfast of eggs, bacon and pancakes while Derrick, Josh and Eli finished setting up the tents. Derrick, Polly and Listie would share the big tent and Rani set up a sleeping bag and small air mattress in the back of the truck for her to use. Although the desert sun was intense and the temperatures hovered near 100 degrees during the day, all the campers knew that when the sun went down, it would be much cooler.

By 8:30, the hikers were ready for the day long hike of the Sandal Trail which would take them to the overlook of the Betatakin Ruins. Each wore a well-stocked back pack; hiking required strength and stamina and all of them were prepared for the strenuous but stimulating exercise. It was a two and one-half mile hike to the overlook where one could look down 560 feet into Betatakin Canyon. Rani remembered the short hike she had taken with Josh a couple of weeks earlier that had taken them down into the canyon and where she had seen the drawing inside the alcove below the ruins. Rani was excited about revisiting the alcove; she remembered the cloth bag stored in her back pack among energy bars and bottled water. After seeing it next to the drawing, Rani thought she could make a much better comparison. Hopefully, she would be able to show it to the elders of Old Oraibi before Derrick left for Oregon. Once again, Rani became lost in the silence.

Rani lagged behind Derrick, Listie, Polly and Eli who wanted to be with someone near his age. Josh walked beside Rani, wanting to keep the women and children in between the two men; being with Rani was an extra bonus. Although no words were exchanged, the air was charged with lines of communication that were more powerful than words. Josh studied the exotic woman beside him.

Although born on the other side of the globe with the air of sophistication of someone from New York City, Rani looked as though she had been born in the Arizona desert, connected with the earth and the stone ruins that fascinated her as she hiked this isolated trail. Josh lost all sense of time and space as well. It was as though he had walked into a fourth dimension where the past and future dissolved into only the present. Eli's voice brought him back into the physical present. "Look, Dad! Mom and Dad took us to Pueblo Bonito in Chaco Canyon last summer. We went through the village; are we going inside those today?"

Josh had to take a minute before answering Eli's questions because he had been lost in thought plus his reaction to hearing Eli refer to Chris as Dad. After Emma had Julie, she had asked Josh what he thought about Eli referring to Chris as Dad. Josh had agreed that it made sense and over the years had become quite used to it. Hearing that today somehow intensified the feelings of what Josh had lost. *Would there ever be an experience shared with Eli that didn't have Chris' shadow in the background?*

"No, Son. Those ruins are too unstable to be safe. The public has not been allowed for years. I think there are some officials who periodically go inside to check on the condition. From what I learned on the earlier hike, that village is much like the one at Pueblo Bonito. All of these ruins were once inhabited by the Anasazi people whom the Navajo and Hopi claim as their ancestors."

Josh could see that as he was talking to Eli, Derrick, Listie and Polly were talking in sign. "What are they saying?" he asked. Remembering the last time he had asked that question, Josh stammered, "I, I'm sorry, I didn't mean. . ."

Rani smiled and gently took Josh's hand; both felt the surge of energy. "The last time, you were a detective who seemed to be continuing his investigation. Today, you are a friend who is part of the conversation. Actually, Derrick and Listie are simply telling Polly what you and Eli are discussing." Polly turned and signed something to Rani. In order to answer, she had to let go of Josh's hand. Neither of them wanted that to happen; they both knew it. No words were necessary.

After a short break for water and energy bars, the group continued the hike down into the canyon. Rani remembered this part of the hike before and felt a warm glow sharing this with Josh again. Josh was feeling a twinge of guilt about spending so much time with Rani, but he looked up and saw that his son was not the least bit bothered. Josh smiled. *Puberty. Couldn't have been better if I had planned it.*

Derrick and Listie were perfect, keeping a parental eye on the two adolescents but also allowing them some time to get to know one another. Polly was adept at lip reading so Eli could respond to her simple signs that even speaking people used for communication. *Eli seems to be handling the communication barrier quite well.*

As the group approached the alcove, Listie looked at Rani and said, "Where did you see the drawing?" Both Josh and Eli were getting used to seeing the sign language in tandem with the spoken word. Eli was fascinated and asked more questions about the sign than the ruins.

"It's on the right hand side of the cave, just above some other carvings. Here it is," said Rani as she took off her back pack and reached down into one of the side pockets to pull out the cloth bag. Everyone's attention was focused on the bag. Rani heard a noise. "What did you say?" she asked Josh.

"I didn't say anything," he answered.

"Oh, everyone was so quiet, I thought someone whispered something." Rani took the stone from the bag and held it up to the drawing. Now, she did hear something. It was as if everyone in the room gasped in unison. The drawings were exactly the same!

"Where did you get that?" asked Derrick.

"My mother gave the bag and its contents to me when I left for Arizona. I really didn't know anything about it until then. *Maman* told me that my father had found this in the rubble left from the destruction of the House of *Bab* in Teheran after the radical faction took over Iran. *Bâbâ* (Dad) sewed the stone into the hem of my doll's dress before he gave me the doll on my fifth birthday. He knew the radicals might kill him so he made sure that *Maman* and I, as well as this stone, were safe. When I left New York, my mother gave me the stone because she sensed this stone was somehow connected to the tribal people of the Southwest who are so much like the Bakhtiari tribe of my father's people." Rani studied some of the other drawings while the group passed the stone from one to the other.

After Polly handed her the stone, Rani put it back into the bag and said, "I didn't really look at these other drawings that closely the first time. These drawings are quite similar to those I saw on Prophecy

Rock. I wonder if this rock has the drawing that finishes the one left off the sacred tablet of the Fire Clan about the coming of *Maasaw*. The *Bab* also preached about the coming of the Messiah. Are these two connected? This is crazy!"

"We definitely need to visit the elders at Old Oraibi village before we go back to Oregon," said Derrick. "We can go tomorrow after we break camp before heading back to Kayenta. There should be enough time. Derrick looked at Josh and said, "I know we have to get back so I can meet you at the clinic on Monday."

"If we do no more than leave it with the elders of the Fire Clan, that will be enough for me," said Rani. "I believe that is where this belongs and, unlike others, I have no interest in making money on this." After saying that, Rani shivered remembering the strange "ghost" that had visited her apartment.

"Are you cold?" asked Josh. Listie couldn't help but notice what was going on between this couple. "It is much cooler here than outside."

"Not really, but I think we need to start back. I wouldn't want to be here after the sun goes down. There are too many spirits that hang out here," smiled Rani.

Josh pointed to the outhouses among the trees and said, "I think we should visit these before we head back up."

"Certainly," said Derrick, and the ladies headed toward the female side as the men walked toward the men's bathroom. Josh looked over to the side where he had noticed some disturbed earth before. *Why does that still look as though it has been freshly dug! I'm starting to feel this spirit thing myself,* he thought.

It was almost four when the tired hikers returned to camp. Listie, Polly and Rani prepared another large meal for the hungry hikers while Derrick, Josh and Eli rested since they would be cleaning up afterward. As the sun receded, the camp fire began to glow and create shadows that seemed to move as though the Kachina spirits were dancing in a mystical ceremony. Josh pulled out some brochures he had brought with him and he and Eli were reading those aloud for a while. When darkness took over the camp, Eli stopped reading aloud and took the brochures and sat next to Polly.

The two of them read silently by the light of a single lantern and seemed quite content sitting next to one another in the silence.

Derrick and Listie went into their tent and Rani sat next to Josh in front of the fire. Neither spoke for a few seconds; Josh stirred the dying coals with a stick and added another branch to the fire. "You look so beautiful in the firelight," he said. "What are you thinking?"

"It seems strange, but I was thinking about that night so long ago when everyone was dancing around a fire similar to this and then . . ."

Josh took her hand and said, "No need to finish."

"But I need to finish," said Rani. "It seems as though I never left that place, that all the years in between then and now have vanished. I can feel my father's presence and hear him saying, 'Run to the barn, Bedar. You and Rani will be safe there. I have made arrangements for you to go to America; don't look back, never look back. Your hope is in the West.'" Rani retrieved the stone from her backpack and looked at it again. "Somehow, I think the answer to my questions as well as to your murder investigation are connected to this stone."

"I don't know if I can be that mystical, but this I do believe," said Josh. At that, he took the stone from Rani and laid it next to the bag. He took both Rani's hands and pulled her up into his strong, loving arms; the kiss was magic. Rani melted into his embrace and as she did, the invisible wall started to crumble. There was no fear great enough to challenge the comfort she felt in this man's loving arms. No matter what happened; she could not allow fear to keep her from this experience.

"Hey, Dad!" Eli's words brought the two lovers back to reality and Rani pulled away, feeling the heat rush to her face at the sight of Eli's knowing look.

"Where's Polly?" asked Josh.

"She's in the tent with her mom and dad. I think it's time for bed." Eli smiled. "That's different. Me telling you to go to bed!" he said.

"Okay, Son. You go in the tent. I want to make sure Rani is okay before I turn in." Rani was picking up the stone and putting it back in the cotton bag. Josh dowsed the fire, covered it with dirt and walked with Rani to the camper. "Are you sure you will be all right here? All this talk of spirits and murder makes me a little jittery. You know you could sleep in the tent with Eli and me." Josh rubbed her arm and felt the energy and sighed. "You know I would be a perfect gentleman," he smiled. Despite his words, Josh pulled Rani into his arms for another long, kiss.

This time excitement almost overtook both of them, but they both heard the crack of a twig snapping somewhere in the distance. "What the?" asked Josh as he motioned for Rani to be quiet. Josh nodded in the direction of the Stratton's tent and Rani moved quietly in that direction while Josh ran back to his tent to get his gun. Eli started when he entered. Josh whispered for him to go with Rani to the Stratton tent as he pulled the holster from his backpack and put it on his shoulder. By that time Derrick had come running toward Josh.

"I'm coming with you," he said.

"No, I think it's best that you start packing the truck and maybe even wait in the truck for a quick exit if need be. We don't have any cell service here. Keep as quiet as possible, though." Taking the gun from its holster, Josh started walking silently in the direction of the sound. Watching Josh leave, Rani flashed back to her time in the barn those many years ago.

"Will do," said Derrick who went back to the tent and started signing instructions. Eli just followed their lead; they all knew how important the silence was.

And then they heard the gunshot.

CHAPTER

15

"**A**ny luck getting in touch with Overton?" asked Chief Nat'aanii as George Yazzie came into his office.

"No, Sir. They are probably out far enough to have lost any cell service. Can't get in touch with Beneè either. Not unusual, he spends a lot of time in the back country on his time off."

The Chief picked up his phone and called Federal Marshall Hardwick, still in St. Louis. "No luck contacting Overton," said the Chief. "I wanted him here to receive your report at the same time. Guess we'll have to wait. So, what have you found out?"

"The St. Louis police dispatched the composite drawing of the sketch done from Overton's description of the man who burgled his hotel room to state officials from Missouri to New Jersey. Yesterday afternoon, a person who lives in the same complex as Stewart Campbell came forward. The witness identified the man in the drawing as one looking similar to a man who visited Campbell's apartment the day before Campbell disappeared. We got a description of the car the person was driving, a gray sedan with New Jersey license plates."

"Did she get a license plate number?" asked the Chief.

"No, Sir, but after we got the car description we dispatched a bulletin to all state trooper offices from Missouri to New Jersey to be on the lookout for a car with New Jersey plates that fits the description. This morning, a state trooper in eastern Kentucky pulled over a car driven by a man that matched the description in the drawing. They're in the process of extraditing him and sending him back to St. Louis. Officials hope he will be here by Monday afternoon. Since he's a person of interest in the disappearance of

Campbell, he'll have to be questioned and held in St. Louis unless Overton has found something to connect him to Ole Jack's murder," said Hardwick. The last statement was more of a question.

"That's why I wanted to get Overton on the phone," said the Chief. He left to hike the back country of the Navajo Monument with his son and must not have cell service. I have been trying to locate Robert Beneè so I can send him out to look for Overton. Beneè knows the back country around the Monument like the back of his hand. Worked there as a guide for years before joining the police force, but we haven't been able to reach Beneè either. He wasn't on call this weekend so I guess he is also off on the reservation somewhere. Don't want to send anyone else on a wild goose chase; we'll just have to wait until Overton checks in – probably Sunday evening after he has taken Eli back to Flagstaff. Is there word from Perkins in New Jersey?" asked the Chief.

"Officials have started investigating the Energy Development West off-shore account for a link to any of the Giovanni Family businesses, legal or illegal. So far, no connection has been found. Alfredo Giovanni is well represented and until we have any physical proof to connect him to the off shore accounts we can only question him about Halverson's allegations. I told Perkins to run financials on any and all legal operations run by the Giovanni Family so we can get the physical evidence we need. Halverson's testimony about the Giovanni Family is only hearsay at present. Perkins says to have someone in Tuba City run a check on all of Kellogg's and Halverson's phone records to see if there is any number there that could provide a link, no matter how small, to the Giovanni Family. Also go back and look at Munson's phone numbers and emails from his business as well as personal files and see if something pops up," said Hardwick.

"Hear that, George?" asked the Chief.

"On it," said Yazzie.

Yazzie went back to his desk in the briefing room and pulled up financial and phone records for everyone involved in Ole Jack's murder. That included Halverson, Munson, Kellogg and most recently, Stewart Campbell. Nothing showed up on any suspicious calls on records for Halverson and Munson. *Those guys were careful. Any burner phones the two had were gone. If Kellogg had a burner phone, it probably was taken by whoever killed him. What about Campbell? Still missing. Wonder if there might be phone records available from Peabody. Campbell worked there.* Yazzie filled out a request for Stewart Campbell's Company phone records and sent it to Virginia Carroll at Peabody Headquarters hoping to have a response by early Monday morning. He sent a text to Josh Overton and looked at his watch. 6:00 pm. *Nothing more can be done until we hear from Josh. Might as well go home.*

*   *   *

Rani was in the back of the camper truck when she heard Josh's phone signaling a text. *How fast is Derrick going?* Eli looked at her and said, "Should we read that?"

"You just keep holding your dad's hand, Eli. I'll look at it." Eli sat on the floor of the truck, bracing himself on one side while holding onto his dad's hand. Josh was unconscious and bleeding profusely from a wound in his stomach. Derrick had done what he could to stem the flow and bandage the wound before moving Josh to the air mattress in the back of the truck. Eli had refused to leave his dad; Listie and Polly were in Josh's SUV and Derrick was flying down SR 564 to the closest help he knew for Josh – the clinic Eleanor Parker operated off Highway 163 near Kayenta.

Hearing the text signal on Josh's phone alerted Rani to the fact that they must now have cell service. Instead of reading the text immediately Rani picked up Derrick's phone to call Dr. Parker. *Please be there! Please be there!* Rani breathed a sigh of relief when she heard Dr. Parker's voice saying, "Dr. Parker's Office."

"Hello, Dr. Parker. This is Derrick's friend Rani."

"Call me Eleanor," said the voice on the other end not yet picking up on the distress in Rani's voice.

"Yes, certainly. I'm afraid we need your help. There's been a shooting at the Navajo Monument. . ."

"Oh, no. Who? What? Derrick? Listie?"

"No, Derrick, Listie and Polly are okay. The FBI agent Josh Overton has been shot. Someone or something was skulking around our campsite and he went to investigate and. . ."

"What do you need me to do?" interrupted Eleanor. The doctor's lifesaving adrenalin was now fully functioning and all she needed now was to know how to get to the wounded party.

"We're about five miles from the clinic now. Josh has a gunshot wound to the stomach and is unconscious."

"What are his vital signs?"

"Derrick didn't take the time to take them, only to stem the flow of blood and get Josh in the truck so we could get him to you."

"You say you're five miles out now?"

"More like two. Derrick is flying."

"Okay, I'll have the exam room prepared for emergency surgery. See you when you get here." Before Rani could say anything the line was dead and the truck was pulling into a parking space in front of the clinic. Listie was right behind.

Derrick jumped out of the front and yelled at Listie, "Take the children to the front room and settle them." Eleanor Parker came from the back of the house pushing a gurney. "Good," sighed Derrick. "Help me get him on the gurney, then you go join the rest in the front of the house and make the necessary phone calls."

Rani didn't want to leave Josh. She flashed back to that time so long ago when she didn't get to say goodbye to her father or leave him without a proper burial. *Why did I get involved again? I should have stayed in New York!* Although Rani felt as though her insides were being torn apart, she appeared calm as she walked around to the front of the house and into the front room. Eli had his face buried in Listie's right arm; her left arm encircled Polly. "Stay put," said Rani. "I need to make some phone calls." The first call was to Emma.

The voice that answered was pleasant and friendly, "Hello, this is Emma," she said.

"Hello Emma, you don't know me but . . ."

"Has something happened to Eli?"

"Oh, no. I should have told you immediately; Eli is fine physically."

"Josh?"

"Yes, Josh has been shot. I want you to know Josh never intended to put Eli in danger. Someone or something came to our campsite last night and when Josh went to investigate he was shot."

"Someone or something?"

"I know that sounds strange and I am sure whoever it was is somehow connected to the murder investigation, but at this time, we don't know who it was. We were focused on getting Josh the medical attention he needs," said Rani.

"Of course," said Emma, her voice wavering. Rani could hear questioning in the background.

"Take your time to explain to your husband, then we need to discuss how to get Eli back to Flagstaff."

Upon hearing this, Eli said, "I don't want to leave until I know my dad's going to be okay."

Rani smiled wanly as she said, "I'm sure your parents will do what is best for you Eli."

"Let me talk to Mom," he said.

"Of course," said Rani as she handed Josh's phone over to Eli.

Rani walked over and sat down in a chair near Listie and Polly until Eli looked up and said, "My mom wants to talk to you again."

Rani took the phone. "Eli is insistent on staying with his dad, and Chris and I think that is where he needs to be right now. Josh told me he knew a lady who could help him with Josh if need be. You think Eli could stay with you for a few days until we know what's going to happen? He doesn't need to be back until August 15th for registration for school."

"Would he be old enough to stay by himself?" asked Rani. I do have to go to school next week."

"That shouldn't be a problem," said Emma. "Just a couple of days anyway. That will give us time to know about Josh and make arrangements for me at least to come to Kayenta to pick up Eli and bring him back home. I'm really grateful; I know Josh would want it this way. He really likes you."

"I like him, too," said Rani. At this point tears started flowing and Eli took the phone.

"Thanks, Mom," he said in a surprisingly adult voice. "I'll keep you up to date and don't worry about me." After the call ended, Eli handed the phone back to Rani. She was about to check the text message and call the Justice Center when Derrick came into the room. He was dressed in scrubs prepared for surgery.

"Josh's vital signs are not bad. Eleanor has cleaned up the wound and sedated him. The bullet lodged around the spleen near the stomach. Missed the heart and lungs. She thinks she can remove the bullet here, but you need to call the Justice Center and alert them and make arrangements to have Josh moved to the hospital in Tuba City sometime tomorrow."

"All right," said Rani as Derrick walked back into the clinic.

Rani finally took the time to look at the text on Josh's phone. It was from Chief Nat'aanii and had been sent sometime yesterday afternoon.

> *Hardwick phoned with message about the composite drawing. Man matching the description has been picked up by state troopers in Eastern Kentucky. Extradition to Missouri. Need you to call ASAP.*

Rani found the Chief's number in Josh's contact list. She sat down; her hands and legs were shaking – the only visible sign of her stress. As she dialed the number, she thought, *I have to keep myself together for Eli!* As Rani thought this she began to understand fully what her mom had experienced that night so long ago. Having Eli to consider helped Rani take the focus off herself. She began to realize that one of the things that is comforting during the loss of a loved one is having other people to love as well.

Suddenly, Rani realized she had been not been able to let go of her father because she had not allowed herself to grieve his loss and move on with gratitude for the short time he was part of her life to acceptance of the love of another "father" to take his place. Loving Craig as a father did not take away from the love Eli had for his biological father. Keeping other love out by closing off and holding too tight to a memory had kept Rani imprisoned all these years.

Rani looked at Eli, so mature for such a young man. Faced with the loss of his dad, Eli was upset, worried and afraid and if his dad died, Eli would grieve that loss. But, eventually, Eli would move on with wonderful memories of his time with his dad, but open to the love he knew he had from Craig. Rani had opened herself to love and now was faced with the possibility of losing the love before it really blossomed – much like her father. She looked at Eli again; he smiled bravely and took her hand. Rani felt a flood of peace fill her, calming her shaking limbs. There would be no looking back, no matter what happened except to cherish the memory with gratitude. She pulled up Nat'aanii's number and punched the call button.

The first thing Rani heard was the voice of the Chief saying, "Overton, where are you?"

"Is this the Justice Center in Tuba City?" asked Rani.

"Yes, who are you and why are you calling from Josh Overton's phone?" asked the Chief.

"My name is Rani Bijan, I am a friend of Josh and Derrick and Listie Stratton. We ran into Josh and Eli when we reserved the campsite next to theirs at the Navajo National Monument. I'm sorry to tell you Josh has sustained a serious gunshot wound to the stomach. Derrick Stratton, as you probably know, works at the clinic run by Dr. Eleanor Parker just outside of Kayenta Township. Derrick drove us to the clinic and Josh is stable and is now in surgery. Dr. Parker said to call you and let you know what has happened. At present, Josh is still in surgery, but if all goes well, Dr. Parker thinks Josh will be able to be moved to the hospital near the Justice Center in Tuba City tomorrow."

"Who the hell shot him?" asked the Chief.

"We don't know. Josh heard a noise that sounded like a person walking near the campsite. It was dark, so he told all of us to go to a central location while he investigated. We were packing up our gear when we heard a gunshot. Listie and I helped the children get the truck packed while Derrick went to investigate. Derrick found Josh unconscious and bleeding. Since Derrick has had medical training, he cleaned the wound and stopped the bleeding. Josh was unconscious all the way to the clinic and is now sedated. No one will be able to question him until tomorrow at the earliest." Rani heard a heavy sigh on the other end of the phone.

"Update me when Josh is out of surgery. I'll get Yazzie to come to the clinic with the paramedics in the morning. Thanks."

"You're welcome," said Rani. Just as she hung up the phone, Listie handed her a cup of hot tea.

"Thought this might help," she said. "I looked in Eleanor's fridge and found some deli meat and sandwich fixin's. Would you like a sandwich?"

"No, I'm too nervous. You go ahead and feed yourself and the kids. I need to sit here and drink the tea. He has to be all right, Listie."

"I know," she said softly as she stroked Rani's arm.

"Rani," Derrick's hushed voice and gentle tap on her shoulder woke Rani from a sound sleep. Rani was happy to be awake because she had been having a nightmare that mixed images from the night her father was murdered with dancing, masked Kachinas trying to protect her from bandits raiding the circle and wielding scythe like swords. Josh stood just outside the circle with arms extended in an effort to grab her and take her to safety. "Josh has made it through the surgery. He is still asleep, but should be able to talk after the sedatives wear off in about an hour."

Rani sat up, shook her head and said, "What time is it?"

"It's 2:00 am. Listie and the kids are asleep in Eleanor's bedroom. I'm going to get Eli when his dad is awake. You need to call Tuba City?"

"It's too late to call. I think I'll send a text." Eleanor Parker came up behind Derrick.

"I think Josh will pull through; I saved the bullet we retrieved to give to ballistics. You and Eli can talk to him when he is awake, but keep it short. He needs rest."

"Okay," said Rani. "Listie made some sandwiches and coffee. You want some?"

"Sure," said Derrick.

Eleanor put a hand on Rani's shoulder. "You just sit there and make your phone call. We can take care of ourselves."

"Okay," said Rani as she pulled Josh's phone from her purse.

Rani put Josh's phone back in her purse and walked into the kitchen where Derrick and Eleanor sat eating the sandwiches Listie had made earlier.

CHAPTER

16

Chief Nat'aanii heard the beep on his phone next to his bed; he looked at the clock *2:30*. He sat up quietly so as not to disturb his wife. *She's learned to sleep through anything,* he thought. Putting on his glasses, he pulled up the text message and breathed a sigh of relief. He then dialed the number for the emergency room at the Tuba City Medical Center as he walked quietly into the bathroom, turned on the light and shut the door. He asked to speak with Dr. Begay, the night shift physician.

"Sandy, Chief Nat'aanii here. Agent Josh Overton was shot last night and had emergency surgery at Dr. Eleanor Parker's clinic outside Kayenta Township. The doctor says he is stable and can be moved to the hospital after 10 am this morning. Can you make arrangements to send an ambulance to pick him up at Dr. Parker's clinic?"

"Will do," said the doctor. We'll need some time to examine and admit him. I'm sure you will want to talk with him as soon as he is able, but let us call you and tell you when that can happen. Sometimes, you police officers get in our way."

"Call me as soon as we can talk with him. In the meantime, I'm going to have my men bring in everyone who was with Overton so that we can find out what they know before we talk with Josh."

"Don't get so involved in talking with witnesses that you forget there are people who care about Overton who might want to stay with him until he is situated in the hospital."

"I think his son and a lady friend were there. They can accompany Overton to the hospital, but the others need to report to the Justice Center for questioning before going anywhere else. My officers and I will make those arrangements. I understand Mr. Stratton will be bringing the bullet used in the shooting for ballistics testing. When we come to talk with Overton and retrieve the bullet, we can talk to Ms. Bijan. We'll need Josh's approval to talk with his son anyway." The chief hung up the phone and sent a text to George Yazzie.

> *Will need you and Beneè to go to Navajo Monument after talking with Overton. Keep trying to find Beneè. I will call and send a text as well.*

The Chief dialed Beneè's number which went straight to voice mail. *Where is he?*

> *Report as soon as possible. Overton's been shot, need you to go with Yazzie to interview Overton and then accompany to Navajo National Monument.*

The Chief heard his wife stirring in the bedroom. "Are you leaving?" she asked.
"Yes, I need to get to the center."
Damn that Beneè. Where is he?

*   *   *

George Yazzie was waiting for the Chief when he arrived at the Justice Center. "Anything from Beneè?" asked the Chief.
"No, I was hoping you had heard from him. Do you still want me to go to the Navajo Monument after I interview Overton? The hospital ambulance just left to go get him."
"Keep trying to get in touch with Beneè until the hospital calls. Call Beneè's family in Kayenta to find out if anyone there knows where he might be. Also, get Ranger Benally to go to Beneè's apartment here. I've told the Stratton's to report to the Justice Center after they get to Tuba City; Rani and Eli will stay with Josh. You can question the Stratton's, then go and talk with Overton, his son and the lady friend. Hopefully, Beneè will have shown up by then and you two can visit the site of the shooting," said Nat'aanii.

"Hardwick has flown to St. Louis and will be questioning Lucas Fowler. That's the name of the man picked up in Kentucky," he continued. "Quite a record. This man is a former sniper for the military in Afghanistan. I suspect he may be an assassin for the CIA turned mob assassin. The Missouri police is running financials and checking phone records. We'll have to wait until Hardwick gets to Missouri and reports on the findings there. Where the hell is Beneè?" The Chief's phone rang.

"That was the hospital. Overton just arrived and is being admitted. The Stratton's are on their way here." Just as the Chief hung up the phone, Derrick, Listie and Polly Stratton arrived.

George Yazzie greeted the family and told Listie and Polly to wait in the lounge area until he finished questioning Derrick. "Would you like something to drink?" he asked and noticed that Listie was signing something to her daughter.

"Maybe a cup of water for the two of us," said Listie.

"I'll have some water also," said Derrick as he followed George and Jeanette to the interrogation room. A woman police officer appeared with two cups of water and motioned Listie and Polly to seats in the waiting room.

Yazzie introduced Derrick to the court reporter who would be recording his statement. "Take a seat at the center of the table facing the reporter," said Yazzie.

Jeanette turned on the video recorder as Yazzie said, "You are here as a material witness to the shooting of FBI agent Josh Overton on the evening of August 2nd of this year. Please answer all of the questions as truthfully and accurately as you can. Let's begin. Why were you at the campsite at Navajo National Monument on the weekend of August 1st and 2nd?" asked Yazzie.

"My wife and daughter had come back from Coos Bay, Oregon to visit me and our friend Rani Bijan during the time I have been detained here."

"Why were you detained?"

"There was some question as to whether or not I was involved in the murder of Ole Jack since my fingerprints were found on the murder weapon. The authorities told me to stay here until that case was solved or until I was exonerated," said Derrick.

"Have you been exonerated?"

"Not entirely. Mr. Overton had scheduled a meeting with Dr. Eleanor Parker and myself on Monday, August 3rd to clear up a few more details before releasing me to go home with my wife and daughter this week. We decided to accompany Rani on a hiking trip to the Navajo National Monument since she is new to the area and wanted to camp overnight before the weather turned too cold and before we returned to Coos Bay. My wife and I thought I would be released to go home with her and our daughter at the end of this week – and then this happened," said Derrick.

"When did you first see Mr. Overton?" asked Yazzie.

"Josh and his son were already at the campsite when we arrived. We had only reserved one of the two campsites and were surprised to see Mr. Overton and his son. We were happy since Eli is almost the same age as our daughter Polly, and we decided we would hike to the Betatakin Ruins together. Rani had a stone with a drawing similar to one she had seen on the inside of the alcove on her first hike and she wanted to compare the two. After the hike we returned to the campsite and Rani decided she wanted to go to Old Oraibi and show the stone to the members of the Fire Clan to see if they could tell her more about it."

"Where did Ms. Bijan get the stone?" asked Yazzie.

"You will be questioning her later. I prefer she tell you," said Derrick.

"Fair enough. What happened after your hike?"

"We built a campfire, had dinner and spent the remaining daylight reading brochures about the Monument."

"Tell me about the shooting," said Yazzie.

"My wife and daughter and I had just gone to our tent for the evening. Eli went into his tent and Josh walked Rani to the truck where she was going to sleep. Not long after that, Rani came back to our tent with Eli and said we were to stay together in the tent while

Josh went to investigate a sound he had heard. I wanted to go to help, but Rani said we were to stay there and start packing in case we had to leave in a hurry. Not long after that, we heard the gunshot.”

“What did you do then?”

“I told the others to get everything in the truck while I went to investigate.”

“Did you have a gun?”

“No, I don’t own a gun. I took a big stick with me.” At this point Derrick grinned at the image that popped into his head, but became serious again when he described finding Josh. “I heard a sound like the wind brushing against a bird’s feathers and walked slowly in that direction. Just as I approached Josh who was lying there bleeding and unconscious, I saw a dark bird like figure running away.”

“Did you try to stop the figure?”

“No.”

“Why not?”

“My first thought was to take care of Josh. I rushed toward him and tore my shirt to make something to stem the flow of blood. Then I ran back to the campsite, told everyone else to pack up and leave and drove Rani and Eli to get Josh.”

“Did you see the figure again at any time?”

“I can’t say that my mind was on apprehending a criminal; I wanted to take care of Josh. I didn’t see any more of that figure, no.”

“What happened next?”

“After I stopped the bleeding, I ran back to the campsite and got the truck to go and get Josh. Rani and Josh’s son came with me. I told my wife to finish throwing things in our SUV and then to follow me to Dr. Eleanor Parker’s clinic in Tsegi. As soon as we had cell service, Rani called Dr. Parker to alert her of the need for emergency surgery. Dr. Parker met us when we arrived, examined Josh and then did the surgery to remove a bullet from a wound in the stomach. I assisted her while the others waited in the outer area. After Josh was stable, Dr. Parker called the hospital in Tuba City and made arrangements for him to be transported there today. I put the bullet in a plastic bag and brought it with me to this interrogation and gave it to a Jeanette Duffy upon arrival."

"Did you notice a gun at the site of the shooting?"

"As I told you before, all I could think about was getting Josh to Dr. Parker's office. I wasn't thinking about collecting evidence. I also wanted to get Rani, Eli and my family to safety as soon as possible."

"That will be all. You may leave, but don't discuss anything with your wife before we have a chance to record her story," said Yazzie. "Jeanette, go and get Mrs. Stratton and her daughter."

Derrick smiled at Listie and Polly as he walked past them toward the waiting area. Listie's voice awakened him about 30 minutes later. "We're ready," she said.

"We can go?"

"Ranger Yazzie said we could go home, but not to talk to anyone, including Dr. Parker, until everyone has been questioned. With that, Derrick, Listie and Polly headed toward their SUV to go home for some much needed rest.

"What do you make of the stories?" asked the Chief.

"Not much help except for one thing," said Yazzie.

"What's that?" asked Nat'aanii?

"Mr. Stratton told us about a stone tablet Ms. Bijan had that matched one of the drawings in the alcove at the ruins. He said the drawing was exactly like one of the petro glyphs in the cave. She had intended on taking it to the Fire Clan in Old Oraibi Village today, but, of course that didn't happen," said Yazzie.

"So she still has the stone?" asked the Chief.

"I guess so," said Yazzie.

"How did Ms. Bijan get the stone?"

"Stratton didn't say, said he preferred that we talk to Ms. Bijan about it."

"We most certainly will," said the Chief. "We will not only question her about it, I want her to bring the tablet in here for me to see when she comes in to be questioned. This tablet could be another stolen artifact that somehow came into Ms. Bijan's possession. This case keeps getting more convoluted."

Jeanette came into the room. "I called Beneè's parents in Tuba City. No one there has seen him, and they had no idea of any friends who may have been in contact with him. Said their son was a loner and that, lately, he was becoming more distant than ever."

"Heard from Benally yet?"

"Benally called just as I was coming to report to you," said Jeanette. He said he had to get the manager to open up Beneè's apartment. It seems Robert left in a hurry without taking too much. His car was gone from the garage and he left the patrol car parked there."

"Do we have a license plate number and description of the car?" asked the Chief.

"Yes," said Jeanette. I have put out a bulletin with a description of the car, license plate number and picture of Beneè and sent it out to states within a hundred mile radius," said Jeanette.

"Better make that five hundred miles. Beneè's been out of touch for over two days."

"Will do," said Jeanette.

The Chief looked at Yazzie asking a silent question. Yazzie shrugged his shoulders and shook his head. "You better get to the hospital; maybe Overton can help us with this." Chief Nat'aanii's phone was ringing as Yazzie walked out the door.

Charlotte Begay heard the sound of a car in the parking lot in front of the manager's office at Rani's apartment complex. She looked up and saw the man she had seen snooping around the place a few days ago get out of his car and walk toward the front door. She stood up to welcome him as he walked through the door.

"Remember me?" he asked. "I was here to look at an apartment the other day and wondered if there was a vacancy yet."

"No, the couple is still here, but they will most likely be gone by the end of this month. Would you like to fill out an application?"

"I really don't want to fill out an application until I see what the apartment looks like," he said. "Would it be possible to see the apartment?"

"All of the apartments are occupied and the couple that rents the one you want has gone on a camping trip and hasn't returned yet,

Mr. ?"

"Oh, Gary Templeton's the name. I'm from Oklahoma and came here to interview for the job at the Peabody Coal Company. You probably have heard about the loss of the plant manager recently. I'm heading back to Oklahoma today, but I wanted to look at the apartment. Not much in the way of housing around here, is there? Is there a similar apartment that I might look at before I leave?"

"The closest one is occupied by a school teacher and she is also gone. She went on a camping trip for the weekend and hasn't returned. That's odd because she had to be at school today. I hope everything is okay."

"Maybe this job isn't all that safe, huh?"

"Oh, I'm sure she's all right – do you have a card so I can call you when I have more information?"

"I'll just call you. I'm not even sure if I will get the job anyway," said Gary as he headed toward the door. Charlotte saw the Stratton's car coming into the complex just as the man pulled out onto the highway. She ran to flag him down, but, evidently, he didn't hear.

Derrick pulled over and said, "Who was that man? He looked familiar."

"Strange," said Charlotte. "Said his name was Gary Templeton, and he's from Oklahoma. He said he was interested in your apartment -been here before, but said he didn't want to even fill out an application if he couldn't see the apartment first. What's going on? I haven't seen Rani yet. Why isn't she with you?"

"The FBI agent Josh Overton was shot last night." Charlotte muffled a gasp. "He's in the hospital now and is in fair condition. I drove him to Dr. Parker's office late last night and she did emergency surgery. Rani's with him and his son Eli at the hospital here now. Listie, Polly and I have just come from the Justice Center where we were questioned. I left the bullet Dr. Parker removed from Josh's spleen with police officers. Name's Templeton, huh?" asked Derrick suddenly changing the subject. "I know I've seen him somewhere before."

"Said he was here from Oklahoma to interview for Pete Munson's job. That's all I know," said Charlotte.

"Well, if he comes back give me a call. I want to talk to him," said Derrick. "Right now, I need to get this car unpacked and I think we need to go to the apartment and rest. It's been a trying two days."

"For sure," said Charlotte as she stepped back upon the sidewalk to let Derrick through the driveway to his apartment.

Chief Nat'aanii was walking back to his office with a fresh cup of coffee when Officer Benally approached him. He had a file in his hands. "Is that the report from ballistics? The lab just called me and said you would be bringing it up here."

"Yes, Sir," said Benally.

"Bring it into my office so I can sit my coffee down," said the Chief. "Have you read it?"

"Yes, and I think you are going to find it most interesting," said Benally.

"Really?" said the Chief as he sat his coffee on his desk and took the file and opened it. After reading the file, he said, "I need to get in touch with Yazzie as soon as possible."

*   *   *

Josh was sitting up in bed with Eli on one side and Rani on the other when Yazzie walked into his hospital room. Although still hooked up to an IV, Josh looked well enough for Yazzie to crack a joke. "I was hoping your job might be available, but it looks like that's not the case." Both he and Josh smiled; Rani looked at Yazzie with a stern look as she walked to the foot of the bed to make room for George.

Josh squeezed Rani's hand before she moved and smiled, "Don't leave on my account," he said. "I was just getting used to your company."

"I'm not going anywhere," said Rani.

"Neither am I. Dad," said Eli.

Josh turned to look at his son and said, "Maybe you both better leave for the moment while I talk with Officer Yazzie. But don't go very far away. I love you both."

Eli kissed his dad and walked toward Rani who took his hand and blushed as the two of them left the room.

"Still the playboy even after being shot," said Yazzie.

"I was serious for the first time in my life," said Josh. "You think I would tell a lady I loved her in front of my son if I didn't mean it?"

"Be careful, Man. Chief heard about that stone she's carrying. He wants her to bring it to him when she comes in for questioning. The lady may be involved with more than just you."

Josh grimaced. Everything he had come to know about Rani convinced him that she was not a part of this criminal activity, but she did possess something that looked as though it was another stolen artifact. "I need to get out of this hospital bed and back on the case now more than ever," said Josh.

"Not so fast. Maybe it's best you are incapacitated for a while. You are a little too close to the lady right now. Start by telling me what you know about the stone."

"I first learned of the stone when I ran into Rani on a day hike to the Betatakin Ruins. We met by accident, but since we were by ourselves we hiked together. We followed the guide to the bottom of the Overlook and went into the alcove to look at the petro glyphs."

"Was there ever a time when Rani was out of your sight?"

"The trail is very narrow and I kept my eyes on her the whole time because I was afraid she might slip. The only time she was out of my sight was when she went to bathroom before we started back up, but that was after she noticed the drawing on the alcove wall. I had heard her gasp when she saw the drawing that was just like the one on her stone, so I asked her about it on the way up. That's when she told me about the tablet."

"What did she say?" asked Yazzie.

"She told me her father had given it to her mother before they left Iran and before he was murdered. Her father had found it in the rubble of a house that had been demolished by the radicals who took over after the Revolution in 1978."

"Really? Sounds mighty farfetched," said Yazzie.

"Yes, it does. But she brought the stone on the second hiking trip to compare it to the drawing. The drawings are exactly the same. Rani planned on taking the stone to the elders at Old Oraibi on Sunday afternoon. Does that sound like someone who wants money? Obviously, she was prevented from doing that. I'm sure she wants the stone to find its way to the rightful owners."

"Well, no matter what she wants, the stone is to be taken to the Justice Center when she goes for questioning. By the way, do I have your permission to interview Eli before I leave? You will have to be present."

"Sure," said Josh.

"Now, tell me your version of what happened." After Josh told his story, Yazzie brought Eli in for questioning; Rani still stayed outside. Both versions of the stories were the same.

Yazzie then called Rani back to the hospital room and said, "I'll need you to go to the Justice Center for questioning and Chief Nat'aanii wants you to bring that stone with you. Where is it?" he asked Rani.

"It's in my back pack. I'll be happy to bring it with me. What about Eli?"

"I've talked with his mother," said Josh. She's on her way to get him. He is to stay here at the hospital and she will take him to get his things before they go back to Flagstaff. By the way, who has his things?"

"The few things he brought with him for camping are in your SUV which is parked at the apartment complex. Listie drove it back; I still have the truck."

"Eli will probably have to leave those things here. The rest of his clothes that he brought for the weekend are at my apartment. I don't think there is much that he will need before I can get those to him. Call me as soon as you get home?" That was more of a question than an order.

"I will," said Rani as he moved toward Josh to take his hand. Before she knew it, she was being pulled toward him for a long, lingering kiss.

"We need to leave," said Yazzie.

"Certainly," said Rani as she blushed again and gave Eli a hug. "Let me know when you get home, Eli," she said.

"Will do." Eli took a chair next to his dad's bed and Rani and George walked out of the hospital room.

"I drove Derrick's truck here. What do you want me to do?"

"I'll follow you to the Justice Center," said Yazzie. "You can call Mr. Stratton once you have finished being questioned and then I believe you will be able to drive the truck back to the apartment on your own."

"Thank you," said Rani. All she could think about was the last kiss from Josh and the words, "I love you." Nothing else mattered just now.

CHAPTER

17

"**Y**ou wanted to see me, Sir?" said Yazzie as he poked his head inside the Chief's office. "I finished questioning everyone but Ms. Bijan; she's waiting outside to talk with you first as you ordered."

"Oh, yes," said the Chief. "I do need to talk with her, but let's get the stone first and send her home. We have something a little more important right now."

Yazzie said nothing but he shook his head and went outside where Rani was sitting. "The Chief can't interview you now, but he wants the stone. You are to go home and wait until someone calls you to come back. Don't talk to anyone about the stone or what happened here. That includes your friends the Stratton's."

Rani's hands were shaking as she reached into her backpack and handed the bag containing the stone to Officer Yazzie. "May I go to work tomorrow?" she asked.

"Yes, but once again it is important that you have no contact with anyone concerned in this investigation or that you discuss this with any of your colleagues until you have been questioned."

"W-What about Josh and Eli?" she stammered.

"We will notify him for you. No contact."

Rani picked up her backpack and purse and silently walked away. Her head was swimming and her stomach was in knots. For a moment, she lost her balance. Officer Yazzie helped her and said, "I know this is scary, but the last thing Josh Overton said to me was that you could be trusted. No matter what, I'm sure you will have him on your side, so just go home, drink some tea and try to rest until time to go to work."

"Thank you," said Rani with a wan smile and she walked away.

Yazzie shook his head and walked back into the Chief's office. "What is it?" he asked.

Nat'aanii said, "Look at this ballistics report."

Yazzie read the report. *The bullet taken from Overton's stomach was from a 10mm from a Glock 20. It is usually used for hunting so we ran a check on all Glock 20's permitted in the state. There was a permit for a concealed carry issued last year to one Robert Beneè of Kayenta Township, Arizona.* The address listed was Robert Beneè's address.

Yazzie looked at the Chief in astonishment. "Robert shot Overton?"

"It looks that way. There's no report of a stolen gun. Maybe Beneè was attacked and had his gun stolen before Overton was shot. That's a possibility. We need to get all available officers to comb the area around the Navajo Monument to check for yet another body," said the Chief.

"I'll get on it, Sir," said Yazzie.

Nat'aanii's phone buzzed signaling a text. *What now? He wondered.*

*   *   *

Charlotte Begay hailed Rani as she saw the Stratton's truck pull into the apartment complex. Rani stopped, rolled the window down and said, "I'm okay, but I'm under orders from Officer Yazzie at the Justice Center to go home and not talk to anyone at this time. Could you call Derrick and Listie and tell them I will park their truck in their parking space, but they are not to talk to me? I haven't been questioned about the shooting yet. Chief Nat'aanii told Officer Yazzie to send me home before they questioned me and I was to wait until they contacted me." Rani smiled politely and drove away.

Charlotte's brow revealed a deep furrow as she walked back to the manager's office. *I needed to tell her about that man! I don't like any of this.* Charlotte sent Derrick a text. *Rani home but under orders from Justice Center not to talk to anyone, including you. She told me she was parking your truck in your parking space, but you were not to talk to her.*

Derrick was just about to go out and talk to Rani when his phone signaled a text. After reading it he showed the text to Listie then stepped outside and waved and smiled. Rani smiled back and walked toward her apartment. "I *just don't like it that she is alone. What has happened?*" Derrick watched until he saw Rani walk around the corner to her apartment and then went back inside.

Listie was sitting silently on the couch with Polly. "Let's call Josh," she said.

"Good idea," said Derrick as he punched in Josh's number.

Josh answered almost immediately. "Hi, Derrick," he said. "Is Rani home?"

"Yes, she is, but she told our apartment manager she can't talk to anyone because she hasn't been questioned yet."

"That's right," said Josh. "George Yazzie called me about some confidential information that needed to be addressed before they interview Rani. Chief Nat'aanii did take the stone tablet from her. All I can tell you is she is under some suspicion now. You sure she is okay? I don't like being unable to help her."

Derrick could hear the concern in Josh's voice. "I watched her walk back to her apartment, but there is something that is bothering me."

"What's that?" asked Josh.

"When Listie and I drove into the apartment complex earlier there was a man leaving. I thought he looked familiar. The manager was standing outside in front of the office, so I stopped and asked her about him."

"Who was it?" asked Josh. He could feel the nervous tension rising; Yazzie had told him about Beneè when he had called.

"Said his name was Gary Templeton and he was from Oklahoma here to interview for Pete Munson's job. Wanted to see our apartment because he was thinking of renting it when we moved out. Charlotte told him we weren't here so he asked if there was another like it that he could see. She told him no but said he could fill out an application and she would start the approval process. The man said he didn't want to fill out an application without seeing the apartment, said he probably wouldn't get the job anyway, then he just left without giving her a card or anything," said Derrick.

Josh was ready to get up and leave the hospital. He had to get to Rani but logic got the better of him. "I need to get this information to Chief Nat'aanii," said Josh. "You go outside and watch her apartment. If you see that man, call the Justice Center. We need to get someone there right away."

"Okay," said Derrick and disconnected the phone.

"What's going on?" asked Listie.

"I don't know, but I think Rani may be in danger. Josh is contacting the Justice Center and said I was to watch Rani's apartment to see if that man we saw comes back."

Listie gasped as Polly watched her parents in amazement.

"Take Polly into the bedroom and lock yourselves in. Do what you need to do to keep her as well as yourself calm," said Derrick as he put on his shoes and walked toward the front door.

He heard Listie say, "All right," as he walked outside and shut and locked the door behind him. Derrick walked around the porch to the laundry room that was directly across from Rani's apartment. He went inside and shut the door, leaving a crack large enough to provide a view of the front door of Rani's apartment. Everything appeared to be quiet.

Inside, Rani sat tied to a chair and gagged as she listened to the man tearing her bedroom apart. He had been inside when she opened the door and had pointed a gun directly at her. She recognized him immediately and said, "What are you doing here, Officer Beneè, and why are you pointing that gun at me?"

"I'm here to get something you have that belongs to my people. Where is it?"

Although terrified and confused, Rani knew what he meant. "You mean the stone, don't you?"

"Yes, where is it. Tell me where it is and then I'll be gone. I have to take your phone and leave you tied, you understand, but I don't want to hurt you. I never meant to hurt anyone; I just want what belongs to my people."

"I don't have it," she said. "The police took it from me."

"I don't believe that," said Beneè who then gagged and tied Rani while he began the search for the stone. Rani heard Beneè throwing things around and she was becoming more frightened. He came back and went into the kitchen and started opening cabinets and moving things around. Frustrated in his search he went back into the living room and told Rani, "Don't scream or I will shoot you, but I'm taking the gag from your mouth. Do you get this?"

Rani's terror was apparent in her eyes. Dark memories from her past came to the surface as she recalled another time when making a noise meant certain death. "Tell me where the stone is," said Robert as he removed the gag but kept the gun pointed at her temple.

"I told you; the police have it. I had the stone with me on the camping trip and after Josh was shot..." Rani paused as everything started to clear. "You shot Josh!"

"Yes, I did and it looks like you may be next. Finish what you started."

"We took Josh to Dr. Parker's clinic in Tsegi for surgery to remove the bullet and then called Tuba City."

"Who's 'we?'" asked Beneè

"Josh and his son and the Stratton family. We ran into Josh and Eli when we arrived at the campsite on Saturday morning."

"That explains it," said Robert to no one in particular as he dropped the gun and started to pace. "You really don't have the stone, do you? And the police probably have already identified the owner of the bullet used to shoot Josh."

Rani thought for a minute and said, "That must be the news they got when they sent me home."

"Stop talking. I've got to think," said Robert. He picked up his phone and punched in a number, then went into the bedroom and closed the door. Rani heard a mumbled conversation and then a sound outside her front door.

*   *   *

Derrick was still standing inside the laundry room when he looked down and saw it – the car the man had been driving was parked in a visitor's slot near the entrance to Rani's apartment! Derrick texted Josh. *I believe that man is inside the apartment with Rani and I just realized where I saw him before. He is an officer with the Tuba City Police Force; I don't remember his name.*

Chief Nat'aanii had mobilized Yazzie and two other officers to go to Rani's apartment as soon as Josh had called him. He was sitting at his desk reading a report from Agent Hardwick when his phone rang. He saw the ID – Josh Overton. "What now?" he asked.

"Stratton just called; he believes Beneè is inside Rani's apartment. Where's Yazzie?"

"He should be there anytime; I'll call and advise him to enter from behind the apartment. Where is Stratton?"

"He's inside the laundry room on the second floor." Almost before Josh finished the Chief had disconnected and was radioing Yazzie the instructions. Yazzie was about two miles out on Highway 163 and after hearing the message, he turned off on a paved road that led to the back of the apartment complex. He and the two officers parked in the back. Some nervous residents saw the police cars and opened their doors to come outside when the officers waved them back inside. Yazzie was glad these residents knew not to run toward a burning building.

Yazzie and the two officers in SWAT clothing walked silently to the corner of the second floor wrap around. Yazzie cautiously looked around the corner. He could see the partially opened door to the laundry room and looked across to Rani's apartment. He had a clear view, but the problem was anyone inside her apartment also had a clear view of him. Yazzie texted the number Josh had given him. *This is officer Yazzie of the Tuba City Police. Shut the door to the laundry room and stay inside.* Derrick's phone vibrated. After reading the text, he cautiously shut the door and waited. When Yazzie saw the door close, he and his men went back downstairs to approach Rani's apartment from the opposite side.

The three officers quietly approached Rani's apartment. The only sound he heard was something like the shuffling of a chair and then a door opening and closing. He motioned his men to move away from the window as he stepped out of view also. *Good thing the blinds are drawn on the inside.* He heard Robert Beneè's voice but couldn't make out what he was saying. The next sound was that of a chair moving and then a woman's voice. *Was he imagining things or was the woman speaking loud enough to be heard?*

"What are you doing; who did you call?" she asked.

"Don't talk so loud," said Robert. "We have to make a little trip. We'll go in your car. Get your keys." More moving around. Yazzie signaled for his men to move around as he stepped back against the wall on the other side. The door opened with Rani walking out first. Robert was behind her with a gun at her back; the two turned away from Yazzie walking in the direction of the stairs where the other two men were. When they reached the corner, Yazzie's men met them with guns pointed. One of the men said, "That's far enough, Robert. This is the end of the line."

Robert showed his gun, now aiming it at Rani's temple once again. "Let us pass or she dies."

"Why would you do that? You shoot her; we shoot you and then you will be tried for murder. Josh Overton's still alive." Robert seemed to be surprised by the news that Overton was still alive. "Did you think he was dead?" Benally asked. *What is that look on Rani's face?* With Robert distracted by conversation, Yazzie was able to approach Beneè from behind. Hearing a noise Robert turned; Yazzie knocked the gun from his hand. Rani broke away and ran around the corner to safety as the two men struggled.

Benally reached for his Taser and soon Robert was down. No shots were fired.

With Beneè handcuffed and Rani safe, Yazzie told his men to escort Derrick back to his apartment. "Tell Mr. Stratton to stay put and not try to talk with anyone connected with this case, including Josh Overton."

He then turned to Rani and said, "You will be coming to headquarters with me, Ms. Bijan. Go back to your apartment and make any arrangements you may need for work tomorrow. You are still under suspicion because of the stone tablet and will be held for 24 hours not only for your safety but also so we can make sense of all this new information we have before we question you. While Beneè was being loaded into the police SUV, Yazzie followed Rani to her car. He would be riding to headquarters with her.

As Rani was unlocking her car door, Yazzie sent a quick text to Josh Overton – *Robert Beneè in custody. On the way to police headquarters to question him and put the pieces of this with the other information we have. Rani will be held in protective custody for 24 hours and then questioned about how she came to possess the stone tablet.*

Emma and Eli had just returned from Josh's apartment with Craig and Julie when Josh received the text. As Emma handed him the keys to his car, he said, "Rani's all right; she is being held in protective custody."

"That's great news. Now we can return to Flagstaff breathing a little easier," said Craig. Craig had driven from Flagstaff with Julie and had met Emma at Josh's apartment. They had come back to the hospital to return Josh's SUV and say goodbye.

Eli hugged his dad tightly; neither really wanted to let go. This incident had affirmed the lasting bond between father and son that no step-parent, no matter how good, could break. Not that Craig had ever wanted to break that bond; Josh knew he had had a lot to do with that. "Call me every day, Dad," said Eli.

Josh heard the concern in his voice. "I will, Son, and after all this is resolved, I'm going to take some time off to reconsider a lot of things. I want to spend a lot of that time with you."

Eli smiled, "I would love that."

"Time to go," said Emma as she touched Eli's shoulder and moved in to hug Josh. Julie did the same and Craig followed with a firm handshake. As the four walked out the door, Josh remembered the soccer tournament and how he had felt like the outsider. Although he knew he would have to share Eli with this family, Josh knew that for the first time he was learning what it was like to be a father and enjoy a father son relationship with a woman like Rani beside him. It had been a long two days and for the first time since the shooting, Josh slept in peace.

CHAPTER

18

Chief Nat'aanii was on the phone with his wife when Yazzie came to his office. The Chief motioned for him to sit down as he ended the conversation. "So, fill me in," he said.

"We have Robert in a holding cell awaiting interrogation. He has a tribal attorney who will be representing him. Rani Bijan will be spending the night with Officer Duffy and returning to the Justice Center tomorrow for questioning," said Yazzie. "I suppose you have news concerning the stolen artifacts?"

"What a day!" exclaimed the Chief. "Hardwick contacted me about the results of the Lucas Fowler case. Finding him has given us just about everything we need to close the investigation involving the murder of Brad Kellogg as well as identifying the players involved in the Energy West Development scheme and the theft of Native American artifacts."

"How does Robert Beneè fit into all of this?" asked Yazzie. Since Overton saw a bird like figure when he was shot, it seems that Beneè at least had possession of the costume. That also makes him a likely suspect in the murder of Ole Jack. We have a DNA profile on the bird feather picked up at the scene. Order a DNA sample done on Beneè as soon as possible." Yazzie nodded in assent and wrote something in the file folder he was carrying.

"After I go over the rest of the evidence with you, said Nat'aanii, "you will understand and then we can start proceedings against Beneè, but there's one more piece you need to know first."

"What's that?"

"Saint Louis police department called us this afternoon. It seems some hikers found a body in a shallow grave on the North River

Front Hiking Trail and called the police. The forensics team recovered the body and took it to the medical examiner's office. It's too soon to say for sure, but they believe it is the body of Stewart Campbell. The person had been strangled with a wire rope in the same manner as Brad Kellogg. The wire rope along with samples from the body have been sent for DNA testing. The DNA tests on the wire rope used to murder Brad Kellogg have come back and we're waiting for the DNA sample taken from Fowler to see if there is a match," said the Chief.

"Wow!" said Yazzie. "So how do Halverson and Munson fit into all of this and do we have anything to implicate the Giovanni Family other than Halverson's testimony?"

"We found a burner phone on Lewis Fowler when he was arrested; he didn't have time to get rid of it. We found records of phone calls from a number registered to the Windstar Casino in Atlantic City, operated by the Giovanni Family. But get this, we also found a call from a phone identified as belonging to Robert Beneè. Guess he didn't think he needed a burner phone."

"Did Fowler give up any information about the phone calls?"

"Not yet. Unless we get a DNA match on the wire used in the two murders, we don't have the basis for a plea bargain. If a match is made, the prosecuting attorney is willing to offer life with no parole in exchange for giving up the Giovanni Family. Giovanni knows we have Fowler in custody and we have Fowler under 24 hour surveillance in St. Louis. We also have surveillance posted at the Windstar Casino in Atlantic City. Unless there is a connection between Fowler and the murder of Ole Jack, he will stay in Missouri."

"What about the missing eagle costume and the stone pestle?" asked Yazzie.

"Can't get any information from him about that until we have something concrete to connect him to the murders of Brad Kellogg and Stewart Campbell. We can process Beneè on the shooting and kidnap charges, so he isn't going anywhere. I suspect he knows where the eagle costume and stone pestle are located. We can question him on that, but can't do anything about Ole Jack until we get a DNA match," said the Chief.

"What about Ms. Bijan?" asked Yazzie.

"She's with Officer Duffy tonight and with Beneè in custody, I don't think she's in any danger. We still need to find out more about how she came to possess the stone tablet. Did you see that thing?"

"Yes, and I have to say I am totally bewildered. The tablet seems to be authentic. We have it in the evidence room and as soon as we retrieve the eagle costume and stone pestle, we will ship to the United Nations people for repatriation to the Hopi. Is that correct?"

"Although I have no doubt that the stone seems to belong to the Hopi people, if Ms. Bijan can prove she brought it from Iran, we will have to do some archeological testing to make certain," said the Chief. "Do you think Ms. Bijan would take a polygraph test?"

"If her story is authentic, she would have no reason to refuse," said Yazzie.

"Make arrangements for that tomorrow and let's try to get that done, before we question her," said Nat'aanii. "After that, you might as well go home for tonight. Oh, maybe you better call Overton. I don't want him taking off from his hospital bed on a knight's errand to save his dulcinea." The Chief had quite a smile on his face when he said this.

"Okay," said Yazzie. He was punching in Overton's number as he left the Chief's office. Josh seemed a bit groggy when he answered the phone.

"What's happening, George?" he asked.

"What's going on with you? You don't seem to be your usual alert self," said Yazzie.

"They have me on a high dosage of pain killers. I suspect the high dosage has something to do with making sure I stay put as well as relieving my pain," said Overton. "Where's Rani?"

"Ms. Bijan is spending the night with Officer Duffy and will be brought back in for questioning and a polygraph tomorrow. Robert Beneè has been charged with deadly assault and kidnapping and we are holding him until we question him tomorrow or the next day. We are waiting for DNA test results on the bird feather found at Ole Jack's murder scene."

"So, you think Beneè did it," said Overton.

"Everything points to it," said Yazzie. George continued to fill Josh in with the information that had come from St. Louis in the past two days.

"I sure wish I could leave this hospital," said Overton.

"Yeah, it's hard not being there when all the pieces come together, huh?"

"Well, that, but I want to be with Rani more than anything. To be honest, I think I need to consider another occupation when all this is over."

"Being shot can do that to you," said Yazzie.

"It's more than that. I've been feeling this way for some time. I think I want to do something a little less exciting and more fulfilling; being shot was part of it though."

"Do you know when you will be released?"

"Doc says by the end of the week if I cooperate."

"So, cooperate," said Yazzie. "You sound like you need to go back to sleep."

Yazzie heard the sound of the phone disconnecting. *Guess he thought so too. Wonder if I need to think about settling down too?*

*   *   *

George Yazzie dropped the file folders on Chief Nat'aanii's desk as though dropping a bombshell. "Results of the DNA tests on the wires and bird feather and comparison to the results from Beneè and Fowler's tests."

"And…?" said the Chief.

"Bird feather DNA and that of Robert Beneè a match — matches to Lucas Fowler on both the wire strands used in the murder of Brad Kellogg, and we now know, Stewart Campbell. Hardwick is starting due process proceedings against Fowler as we speak. We may get enough from him after the interrogation to link the Giovanni Family to the international robbery ring," said Yazzie.

"Get started on due process with Robert Beneè," said the Chief. "Overton is not due to be released from the hospital until the end of the week, but contact him and let him know what is happening. Since he is a victim, himself, I don't think he should be a direct part of the interrogation."

"Okay," said Yazzie. "What about Ms. Bijan?"

"I've turned the stone over to the Fire Clan of the Hopi Tribe in Old Oraibi," said the Chief. "Experts from the archeological office of the Bureau of Land Management will work with them to identify the age of the stone, materials used in the ink drawing connected with any known ancient cultures and any DNA tests that might match DNA findings from current monuments and skeletons. While that is being done, have Benally contact Officer Duffy and tell her to bring Ms. Bijan in for a polygraph test first if she is willing to submit to one. We won't question her until we get the results back from the archaeological testing and the suspects in the murder cases and international theft ring are identified and in custody. Inform Ms. Bijan that she will probably not be able to go back to work for about a week."

"All right," said Yazzie.

*   *   *

Rani had just gotten off the phone with her mother in New York when Officer Duffy received the call from the Justice Center. "George Yazzie wants to know if you would be willing to submit to a polygraph test before you are questioned about how you obtained possession of the stone."

"Do they want to do it today?"

"As soon as possible," said Jeanette.

"I will take the polygraph today, but I don't want to be questioned until my mother arrives from New York; she will verify my story. In addition, my aunt from Albuquerque is willing to come and corroborate my story if needed."

"If you are going to use them to corroborate your story, I'm sure you won't be able to talk with them before you are questioned. When is your mother arriving?"

"The first flight they could get to Albuquerque was not until tomorrow, August 4th. They were going to drive with my aunt from

Albuquerque to Tuba City. That means they won't be here until near the end of the week. How long will it be before I can go back to work?"

"I'm guessing, if you are cleared of any illegal activity, you would be able to go back to work next week. I think you should call the high school and let them know you will be out for the rest of this week at least; the department should be finished questioning you and would probably be ready to question your relatives when they get here. I don't think you will be able to talk with them until after the questioning."

"I'll call and tell my mother and aunt to make reservations at a hotel in Tuba City until after all the investigation is completed."

"Make the call short and then we will leave for the Justice Center."

"Okay," said Rani. Officer Duffy stayed in the room with Rani until the conversation ended, then the two left for the Justice Center. Officer Duffy escorted Rani to the interrogation room where the polygraph examiner was waiting. Duffy strapped the Velcro detectors to Rani's fingers as the examiner explained what was going to happen.

"I will ask you a few nondescript questions to establish a base line. Answer truthfully and relax. After that, I will be asking you questions related to the reason for the polygraph. I may repeat some questions which is normal – just answer the questions. Are you ready to begin?" Rani nodded her head and the examiner began. "What is your full name?"

At the same time that Rani was taking the polygraph, Robert Beneè was being interrogated in another room. Benally escorted a handcuffed Beneè into the room where a court reporter and Beneè's attorney were already seated. George Yazzie turned on the video recorder and began. "Subject Robert Beneè, charged with assault with intent to kill, has been informed of his due process rights and will be interviewed in the presence of legal counsel concerning said assault and will also be presented with evidence connecting him to the murder of Ole Jack on the morning of July 22, 2016. Have you been so advised, Mr. Beneè?"

Robert sat up a little straighter in his chair and answered, "Yes."

"I show you this ballistics' report on a 10mm bullet retrieved from the stomach of FBI agent Josh Overton on Sunday, August 2nd of this year. You will note in the report that the bullet matches that of the bullets from a gun registered in your name. In addition, you were in possession of that gun on Monday, August 3rd when officers arrested you after your attempt to kidnap one Rani Bijan. We have eye-witness reports of a giant bird like creature fleeing the scene after the shooting," said Yazzie.

"What does that have to do with the charges against my client?" asked Beneè's attorney.

Yazzie placed the DNA report from the bird feather along with a report on DNA taken from Robert. "This is a DNA sample from a bird feather found at the scene of the murder of Ole Jack on July 22nd of this year. Next to it is a report on your DNA and you will see there is a match," said Yazzie. Robert and his attorney looked at the report in front of them. Neither said a thing as they looked up at Yazzie.

"We have video proof of a bird like creature stalking the area during the week before Ole Jack was murdered and there is a shadow on the video of the murder that appears to be the arm of a giant eagle. We think this DNA evidence connects you not only to the shooting of Josh Overton but also the murder of Ole Jack," said Yazzie.

"What was the motive?" asked the attorney.

"We have witnesses who saw Robert talking with Ole Jack outside the Blue Coffee Pot a few days before the murder. In addition, Robert's patrol car was seen near the entrance to the Peabody Coal Company about 9:00 on the night of the murder. We know the blackmailer had a meeting with Halverson and Munson at that time. Halverson was unable to identify the blackmailer, however, because of the costume."

"That still doesn't connect my client to Ole Jack, only Halverson and Munson."

"We have Robert's testimony that Ole Jack told him about the eagle's costume in a conversation outside the Blue Coffee Pot just days before the murder. In addition, Robert said he went to the area around the Peabody Coal Company the night of the murder to get the costume. We think Ole Jack told Robert he not only found the eagle's costume, but he wanted to report it to the police," said Yazzie. "We think you told Ole Jack you would check out his story and if it was true, you would go to the police to buy some time. But when you saw Ole Jack alone after you met with Halverson and Munson and had put on the costume, we believe you simply took advantage of the opportunity to get rid of the only person who knew about your connection to the costume."

"If my client has such a costume, where is it?" asked the attorney.

"We are still searching for the costume along with the stone pestle we believe you took from Munson's safe deposit box. The items are not in your apartment, but we have started searching the area around the Betatakin ruins. We think you may have hidden them somewhere around there. Even without the costume and pestle, we think we have enough evidence to convict you of assault with intent to kill, kidnapping and murder. We also have the man we believed killed Brad Kellogg and Stewart Campbell and have been able to retrieve a burner phone which shows several calls placed to that number from your phone number. Lucas Fowler is being held in St. Louis and we think we can get him to give information about the nature of that phone call which will more than likely connect you to the theft and attempted illegal sale of Hopi artifacts."

Robert started to say something but his attorney shook his head and said, "You need to charge my client and have him before a judge within the next 24 hrs. When we appear before the judge we will be asking for bail so that my client can be free to prepare for his trial."

"We'll probably have everything we need within the next 24 hours," said Yazzie. "We believe, however, there is too much evidence to show a flight risk for your client to be released. Tomorrow after you have had time to consult with your client and you have heard the additional evidence, I think you will understand."

"Are we finished for now?" asked the attorney.

"Yes," said Yazzie. He looked at his watch. *Lunchtime.* Yazzie walked to the vending machines to grab something to eat before he checked in with Chief Nat'aanii. As he was walking back to his desk, he saw Jeanette walking past with Rani. "You headin' to lunch?" he asked.

"No," said Jeanette. "I am going back home with Rani. She is under my supervision until the investigation involving the stone tablet is complete."

"Oh," said Yazzie. Now that Beneè was out of the picture, maybe there was some hope for him.

Yazzie was finishing his sandwich and coffee when Benally walked toward his desk. "Here is the report on the interrogation of Lucas Fowler. The Chief has already seen it and he wants you in his office after lunch."

"Okay," said Yazzie. Yazzie opened the file and started reading. He left his half-eaten sandwich and picked up the file and headed toward Chief Nat'aanii's office.

CHAPTER

19

The Chief looked up from the file when Yazzie walked through the open door. "Looks like we have almost everything we need to wrap up this investigation and bring those involved to trial."

"Lucas Fowler's testimony is the key," said Yazzie. "Once he learned of the DNA match to the two dead bodies, he was willing to take a plea. Life in prison with no chance of parole in exchange for testimony against not only the Giovanni Family but also Robert Beneè."

"Fowler admitted he killed Brad Kellogg and Stewart Campbell on orders from Giovanni. He also substantiated Halverson's testimony about the Family's involvement in the bogus Energy West Company being used as a front for the illegal sale of Native American artifacts. The Hopi artifacts were just a small part of a much larger, international theft ring. Fowler admitted Robert Beneè had called him on his burner phone after Beneè had contacted the Giovanni Family with information about the eagle costume and stone pestle; and, get this, he also mentioned a stone tablet that was probably more valuable than any of the artifacts sold to date. The mob boss directed Beneè to Fowler who was to make arrangements to meet with Beneè to obtain the stolen artifacts. Beneè's fate was to be the same as the others. Lucky for him that we caught him, huh?" said the Chief with a sarcastic smile.

"Looks like all we have to do now is present this evidence to Beneè," said Yazzie, "and then turn everything over to the prosecuting attorney. It sure would help if we knew where the eagle's costume and stone pestle were hidden. The search of Beneè's apartment turned up nothing. We have some men from the department searching around the Navajo Monument, but that's a big place and we can't spare the manpower for too long."

"When does Overton get out of the hospital?" asked the Chief.

"The Doc said at the end of the week. That's about the time Rani's family arrives and we will be questioning them in regard to the stone tablet. We should have forensic results that might identify where the stone originated by then also," said Yazzie.

"Call Overton and tell him he is to search for the missing artifacts around the Navajo Monument after his release from the hospital. The case is closed except for the missing artifacts and the investigation of Ms. Bijan. Overton will not be fit for active duty for a while and this will keep him busy and out of our hair while we are finishing the stone tablet investigation," said the Chief. "Oh, and make it very clear he is still to have no contact with Ms. Bijan until we have finished. I don't want any conflict of interest to contaminate our department; Beneè's done enough already."

"Okay," said Yazzie.

*　　*　　*

Josh Overton pulled into the parking lot in front of the visitor's center of the Navajo National Monument. As good as it felt to be alive and have this case nearing an end, Josh was full of nervous tension over not being able to see Rani. He felt helpless not being able to help her prove her innocence and he missed her terribly. He had heard from Yazzie that Rani had passed the lie detector test; that was a relief. Rani's mom and aunt had arrived just before he was released from the hospital. They were staying in a hotel near the Justice Center and were scheduled to also take a lie detector test and be questioned concerning their knowledge of how Rani came to possess the stone tablet.

Rani's mother's testimony was critical because she would swear that her husband found the stone tablet in the rubble around the demolished House of *Bab* in Teheran just after the Iranian Revolution. Bedar would also testify that she gave the tablet to Rani just before she moved to Arizona. Aunt Sizdah would testify that she and Bedar were the only two who knew about the tablet until Bedar gave it to Rani. *I wish I knew the results of the forensics' tests,* thought Josh. That information was being held in strictest secrecy. The newspapers were already sniffing around trying to get information about the mysterious tablet. In fact, Josh had been dogged by reporters since he left the hospital. They had finally left him alone when they got tired of hearing, "no comment."

Josh showed his badge and permit to the clerk at the information desk. "I have permission to conduct a search around the Betatakin Cliffs for the missing Hopi artifacts that have been in the news recently," he said. Your office informed me there would be a special guide to accompany me to insure that the environmental integrity of the area will be respected."

The clerk motioned for a park ranger who came over and introduced herself. "I am Irene," she said. "I will accompany you along the trail into the canyon that leads to the ruins. I am supposed to monitor your search and make sure that the environment and ruins are least impacted by your search," she said.

"I understand. I have an idea of the first place to search and we may get lucky," said Josh.

"Follow me," said Irene. Although Josh looked for any signs of recent disturbance along the two and one-half mile trail, he was focused on getting to one spot, the area behind the portable restrooms at the alcove entrance. Josh remembered seeing a spot where the earth had looked as though it had been recently disturbed on both occasions of his visit there.

As the two approached the entrance to the alcove, Josh alerted Irene to a spot behind the restrooms where the earth still appeared to have been recently disturbed. Irene noticed and walked to the spot and began to gingerly dig into the loose soil. It wasn't long before the outline of a feathered costume appeared. As Irene pulled the costume from the earth, she also saw the stone pestle.

*   *   *

Josh held Rani's hand as the couple walked toward the adobe home of the elders of the Fire Klan, the keepers of the sacred stone tablets. Rani pulled the red scarf over her head in preparation for entering this sacred place. Although Bedar, Sizdah and Craig were also with them, they had stayed behind and Josh would have to turn back at the entrance to the home of the sacred altar.

It was near the end of September; the investigation into the identity of the stone tablets had been completed and the trial of those involved in murder and theft was underway in Phoenix. Derrick and Listie Stratton had returned to Coos Bay just after Rani was cleared of any wrong doing, but the bond between Rani and Listie had been secured before they left. This trip to visit the sacred altar was intended to be a blessing for Rani and recognition that she represented the connection to the *Pahana*, the long, lost white Brother from the East. Her return of the tablet represented the hope that the completion of the Convergence marking the evolution into the Fifth World of Global Harmony was at hand. Rani kissed Josh and walked alone toward the adobe structure. Josh walked back to be with Rani's family, now part of his and Eli's family also.

"What do you think about all this, *Maman*?" signed Josh. Bedar had insisted that Josh refer to her in this manner; learning sign was his choice. Eli was learning sign also.

"I think that this is the completion of the circle, the joining together of the family of humanity to bring about the world prophesied by all the great prophets of all religions of the world. Yours and Rani's work here in Arizona is just part of a global movement toward universal peace and justice. I am happy you decided to retire from the FBI and settle down here with Rani to work with the *Natwani* Coalition. Returning to spiritual and sustainable production of food is the way to create not only healthy humans but a healthy Mother Earth as well. Coaching football at Monument Valley High School is the perfect occupation for you. Both you and Rani will have the summers off to work in Kykotsmovi Village learning and teaching ancient, sustainable practices in food production. I'm also excited that you two will travel to Syracuse and New York City to network with Listie's family and also be part of the United Nations projects around the world that share your ideals."

Bedar stopped when she saw her daughter approaching, her red scarf shining brightly in the desert sun. No words were necessary;

the desert stillness filled them all with peace. As she walked toward the car, Rani thought "We are all part of the same universal family and despite our apparent differences the only thing real is love."